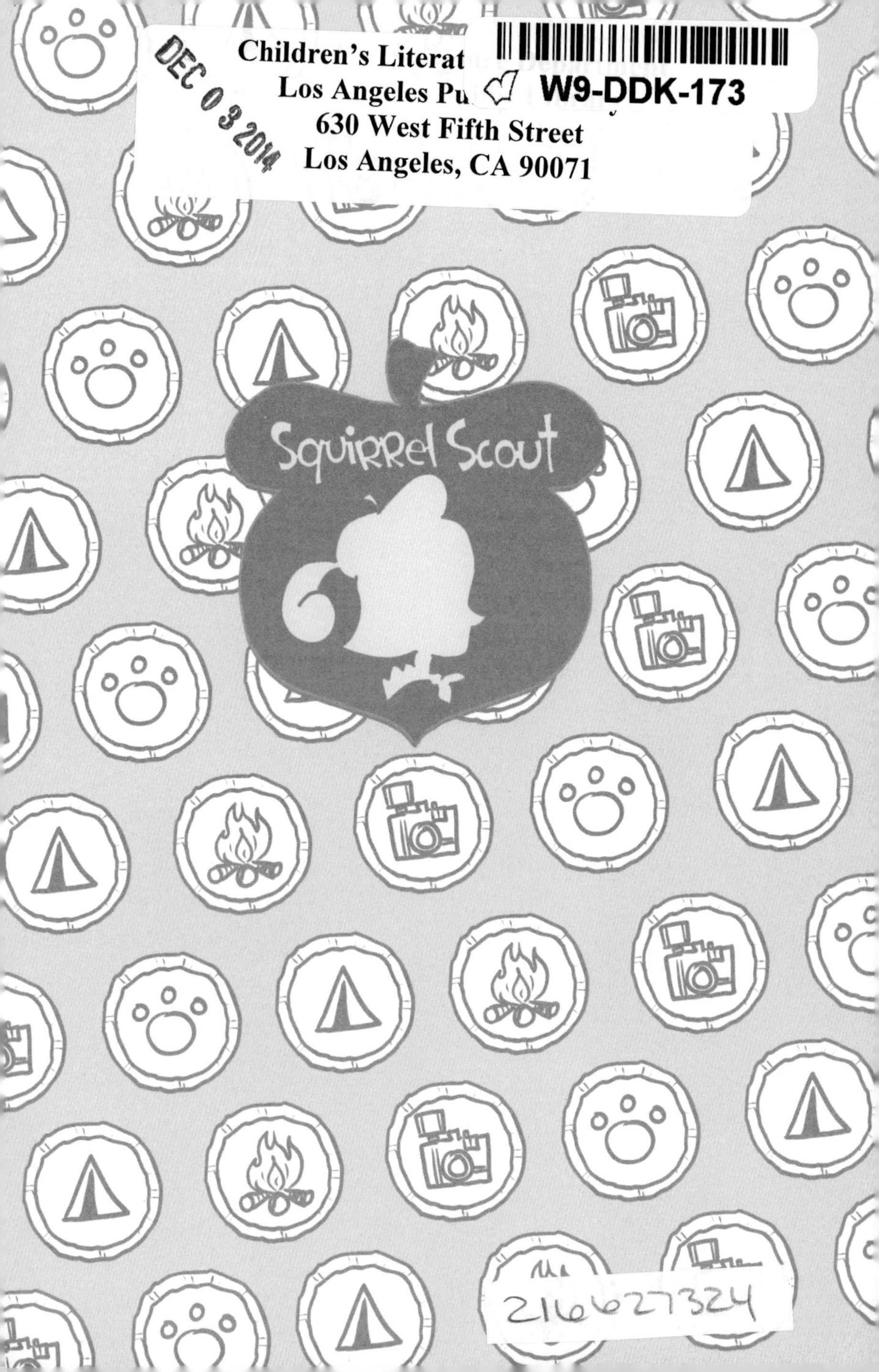
Squirrel Scout

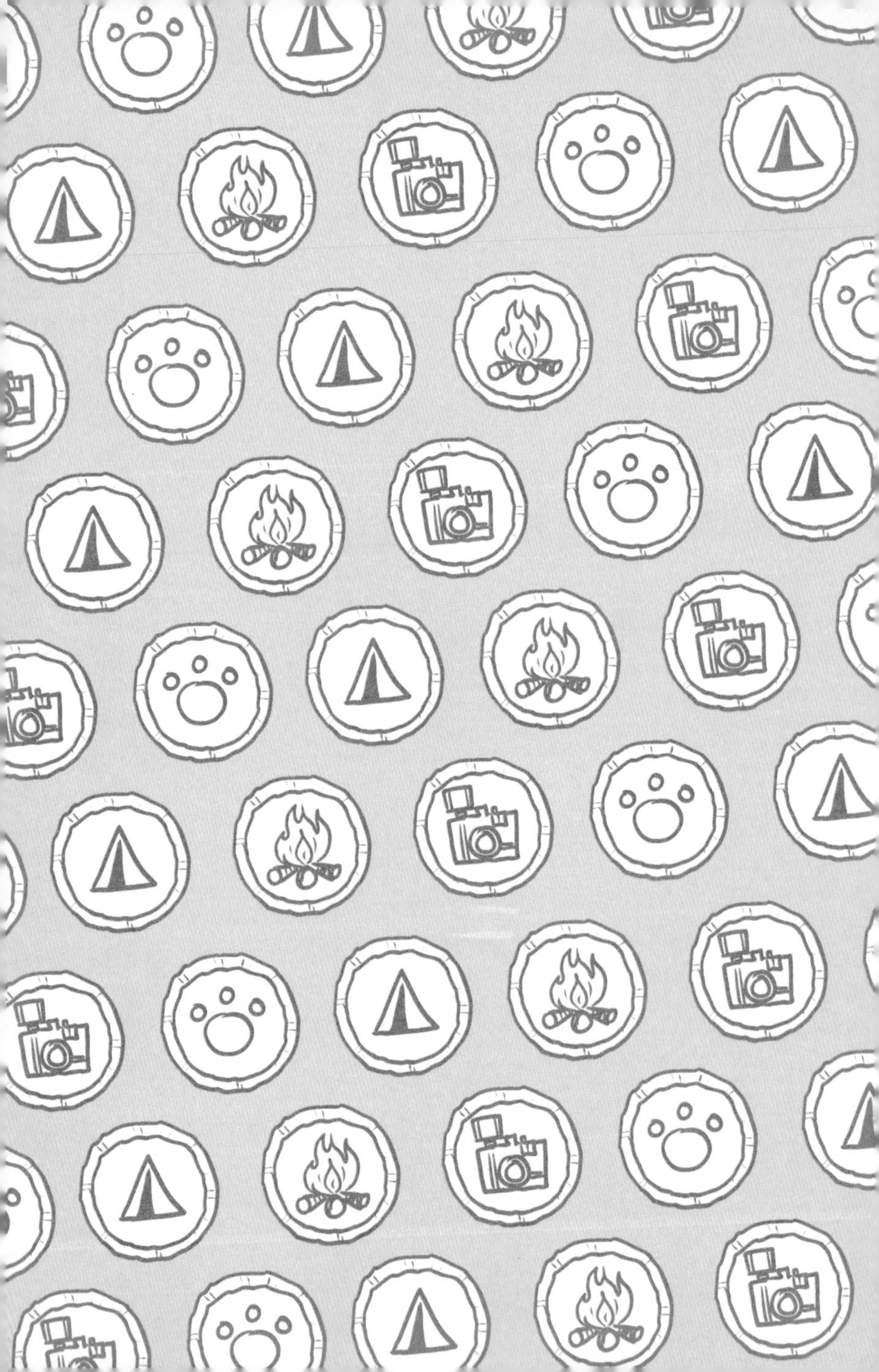

The Misadventures of
SALEM HYDE

3

Cookie Catastrophe

Frank Cammuso

AMU...S
N...

Hardcover ISBN: 978-1-4197-1198-5
Paperback ISBN: 978-1-4197-1199-2

Text and illustrations copyright © 2014 Frank Cammuso
Book design by Frank Cammuso and Sara Corbett

Printed and bound in China
10 9 8 7 6 5 4 3 2 1

Amulet Books are available at special discounts when purchased in quantity for premiums and promotions as well as fundraising or educational use. Special editions can also be created to specification. For details, contact specialsales@abramsbooks.com or the address below.

ABRAMS
THE ART OF BOOKS SINCE 1949

115 West 18th Street
New York, NY 10011
www.abramsbooks.com

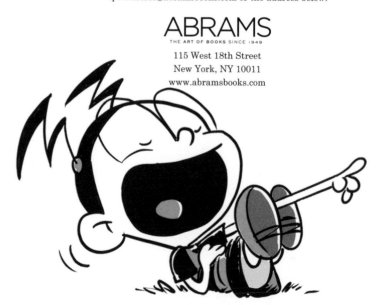

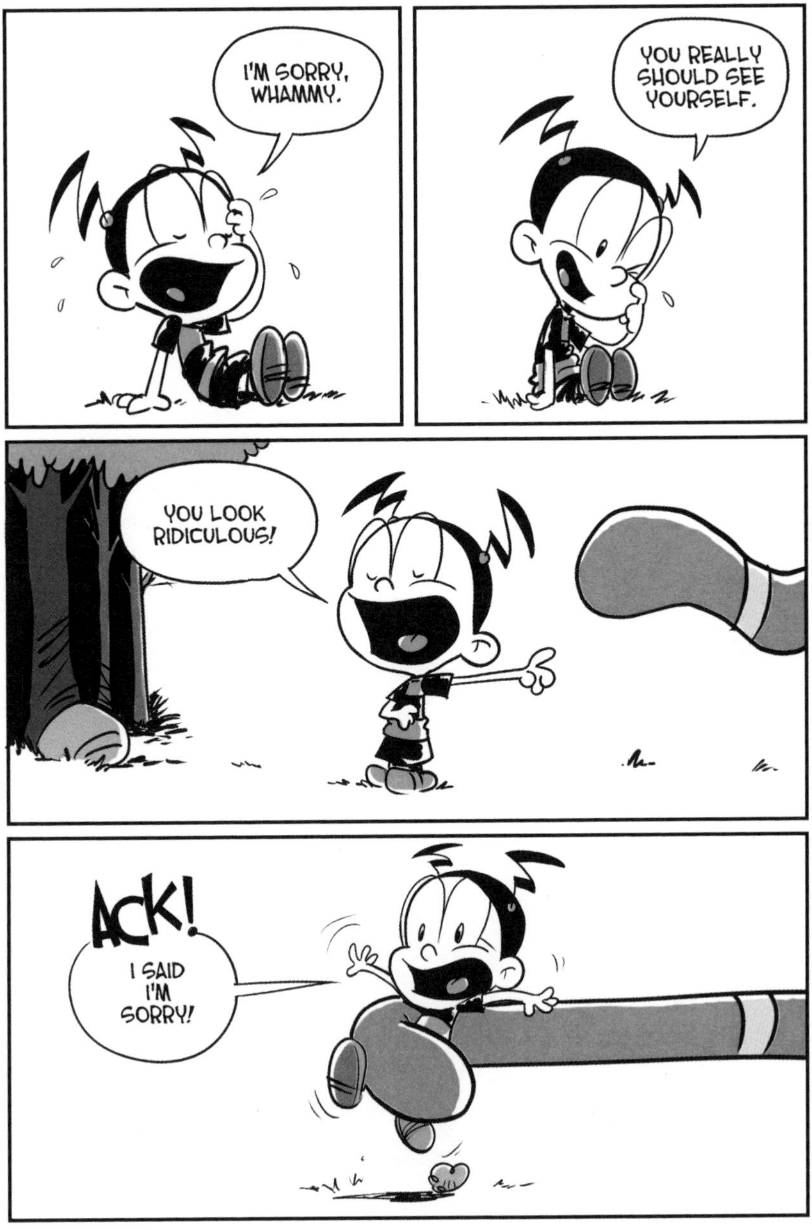
I'M SORRY, WHAMMY.
YOU REALLY SHOULD SEE YOURSELF.
YOU LOOK RIDICULOUS!
ACK!
I SAID I'M SORRY!

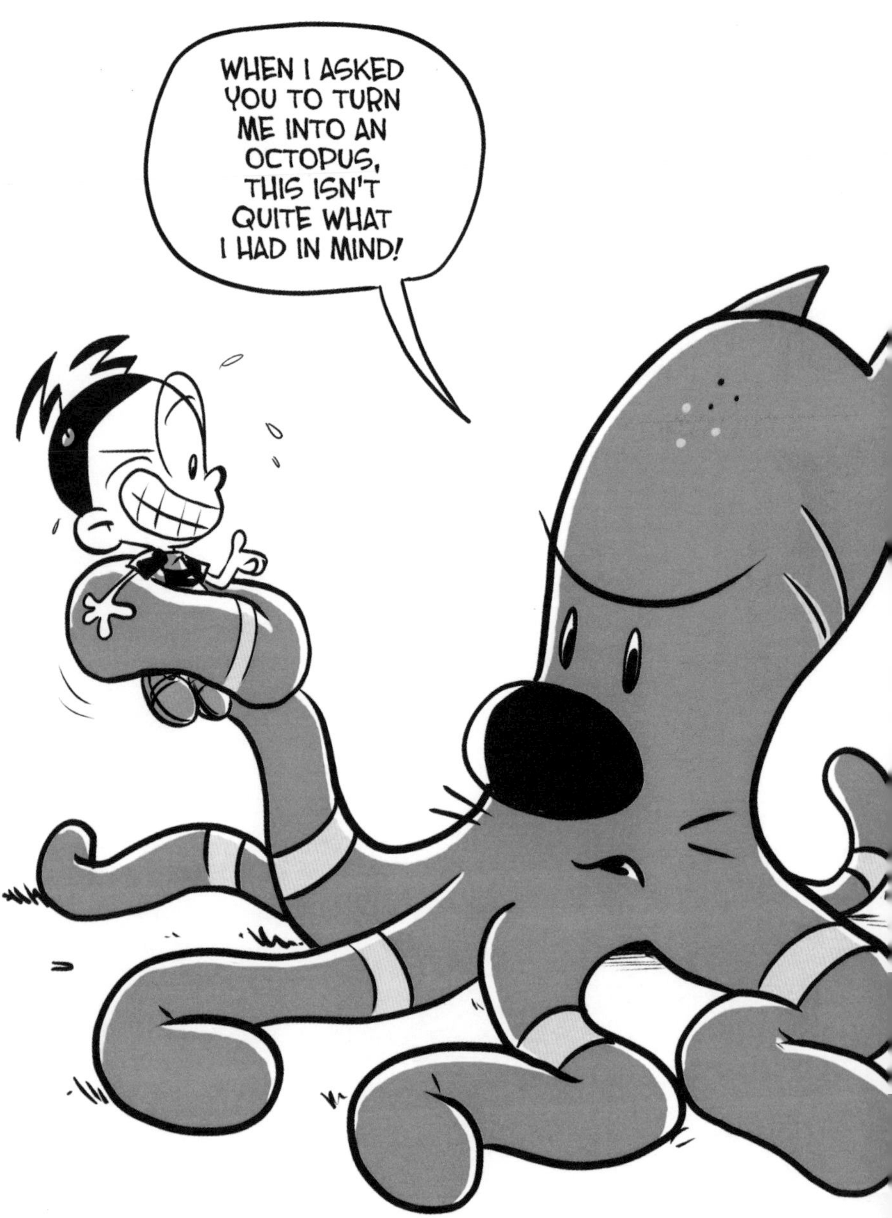
WHEN I ASKED YOU TO TURN ME INTO AN OCTOPUS, THIS ISN'T QUITE WHAT I HAD IN MIND!

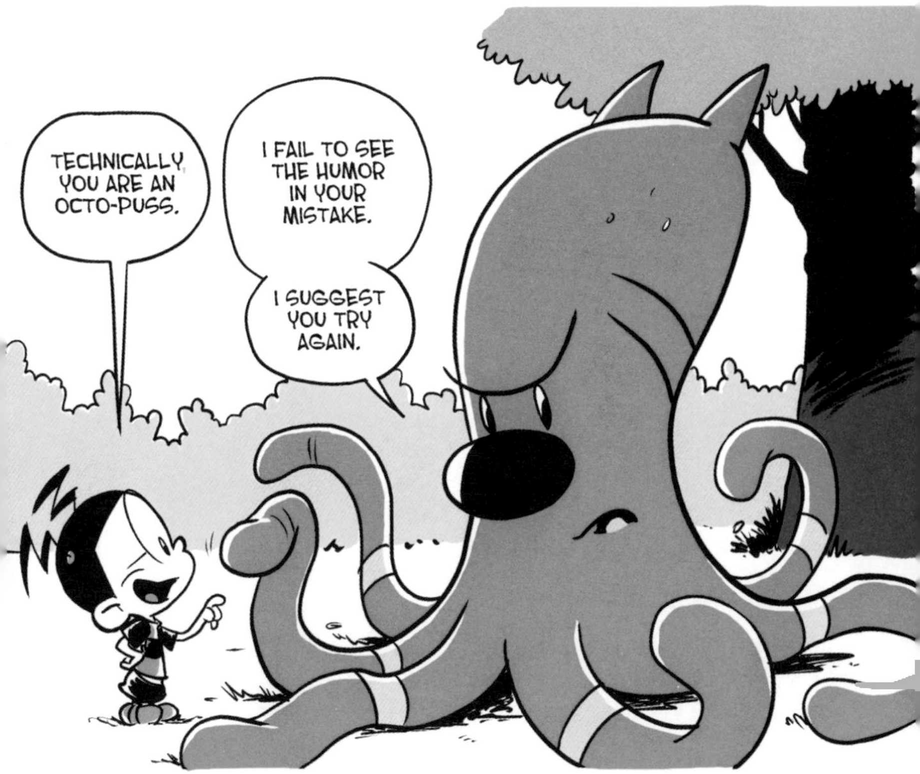
TECHNICALLY YOU ARE AN OCTO-PUSS.
I FAIL TO SEE THE HUMOR IN YOUR MISTAKE.
I SUGGEST YOU TRY AGAIN.

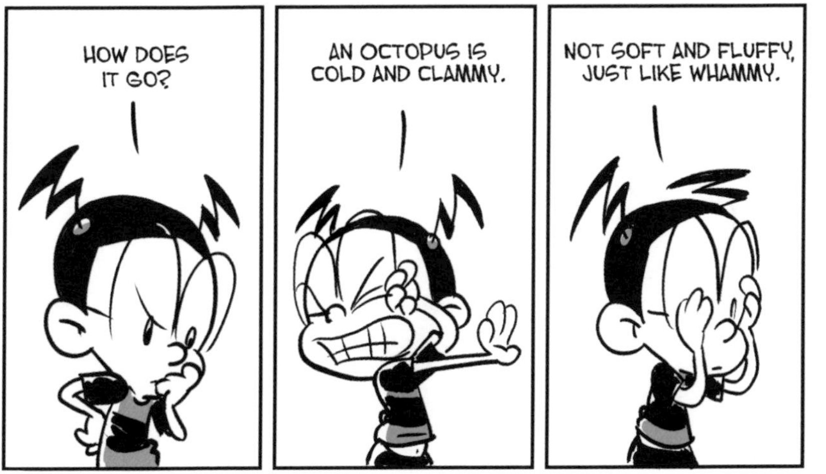
HOW DOES IT GO?
AN OCTOPUS IS COLD AND CLAMMY.
NOT SOFT AND FLUFFY, JUST LIKE WHAMMY.

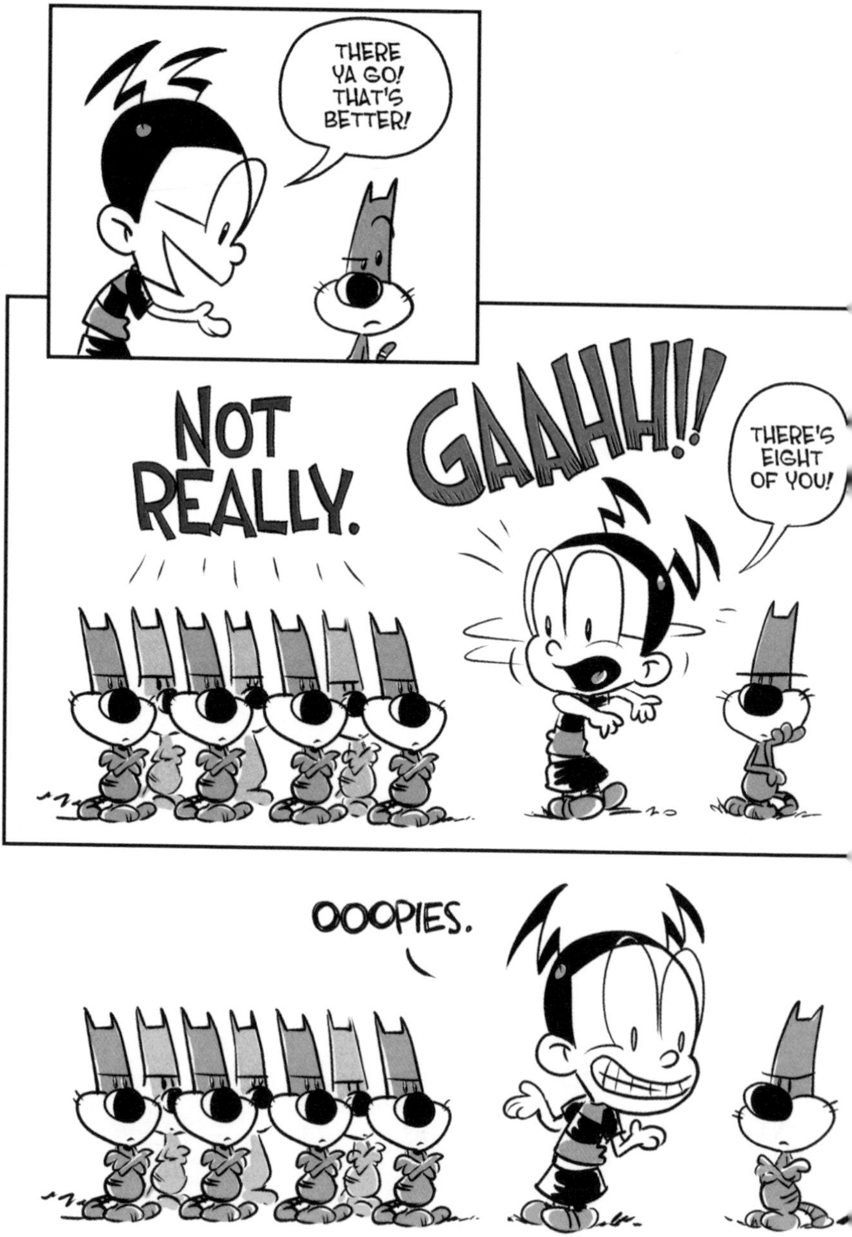
THERE YA GO! THAT'S BETTER!
NOT REALLY.
GAAHH!!
THERE'S EIGHT OF YOU!
OOOPIES.

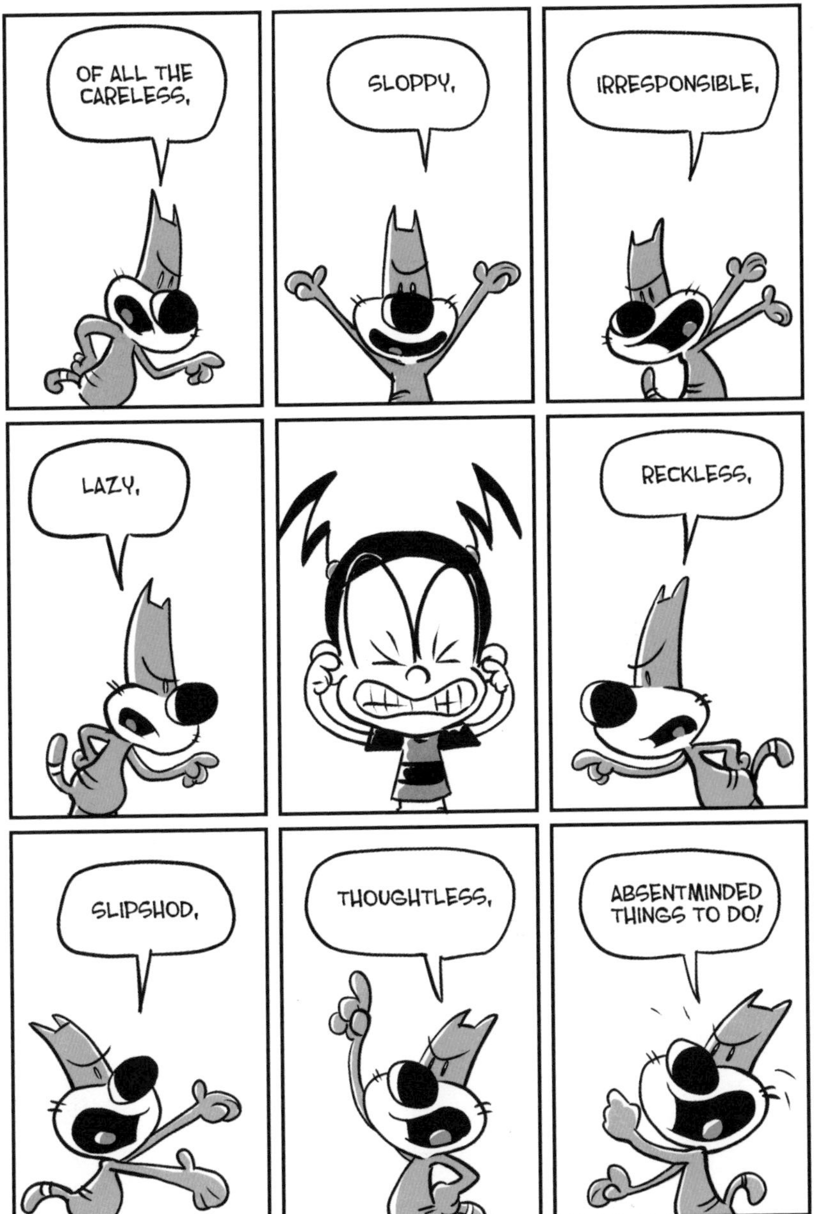
OF ALL THE CARELESS,
SLOPPY,
IRRESPONSIBLE,
LAZY,
RECKLESS,
SLIPSHOD,
THOUGHTLESS,
ABSENTMINDED THINGS TO DO!

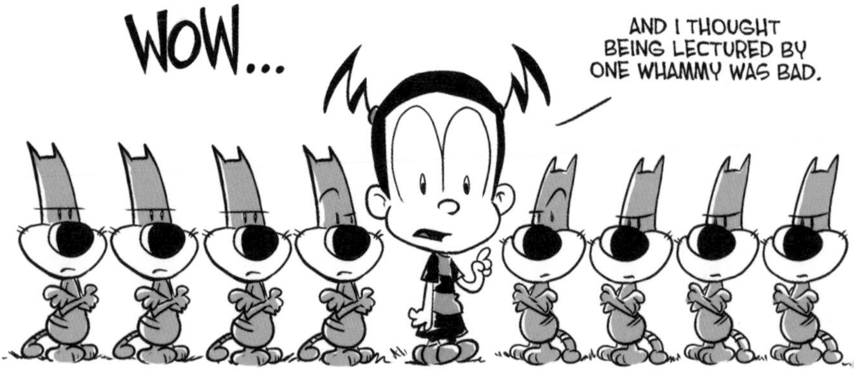
WOW...
AND I THOUGHT BEING LECTURED BY ONE WHAMMY WAS BAD.

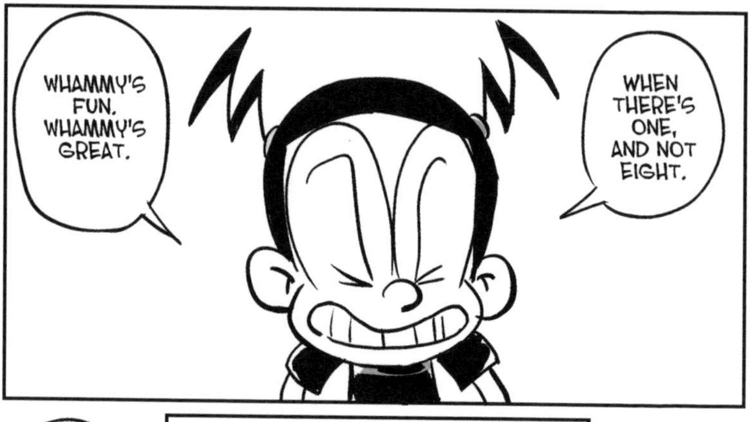
WHAMMY'S FUN. WHAMMY'S GREAT.
WHEN THERE'S ONE, AND NOT EIGHT.

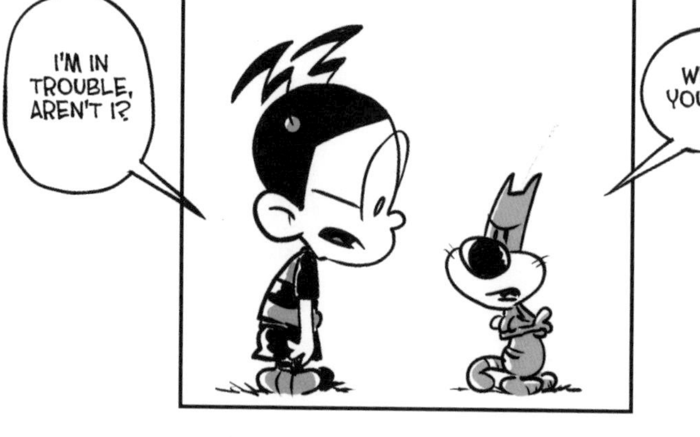
I'M IN TROUBLE, AREN'T I?
WHAT DO YOU THINK?

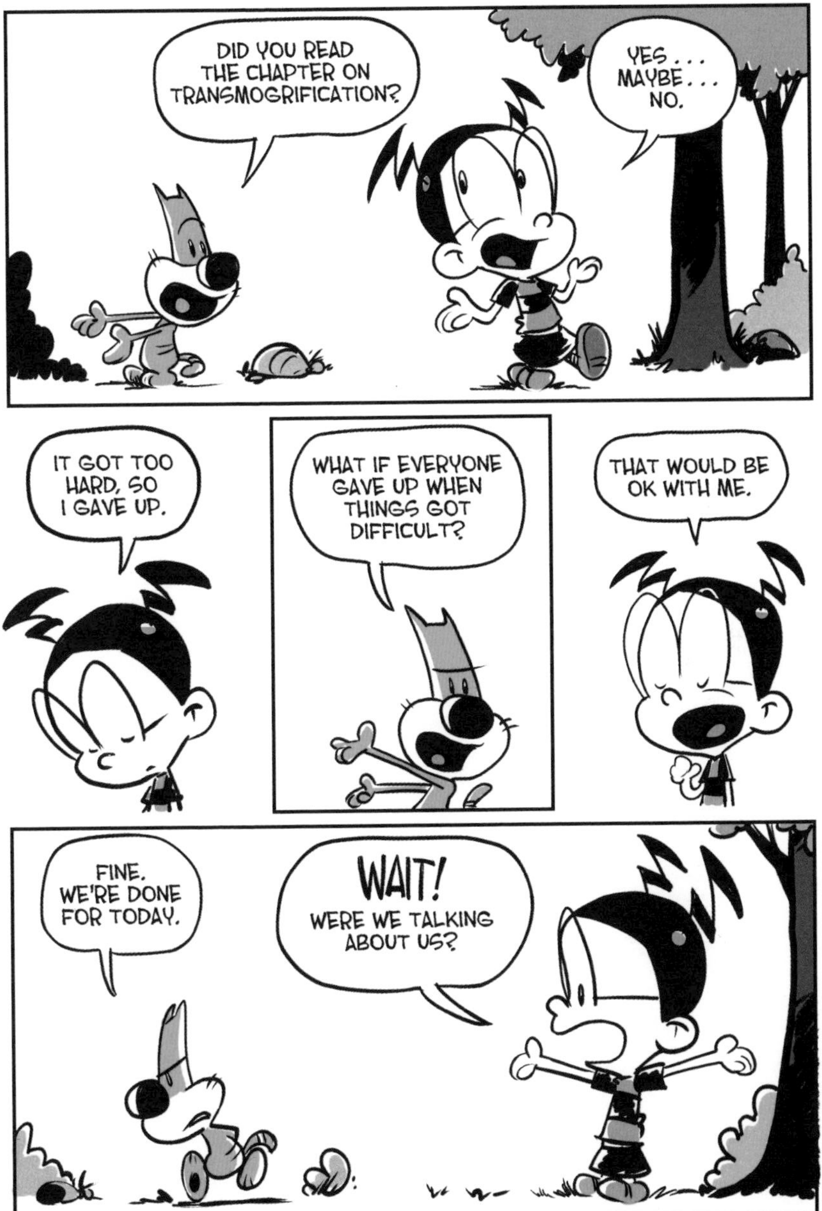
DID YOU READ THE CHAPTER ON TRANSMOGRIFICATION?
YES . . . MAYBE . . . NO.
IT GOT TOO HARD, SO I GAVE UP.
WHAT IF EVERYONE GAVE UP WHEN THINGS GOT DIFFICULT?
THAT WOULD BE OK WITH ME.
FINE. WE'RE DONE FOR TODAY.
WAIT! WERE WE TALKING ABOUT US?

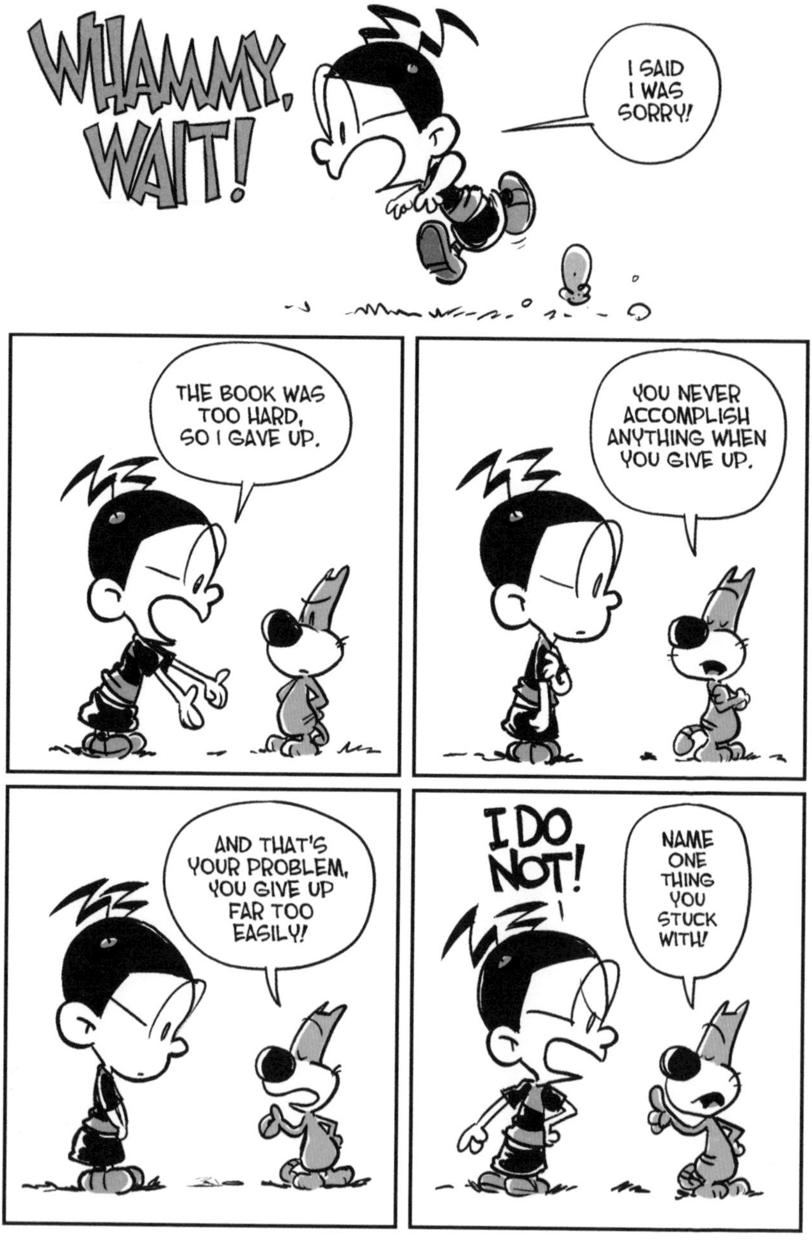
WHAMMY, WAIT!
I SAID I WAS SORRY!
THE BOOK WAS TOO HARD, SO I GAVE UP.
YOU NEVER ACCOMPLISH ANYTHING WHEN YOU GIVE UP.
AND THAT'S YOUR PROBLEM, YOU GIVE UP FAR TOO EASILY!
I DO NOT!
NAME ONE THING YOU STUCK WITH!

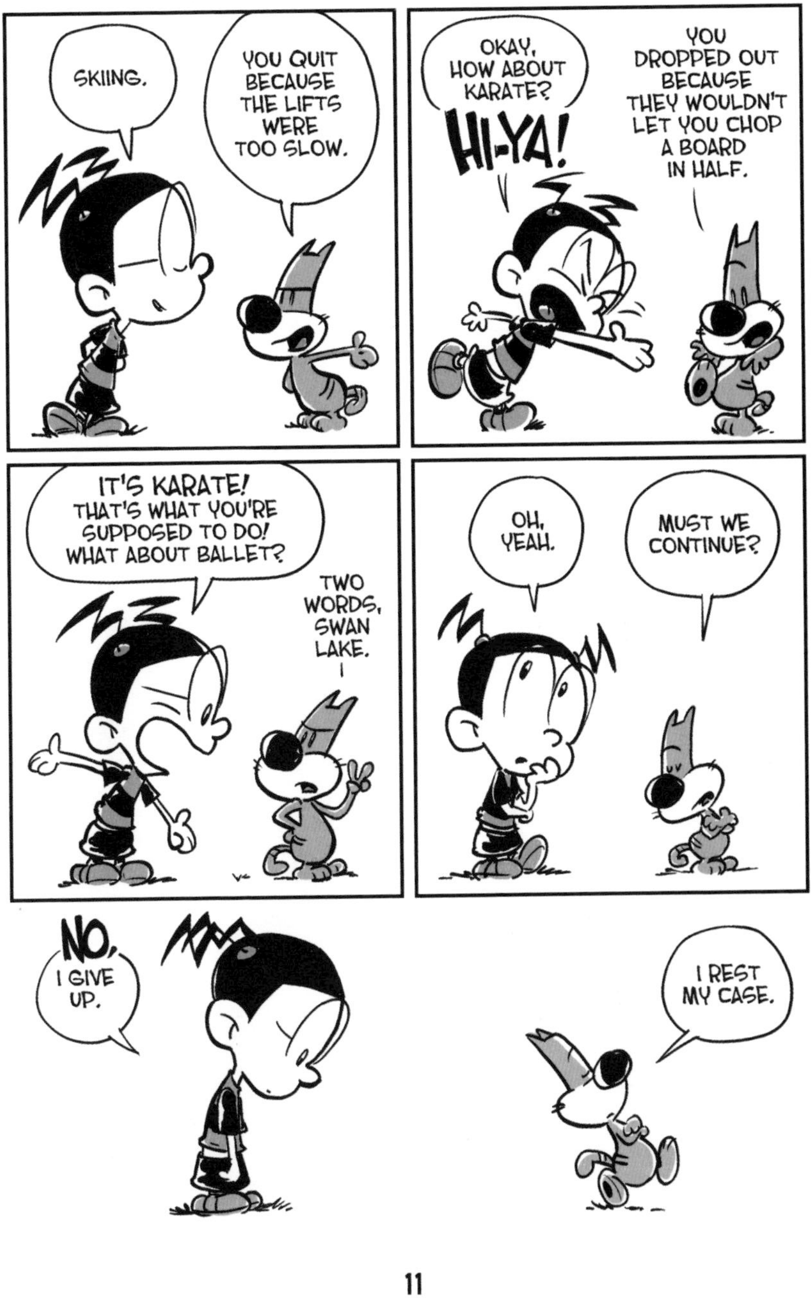
SKIING.
YOU QUIT BECAUSE THE LIFTS WERE TOO SLOW.
OKAY, HOW ABOUT KARATE?
HI-YA!
YOU DROPPED OUT BECAUSE THEY WOULDN'T LET YOU CHOP A BOARD IN HALF.
IT'S KARATE! THAT'S WHAT YOU'RE SUPPOSED TO DO! WHAT ABOUT BALLET?
TWO WORDS, SWAN LAKE.
OH, YEAH.
MUST WE CONTINUE?
NO, I GIVE UP.
I REST MY CASE.

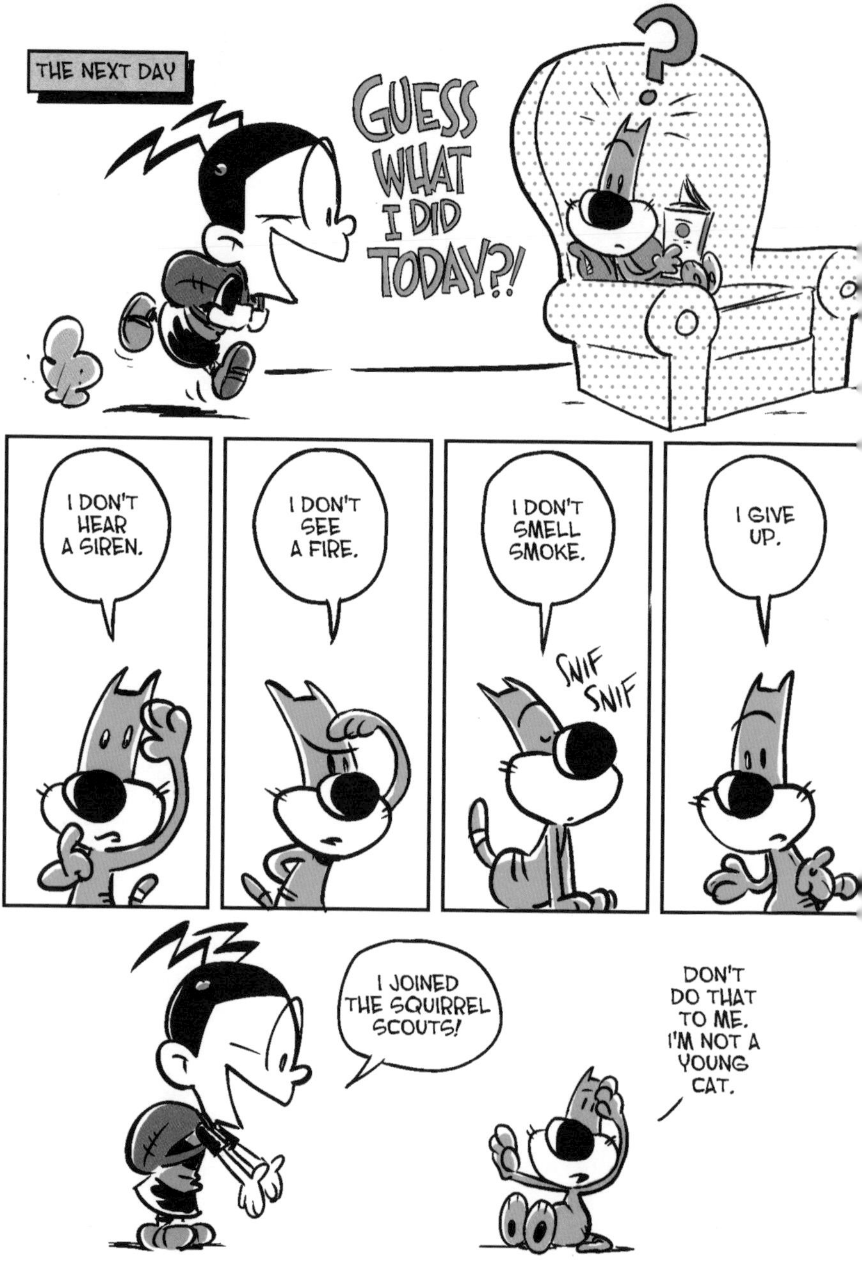
THE NEXT DAY
GUESS WHAT I DID TODAY?!
?
I DON'T HEAR A SIREN.
I DON'T SEE A FIRE.
I DON'T SMELL SMOKE.
SNIF SNIF
I GIVE UP.
I JOINED THE SQUIRREL SCOUTS!
DON'T DO THAT TO ME. I'M NOT A YOUNG CAT.

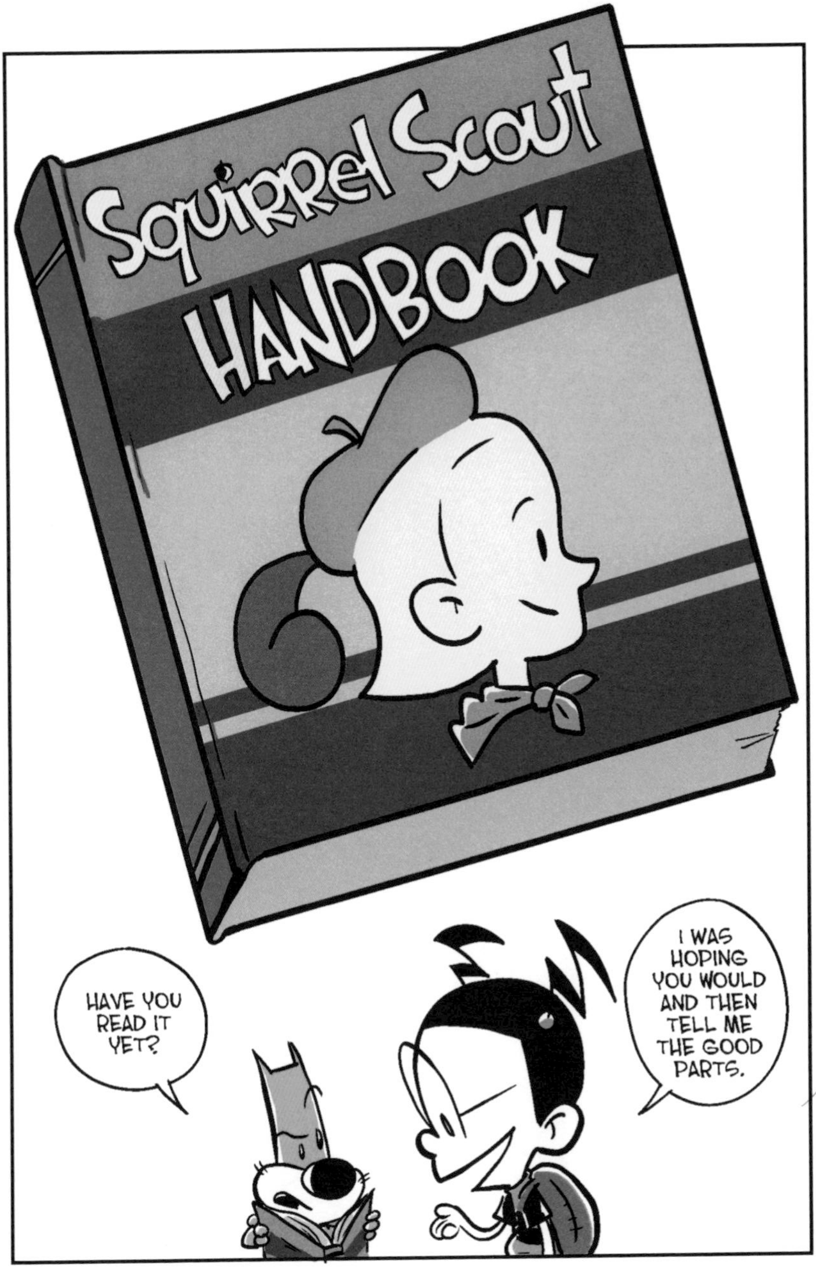
Squirrel Scout HANDBOOK
HAVE YOU READ IT YET?
I WAS HOPING YOU WOULD AND THEN TELL ME THE GOOD PARTS.

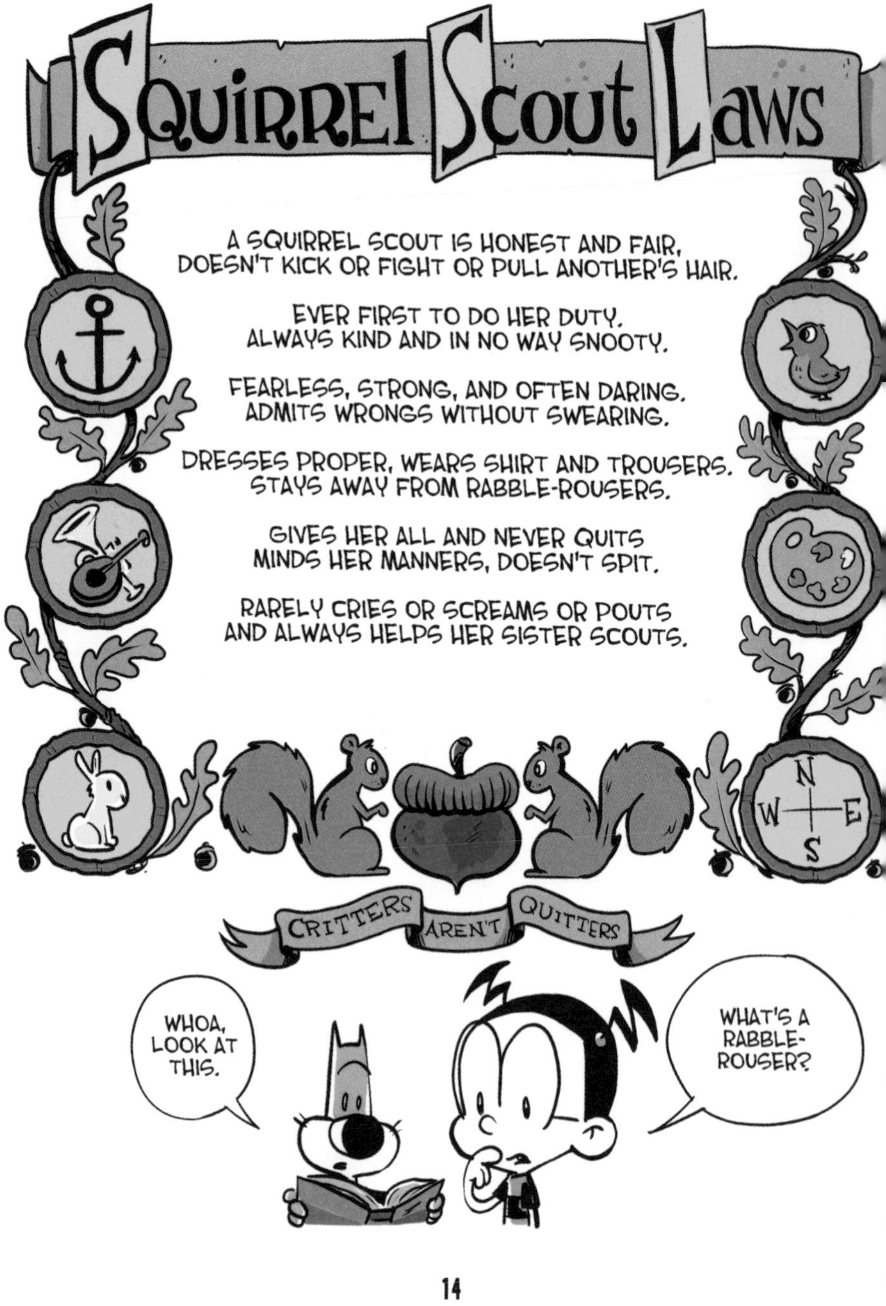
SQUIRREL SCOUT LAWS
A SQUIRREL SCOUT IS HONEST AND FAIR,
DOESN'T KICK OR FIGHT OR PULL ANOTHER'S HAIR.
EVER FIRST TO DO HER DUTY.
ALWAYS KIND AND IN NO WAY SNOOTY.
FEARLESS, STRONG, AND OFTEN DARING.
ADMITS WRONGS WITHOUT SWEARING.
DRESSES PROPER, WEARS SHIRT AND TROUSERS.
STAYS AWAY FROM RABBLE-ROUSERS.
GIVES HER ALL AND NEVER QUITS
MINDS HER MANNERS, DOESN'T SPIT.
RARELY CRIES OR SCREAMS OR POUTS
AND ALWAYS HELPS HER SISTER SCOUTS.
N
W
E
S
CRITTERS AREN'T QUITTERS
WHOA, LOOK AT THIS.
WHAT'S A RABBLE-ROUSER?

PART 1
BECOMING A Squirrel Scout

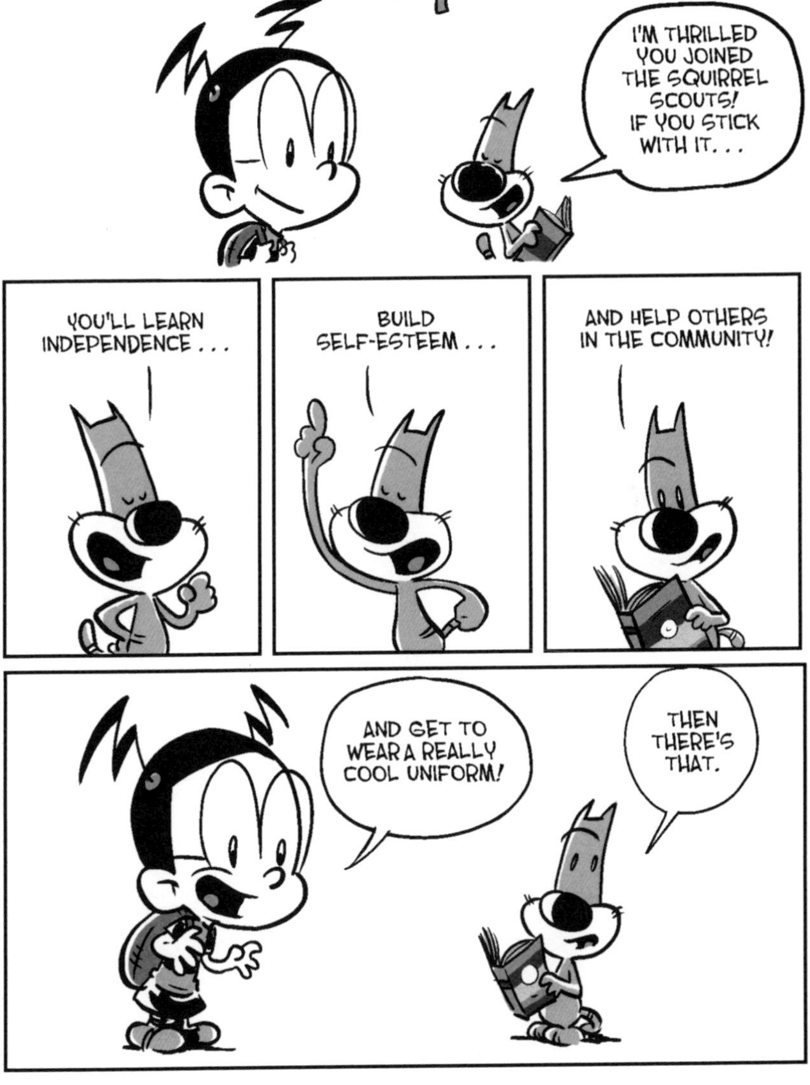

I'M THRILLED YOU JOINED THE SQUIRREL SCOUTS! IF YOU STICK WITH IT. . .
YOU'LL LEARN INDEPENDENCE . . .
BUILD SELF-ESTEEM . . .
AND HELP OTHERS IN THE COMMUNITY!
AND GET TO WEAR A REALLY COOL UNIFORM!
THEN THERE'S THAT.

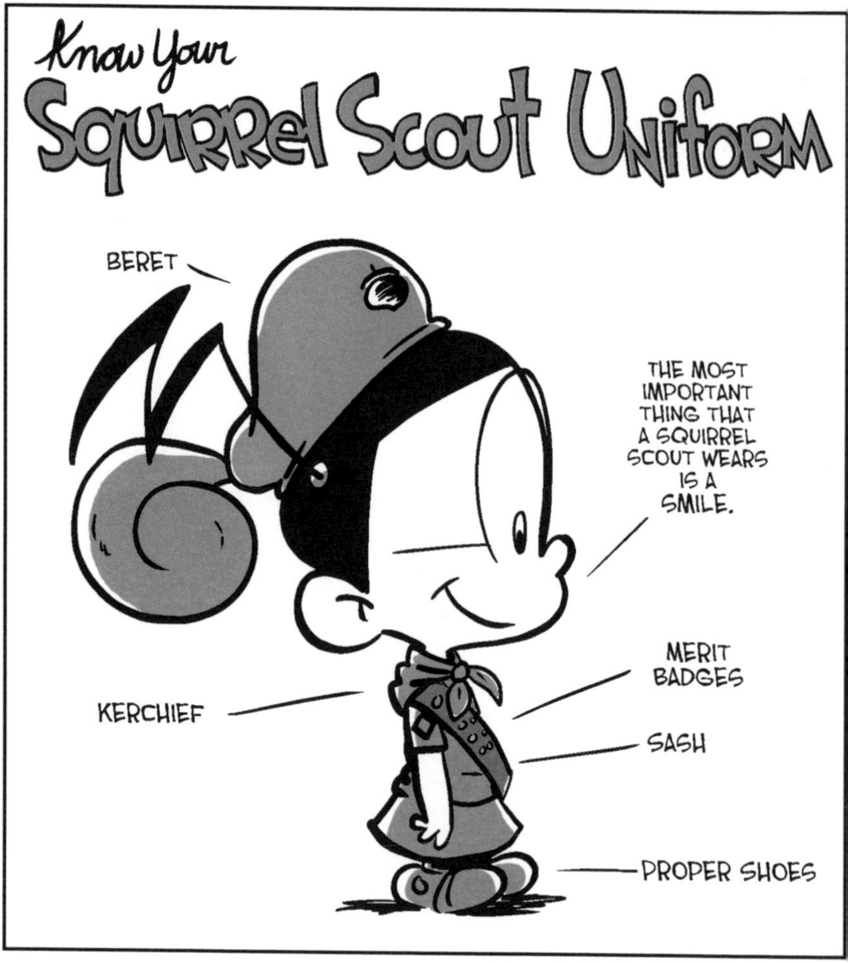
Know Your
Squirrel Scout Uniform
BERET
THE MOST IMPORTANT THING THAT A SQUIRREL SCOUT WEARS IS A SMILE.
MERIT BADGES
KERCHIEF
SASH
PROPER SHOES

SAMPLE MERIT BADGES

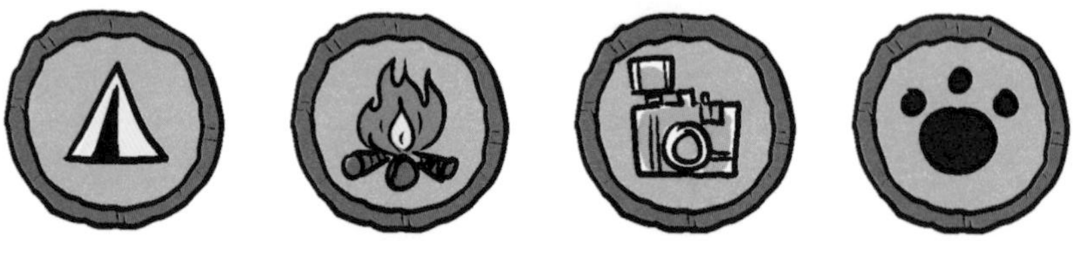

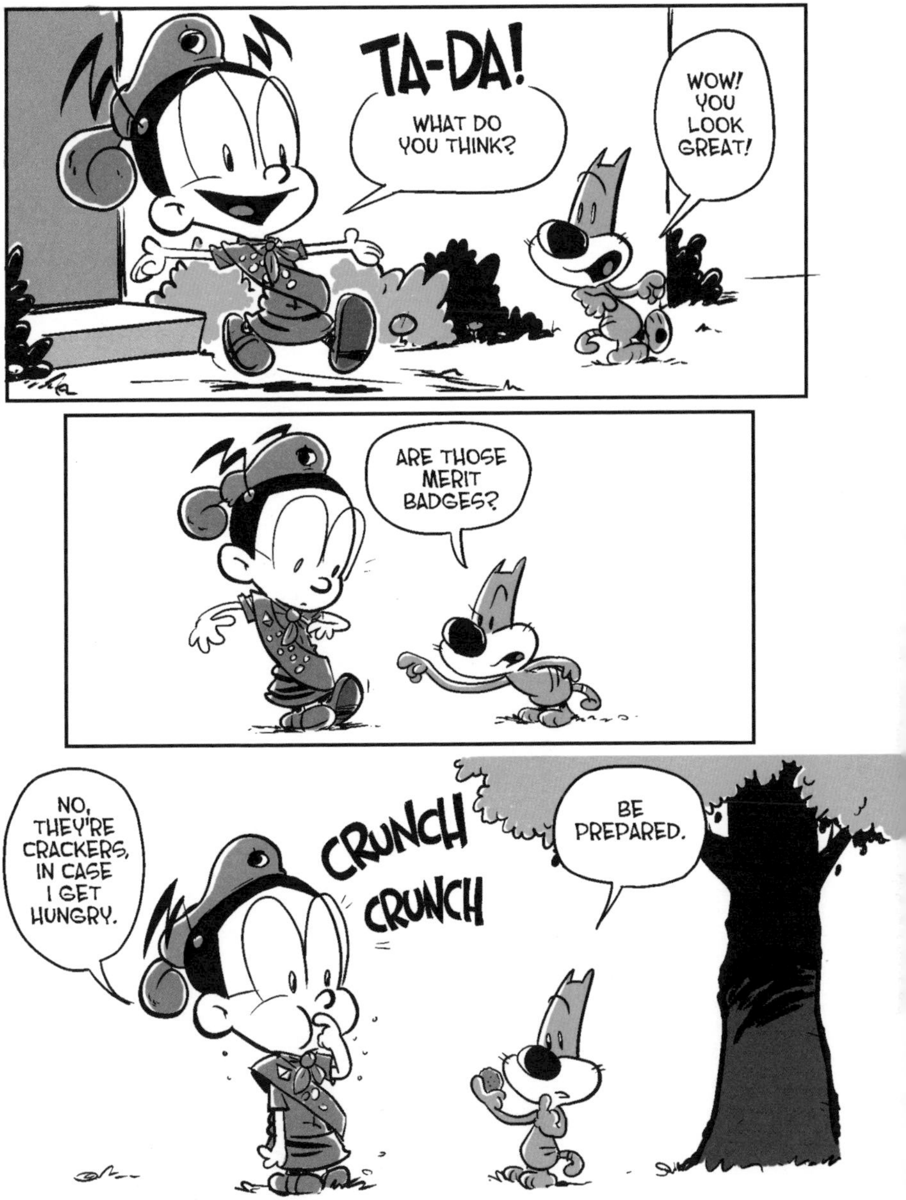
TA-DA!
WHAT DO YOU THINK?
WOW! YOU LOOK GREAT!
ARE THOSE MERIT BADGES?
NO, THEY'RE CRACKERS, IN CASE I GET HUNGRY.
CRUNCH
CRUNCH
BE PREPARED.

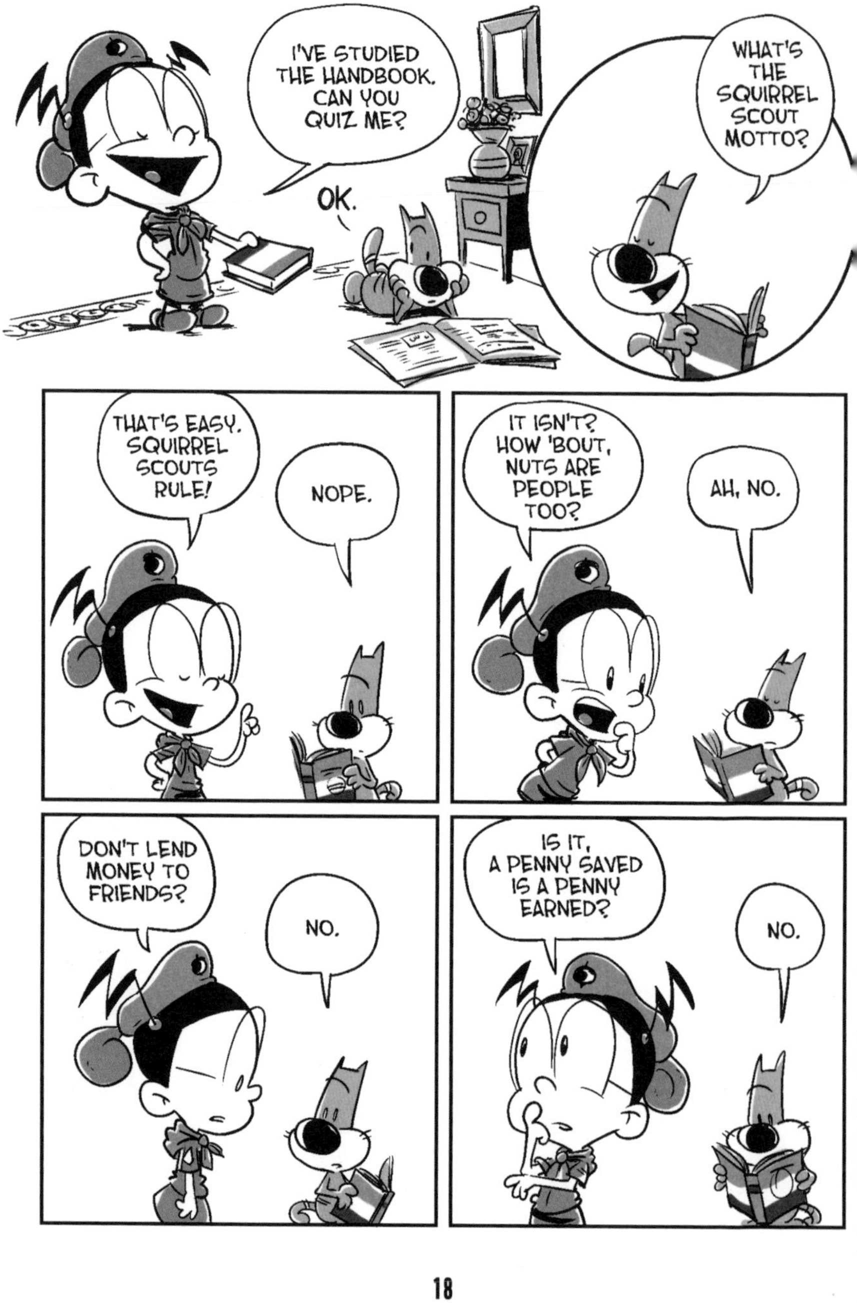
I'VE STUDIED THE HANDBOOK. CAN YOU QUIZ ME?
OK.
WHAT'S THE SQUIRREL SCOUT MOTTO?
THAT'S EASY. SQUIRREL SCOUTS RULE!
NOPE.
IT ISN'T? HOW 'BOUT, NUTS ARE PEOPLE TOO?
AH, NO.
DON'T LEND MONEY TO FRIENDS?
NO.
IS IT, A PENNY SAVED IS A PENNY EARNED?
NO.

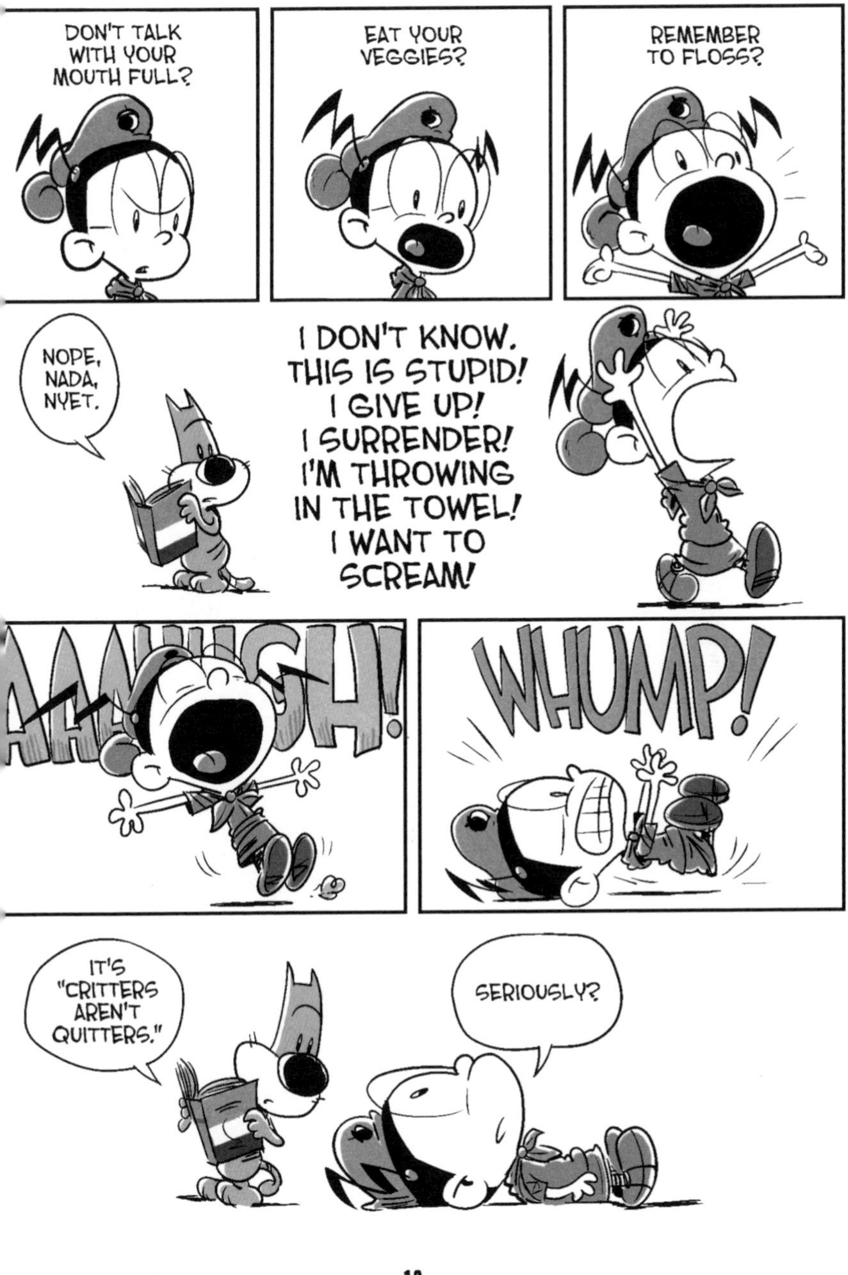

DON'T TALK WITH YOUR MOUTH FULL?
EAT YOUR VEGGIES?
REMEMBER TO FLOSS?
NOPE, NADA, NYET.
I DON'T KNOW. THIS IS STUPID! I GIVE UP! I SURRENDER! I'M THROWING IN THE TOWEL! I WANT TO SCREAM!
WHUMP!
IT'S "CRITTERS AREN'T QUITTERS."
SERIOUSLY?

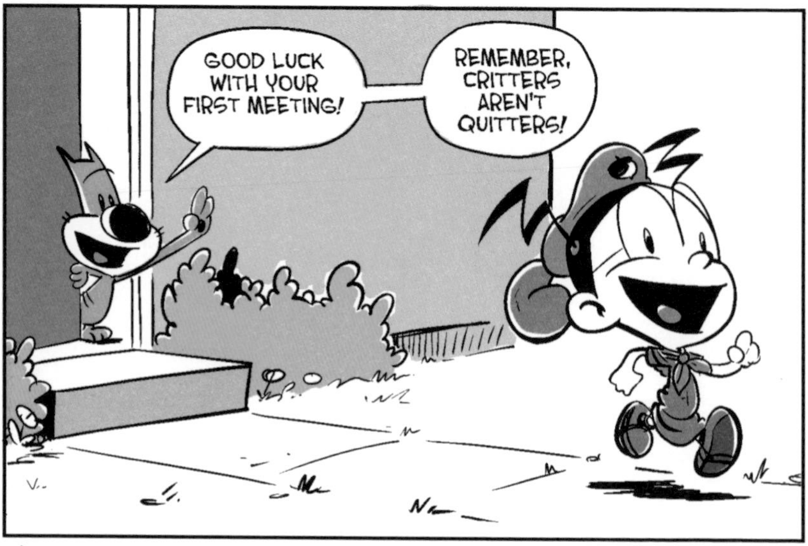
GOOD LUCK WITH YOUR FIRST MEETING!
REMEMBER, CRITTERS AREN'T QUITTERS!

A FEW HOURS LATER...

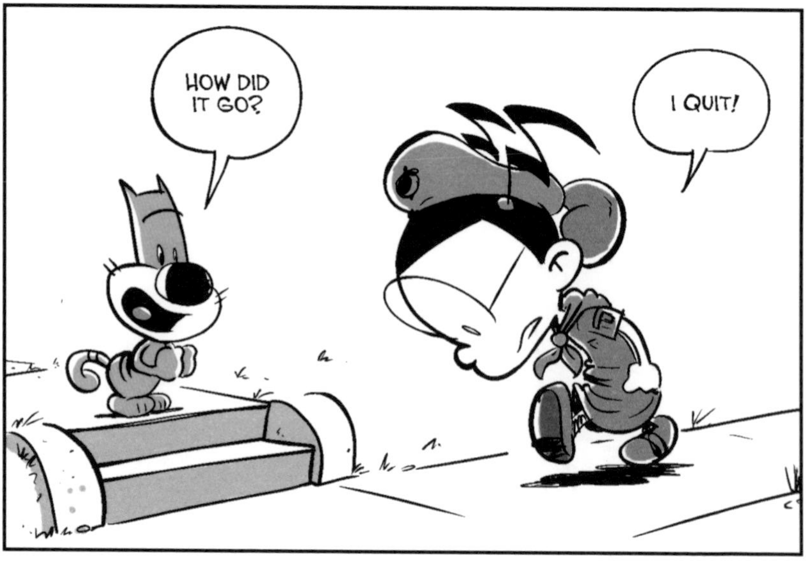
HOW DID IT GO?
I QUIT!

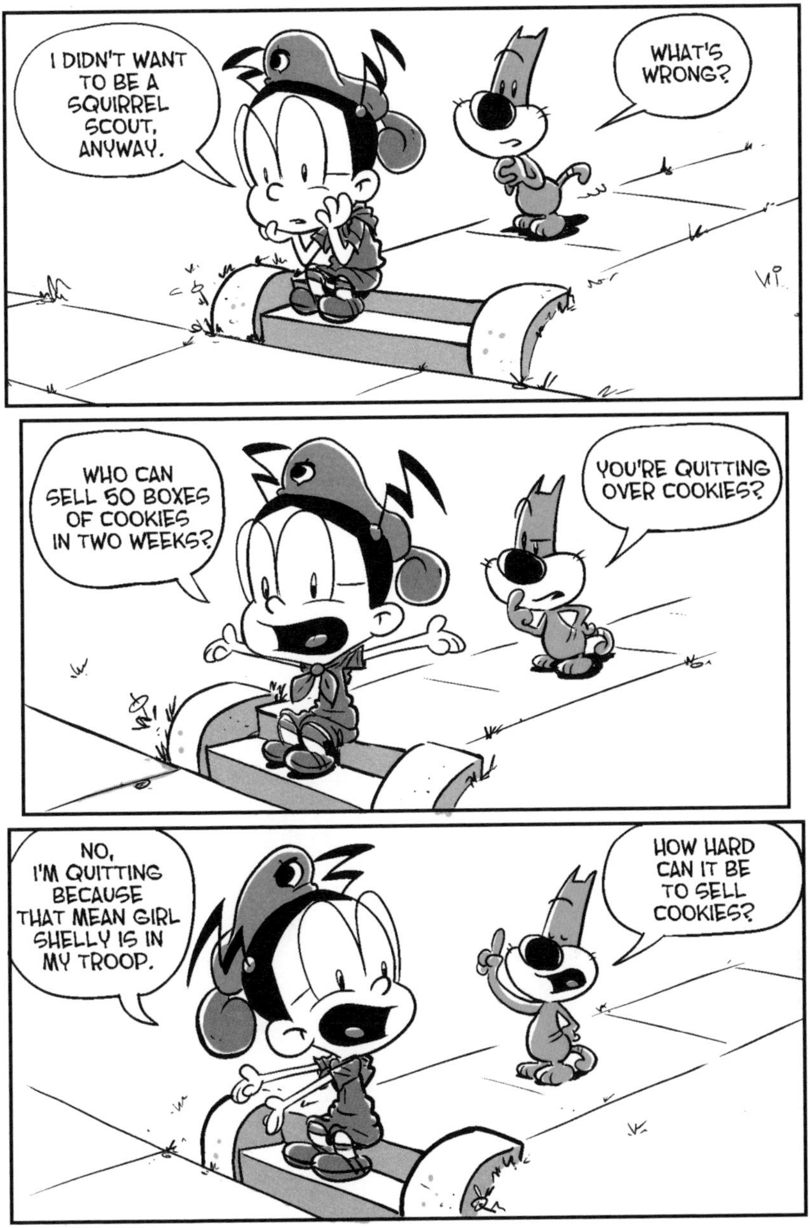
I DIDN'T WANT TO BE A SQUIRREL SCOUT, ANYWAY.
WHAT'S WRONG?
WHO CAN SELL 50 BOXES OF COOKIES IN TWO WEEKS?
YOU'RE QUITTING OVER COOKIES?
NO, I'M QUITTING BECAUSE THAT MEAN GIRL SHELLY IS IN MY TROOP.
HOW HARD CAN IT BE TO SELL COOKIES?

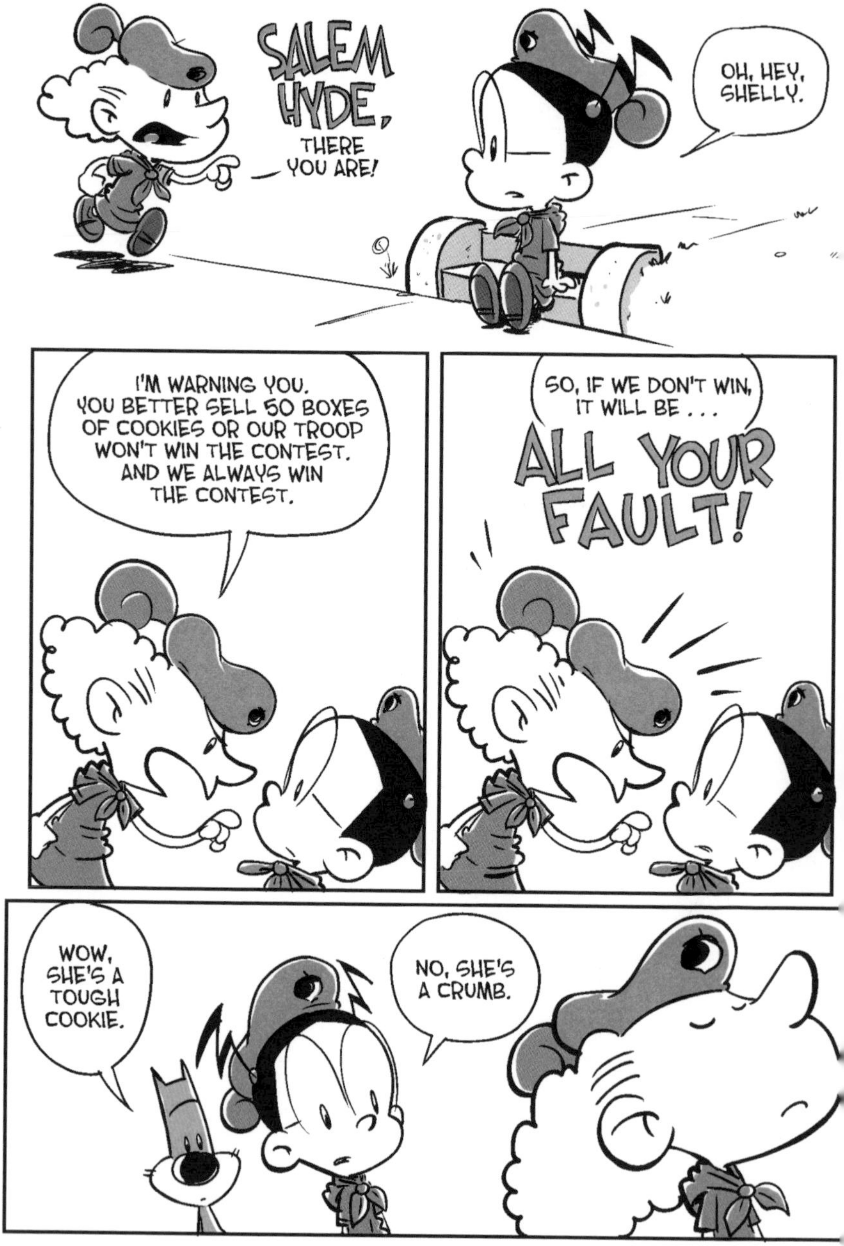
SALEM HYDE, THERE YOU ARE!
OH, HEY, SHELLY.
I'M WARNING YOU. YOU BETTER SELL 50 BOXES OF COOKIES OR OUR TROOP WON'T WIN THE CONTEST. AND WE ALWAYS WIN THE CONTEST.
SO, IF WE DON'T WIN, IT WILL BE . . .
ALL YOUR FAULT!
WOW, SHE'S A TOUGH COOKIE.
NO, SHE'S A CRUMB.

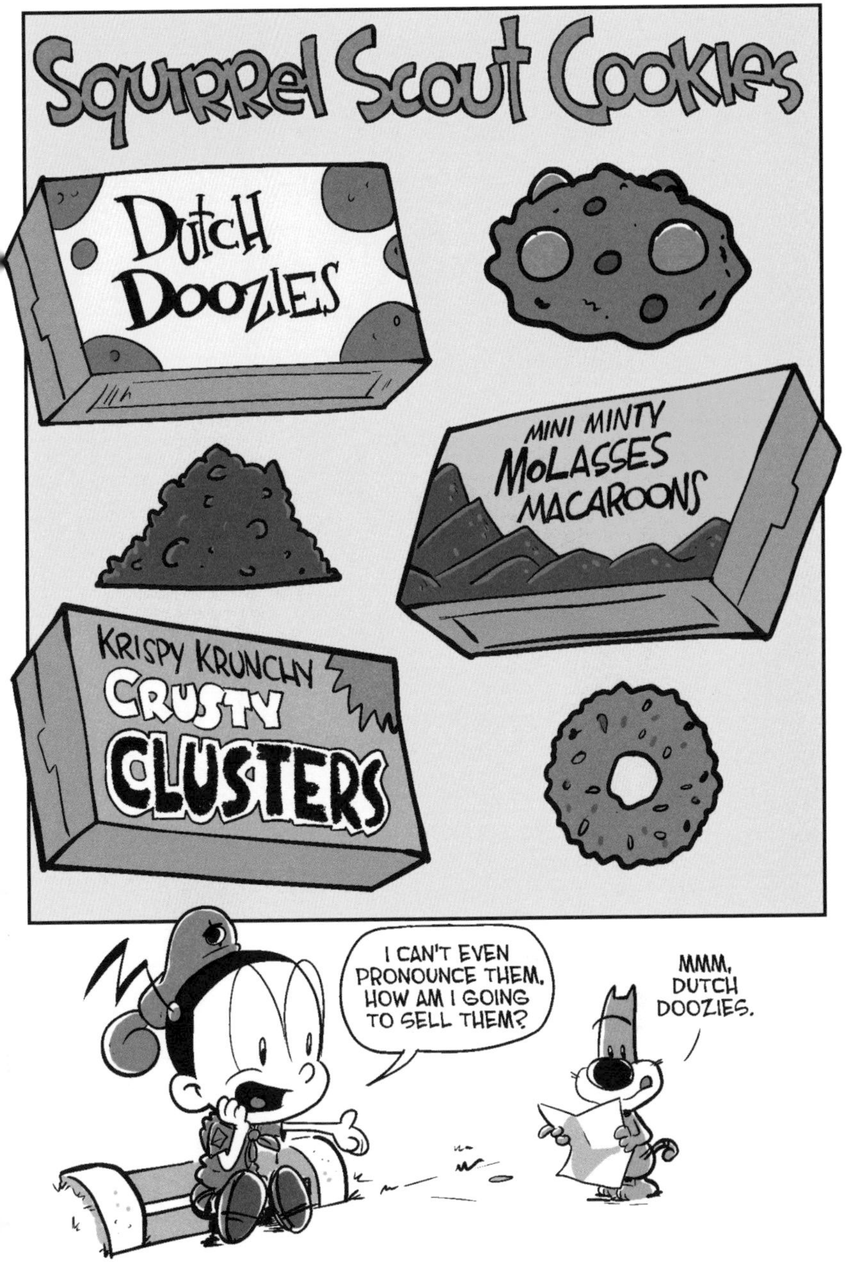
Squirrel Scout Cookies
Dutch Doozies
Mini Minty Molasses Macaroons
Krispy Krunchy Crusty Clusters
I CAN'T EVEN PRONOUNCE THEM. HOW AM I GOING TO SELL THEM?
MMM, DUTCH DOOZIES.

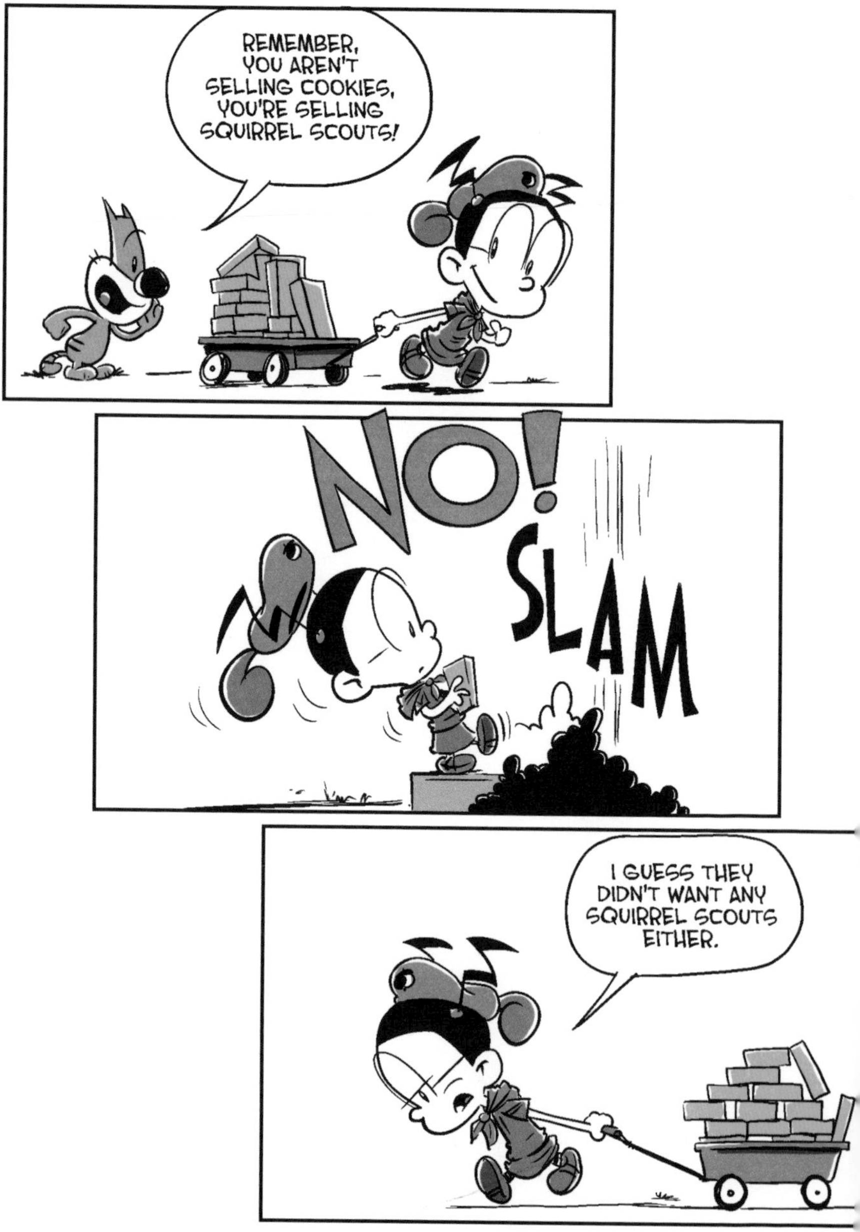
REMEMBER, YOU AREN'T SELLING COOKIES, YOU'RE SELLING SQUIRREL SCOUTS!
NO!
SLAM
I GUESS THEY DIDN'T WANT ANY SQUIRREL SCOUTS EITHER.

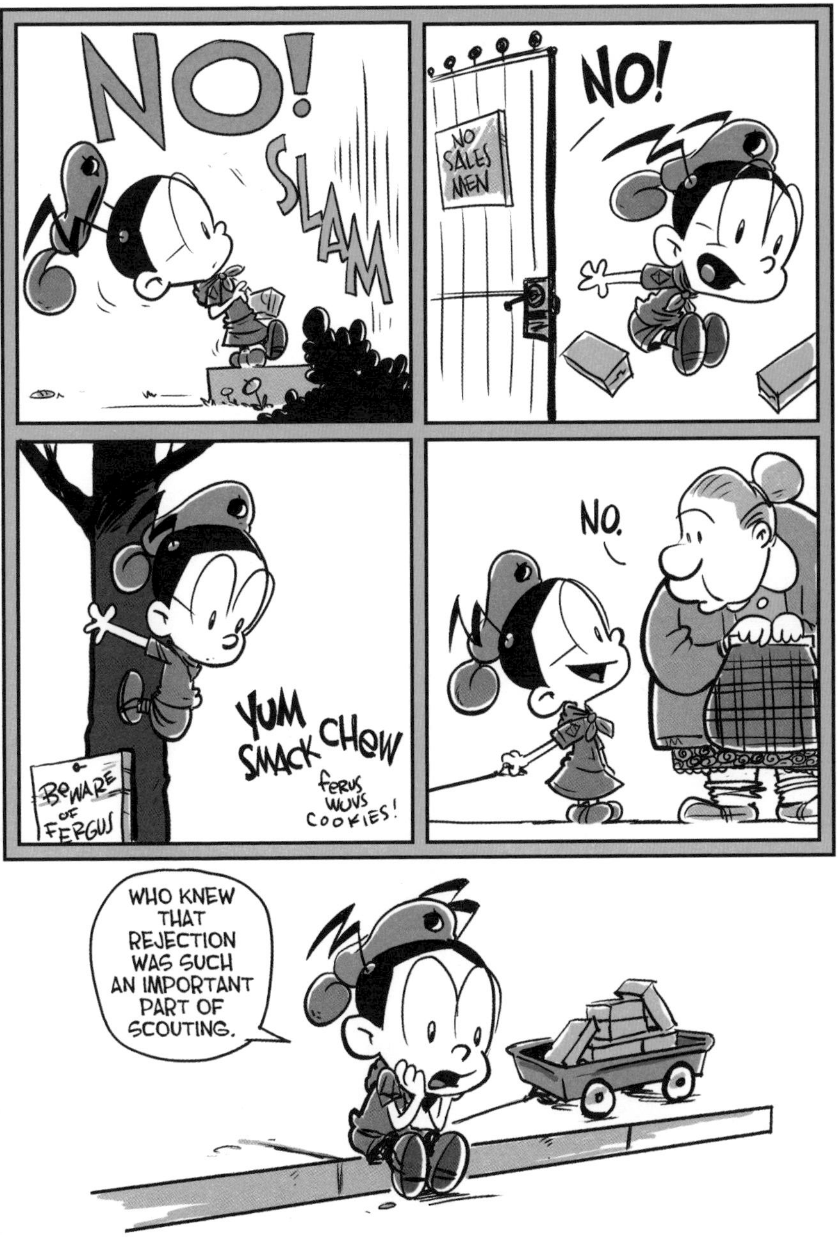
NO!
SLAM
NO SALES MEN
NO!
BEWARE OF FERGUS
YUM
SMACK CHEW
ferus wuvs cookies!
NO.
WHO KNEW THAT REJECTION WAS SUCH AN IMPORTANT PART OF SCOUTING.

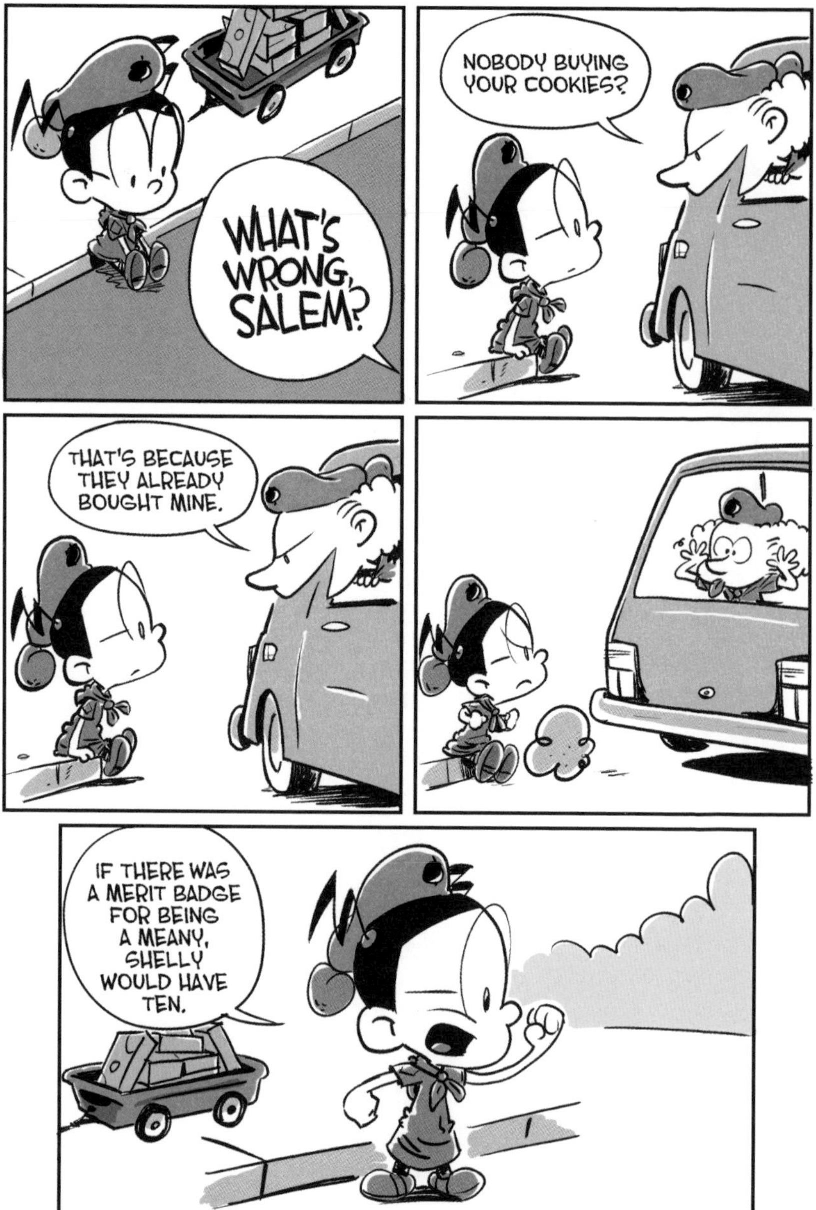
WHAT'S WRONG, SALEM?
NOBODY BUYING YOUR COOKIES?
THAT'S BECAUSE THEY ALREADY BOUGHT MINE.
IF THERE WAS A MERIT BADGE FOR BEING A MEANY, SHELLY WOULD HAVE TEN.

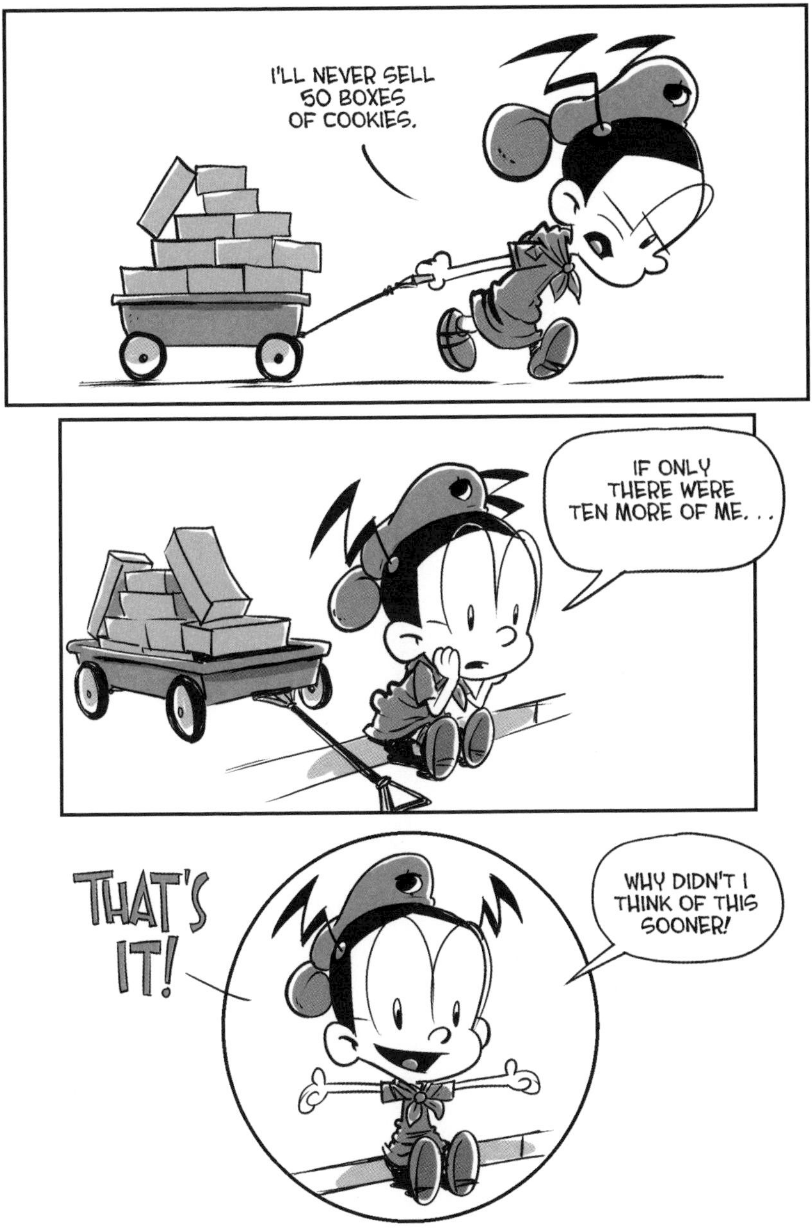
I'LL NEVER SELL 50 BOXES OF COOKIES.
IF ONLY THERE WERE TEN MORE OF ME. . .
THAT'S IT!
WHY DIDN'T I THINK OF THIS SOONER!

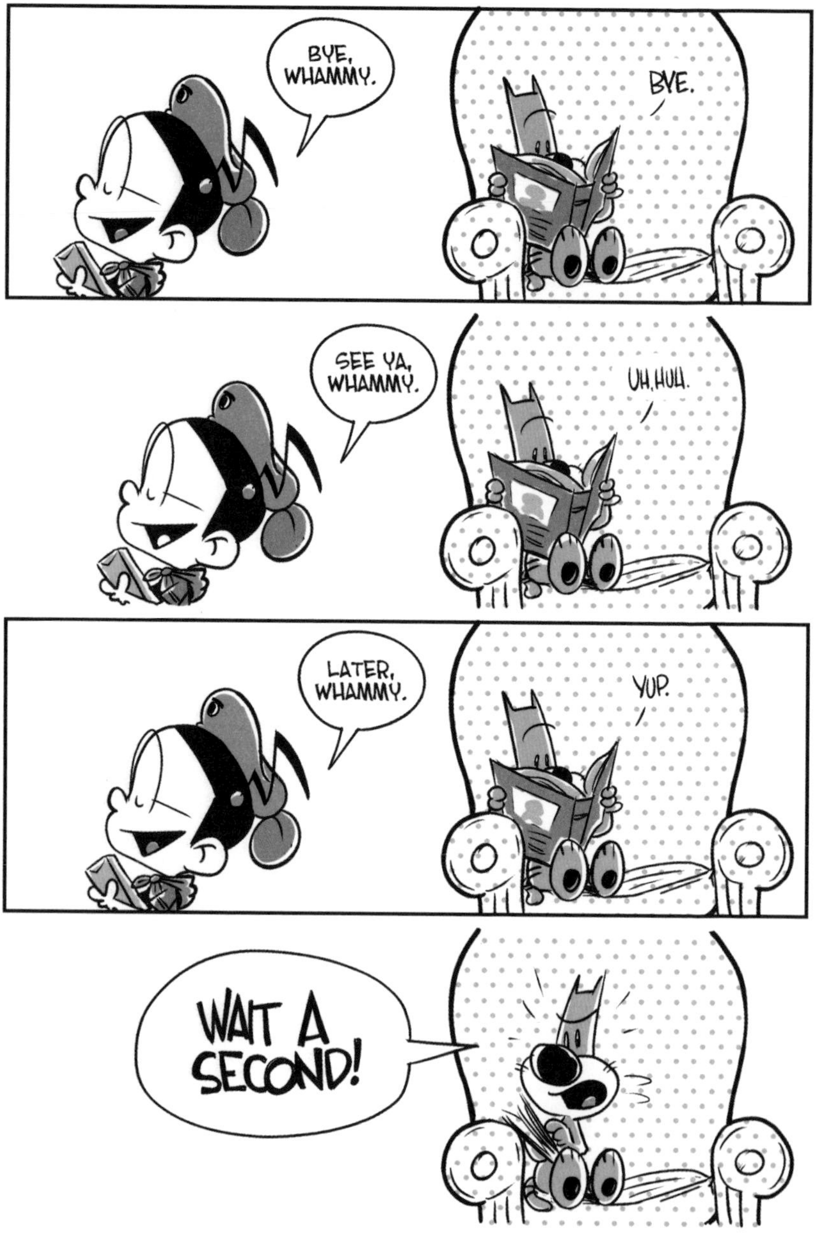
BYE, WHAMMY.
BYE.
SEE YA, WHAMMY.
UH, HUH.
LATER, WHAMMY.
YUP.
WAIT A SECOND!

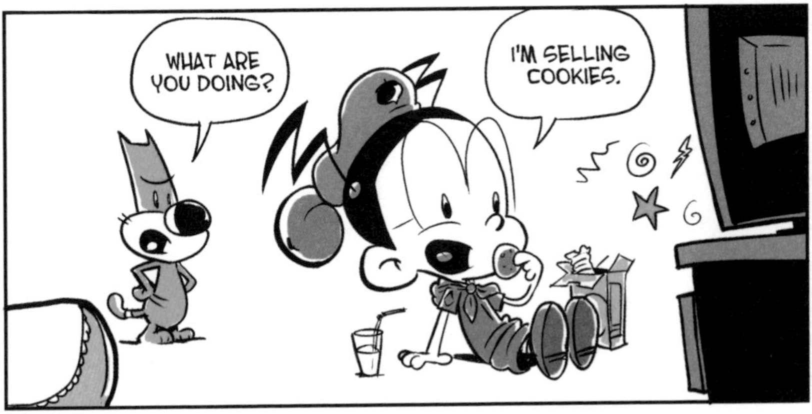
WHAT ARE YOU DOING?
I'M SELLING COOKIES.

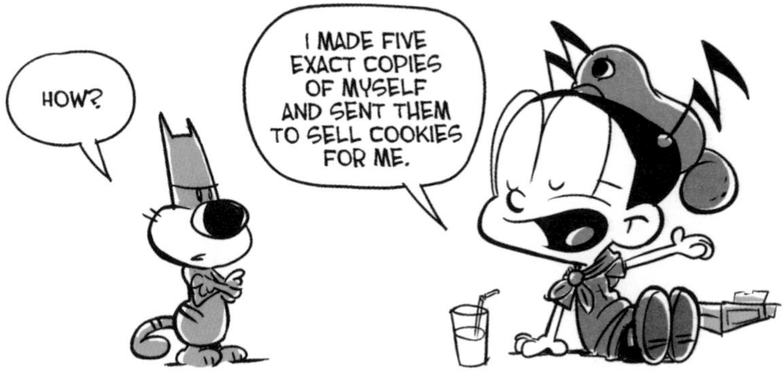
HOW?
I MADE FIVE EXACT COPIES OF MYSELF AND SENT THEM TO SELL COOKIES FOR ME.

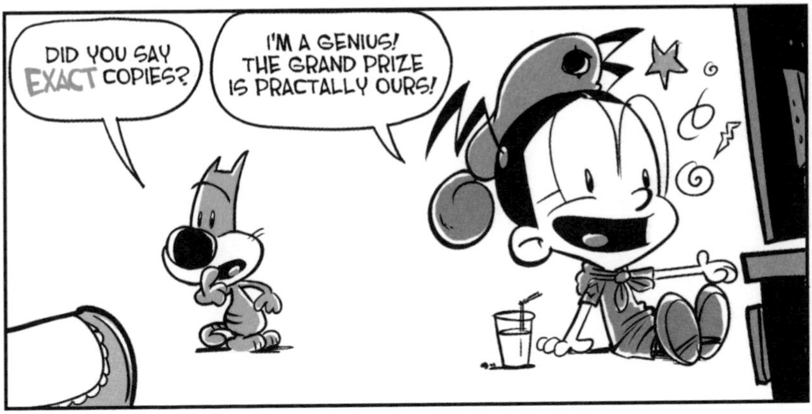
DID YOU SAY EXACT COPIES?
I'M A GENIUS! THE GRAND PRIZE IS PRACTALLY OURS!

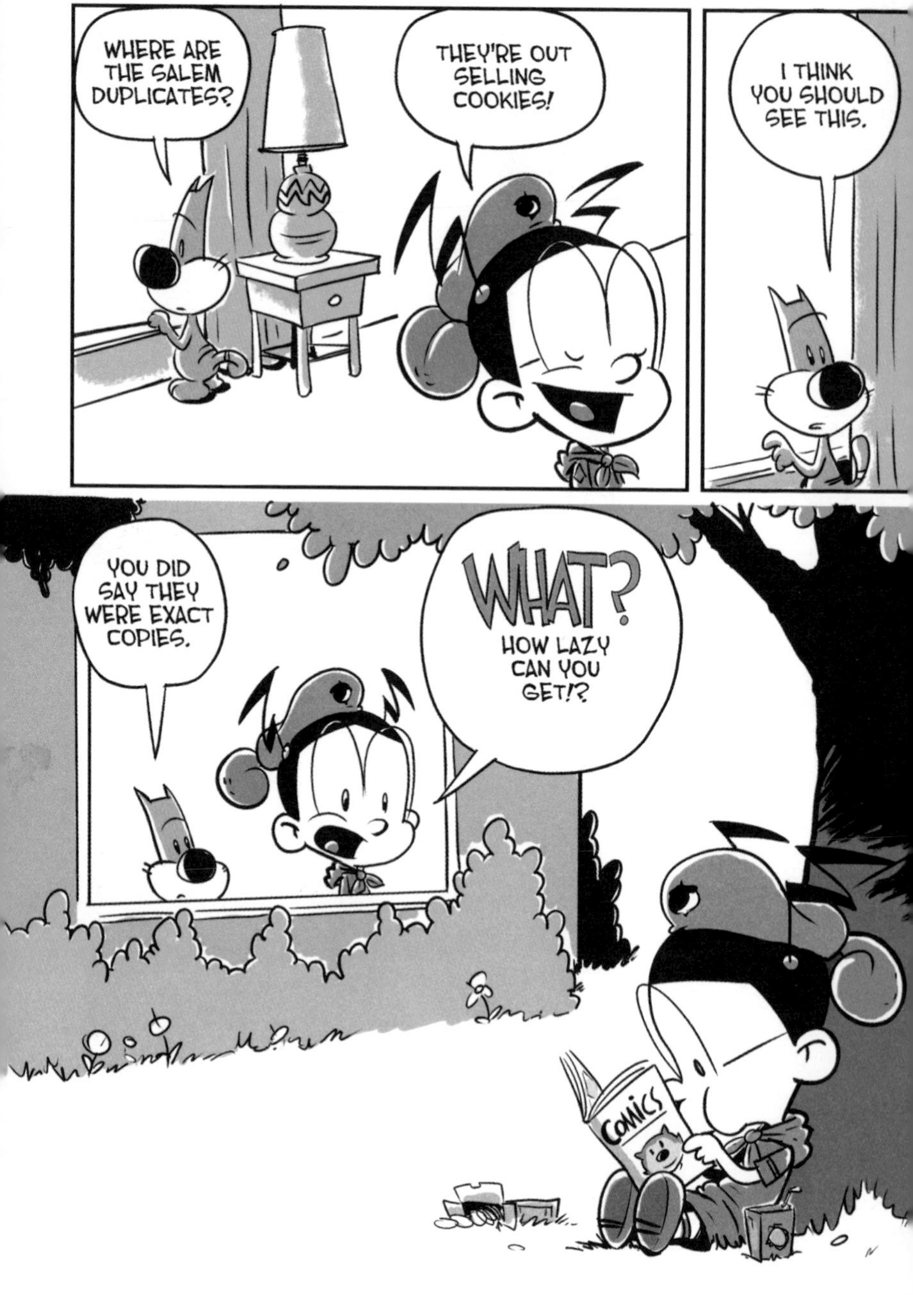
WHERE ARE THE SALEM DUPLICATES?
THEY'RE OUT SELLING COOKIES!
I THINK YOU SHOULD SEE THIS.
YOU DID SAY THEY WERE EXACT COPIES.
WHAT? HOW LAZY CAN YOU GET!?
COMICS

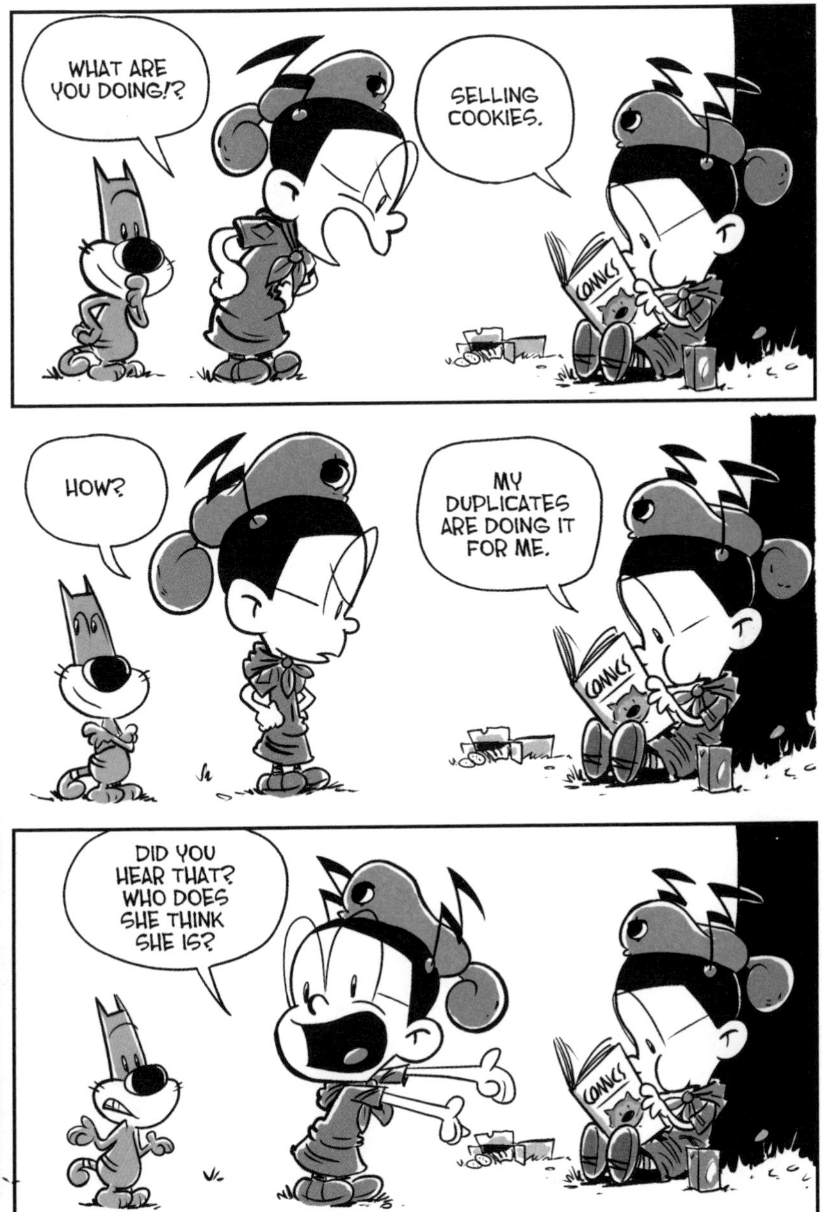
WHAT ARE YOU DOING!?
SELLING COOKIES.
HOW?
MY DUPLICATES ARE DOING IT FOR ME.
DID YOU HEAR THAT? WHO DOES SHE THINK SHE IS?
COMICS
COMICS
COMICS

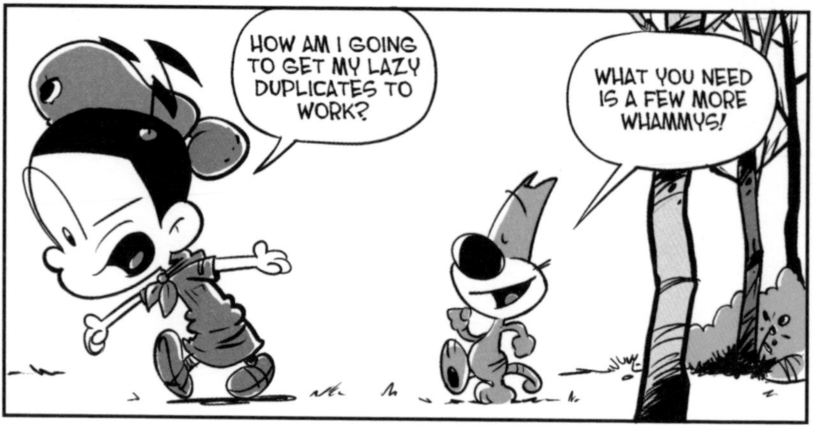
HOW AM I GOING TO GET MY LAZY DUPLICATES TO WORK?
WHAT YOU NEED IS A FEW MORE WHAMMYS!

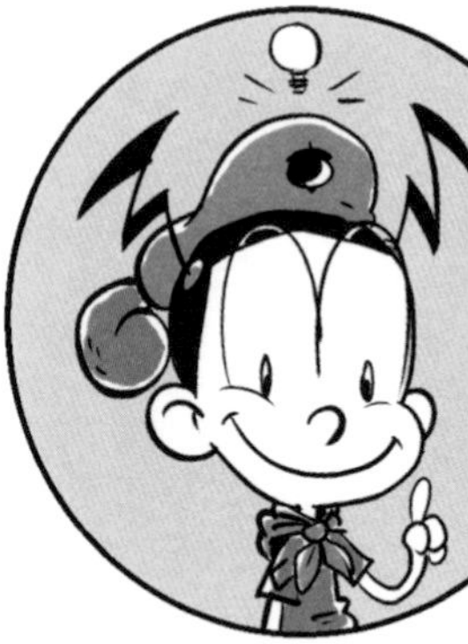

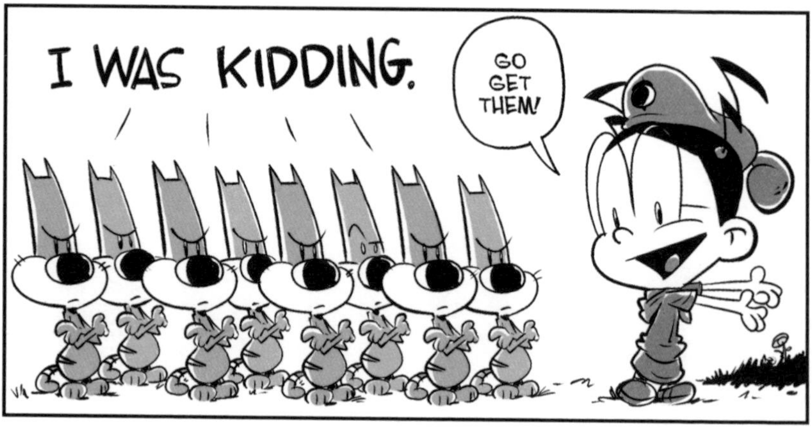
I WAS KIDDING.
GO GET THEM!

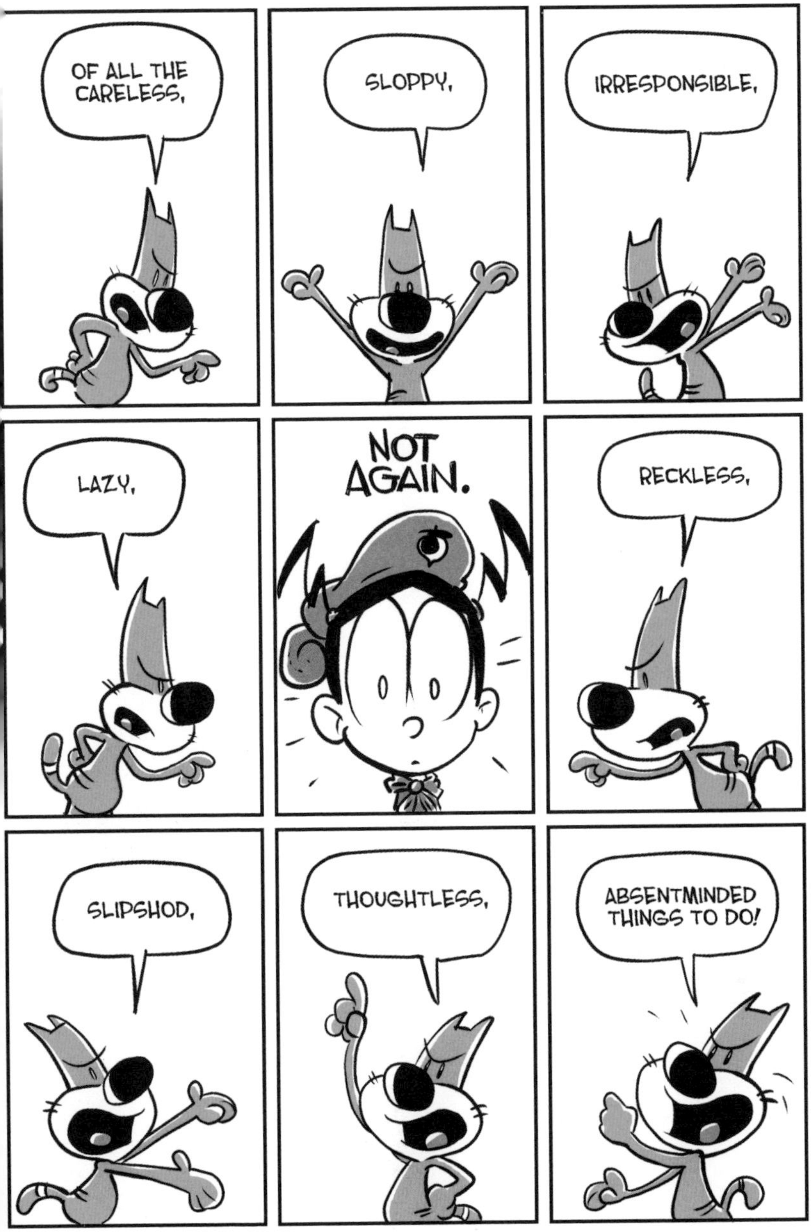
OF ALL THE CARELESS,
SLOPPY,
IRRESPONSIBLE,
LAZY,
NOT AGAIN.
RECKLESS,
SLIPSHOD,
THOUGHTLESS,
ABSENTMINDED THINGS TO DO!

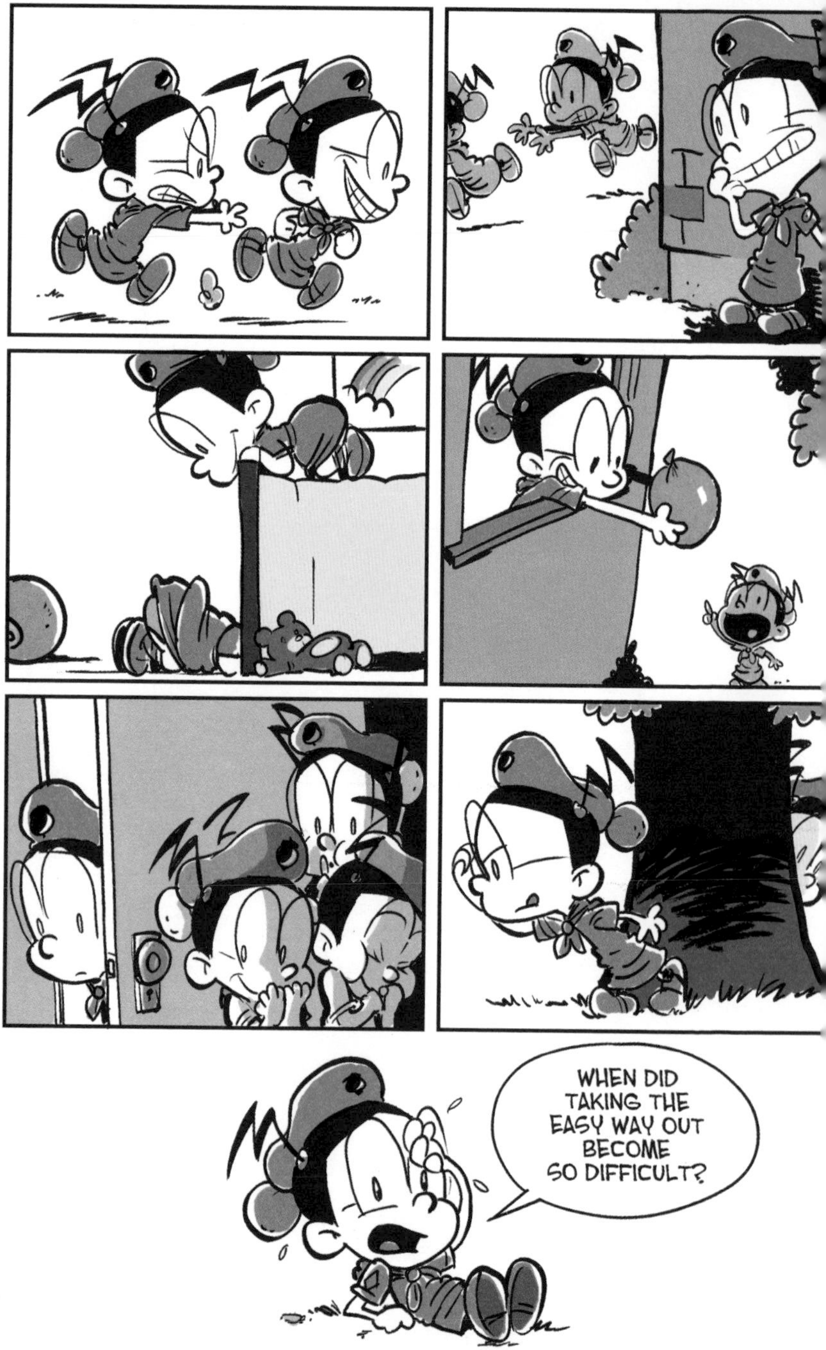
WHEN DID TAKING THE EASY WAY OUT BECOME SO DIFFICULT?

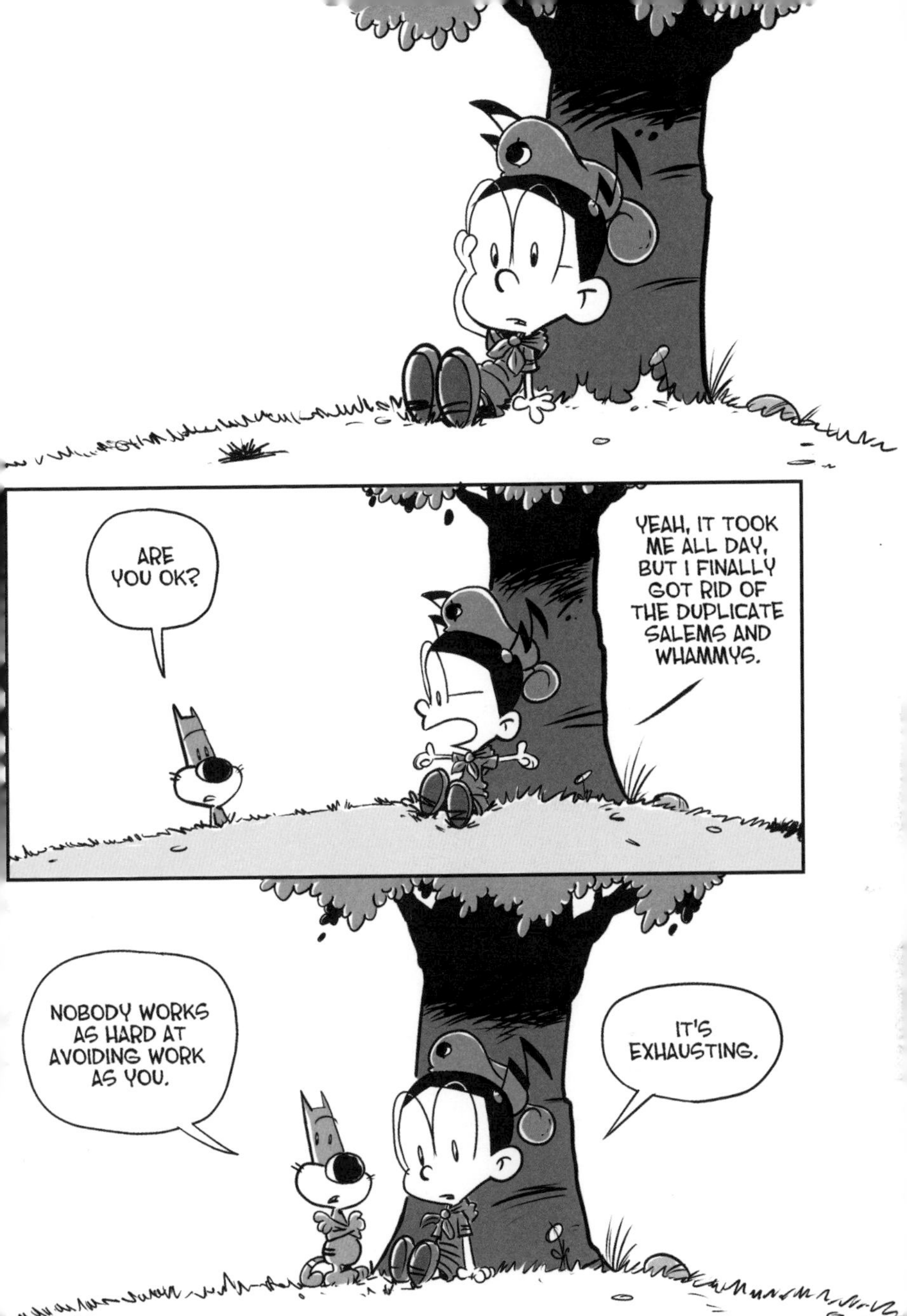
ARE YOU OK?
YEAH, IT TOOK ME ALL DAY, BUT I FINALLY GOT RID OF THE DUPLICATE SALEMS AND WHAMMYS.
NOBODY WORKS AS HARD AT AVOIDING WORK AS YOU.
IT'S EXHAUSTING.

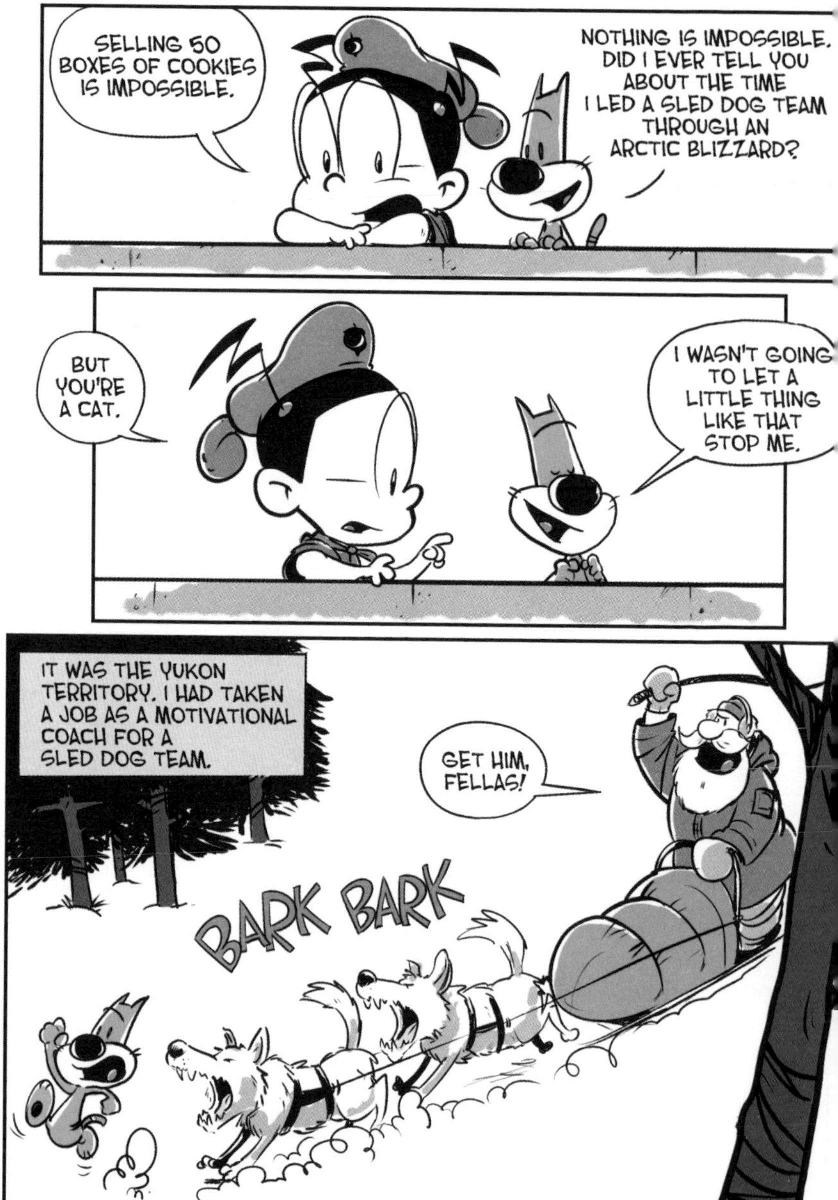
SELLING 50 BOXES OF COOKIES IS IMPOSSIBLE.
NOTHING IS IMPOSSIBLE. DID I EVER TELL YOU ABOUT THE TIME I LED A SLED DOG TEAM THROUGH AN ARCTIC BLIZZARD?
BUT YOU'RE A CAT.
I WASN'T GOING TO LET A LITTLE THING LIKE THAT STOP ME.
IT WAS THE YUKON TERRITORY. I HAD TAKEN A JOB AS A MOTIVATIONAL COACH FOR A SLED DOG TEAM.
GET HIM, FELLAS!
BARK BARK

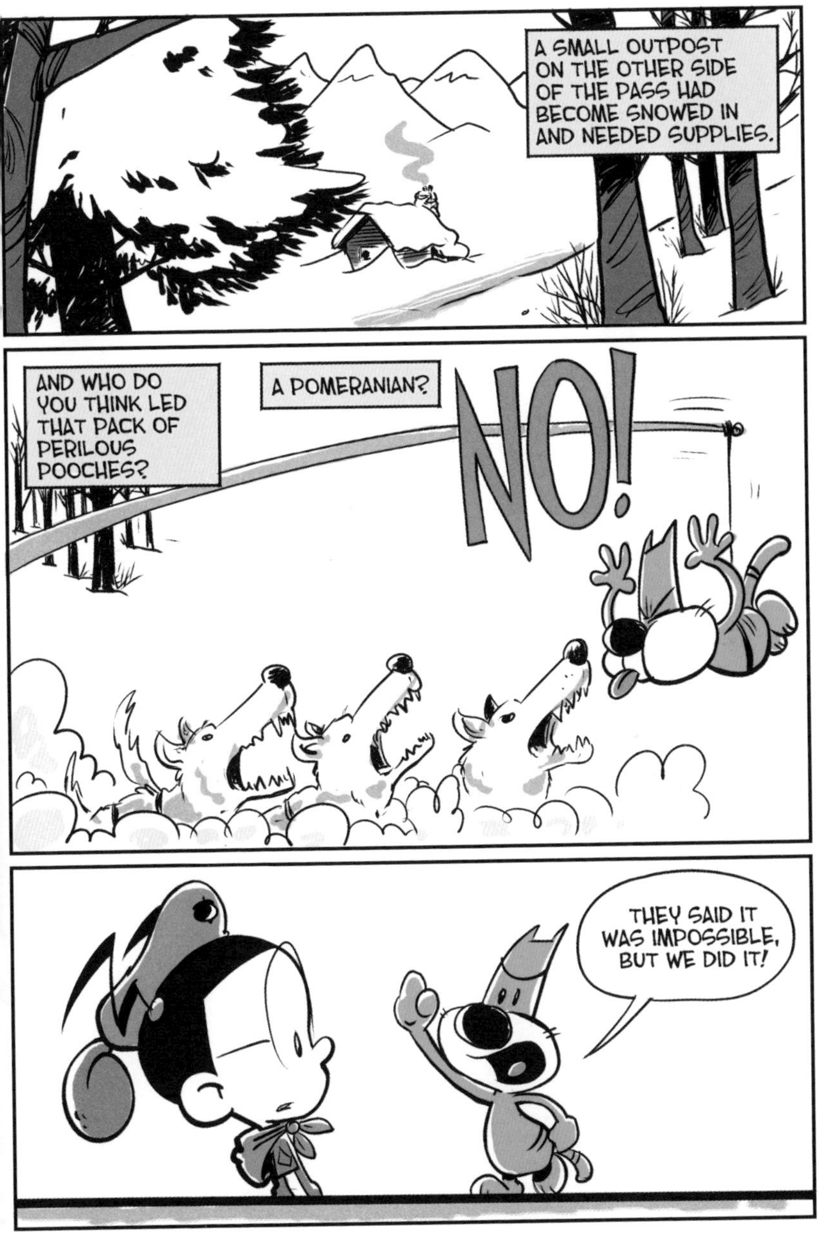
A SMALL OUTPOST ON THE OTHER SIDE OF THE PASS HAD BECOME SNOWED IN AND NEEDED SUPPLIES.
AND WHO DO YOU THINK LED THAT PACK OF PERILOUS POOCHES?
A POMERANIAN?
NO!
THEY SAID IT WAS IMPOSSIBLE, BUT WE DID IT!

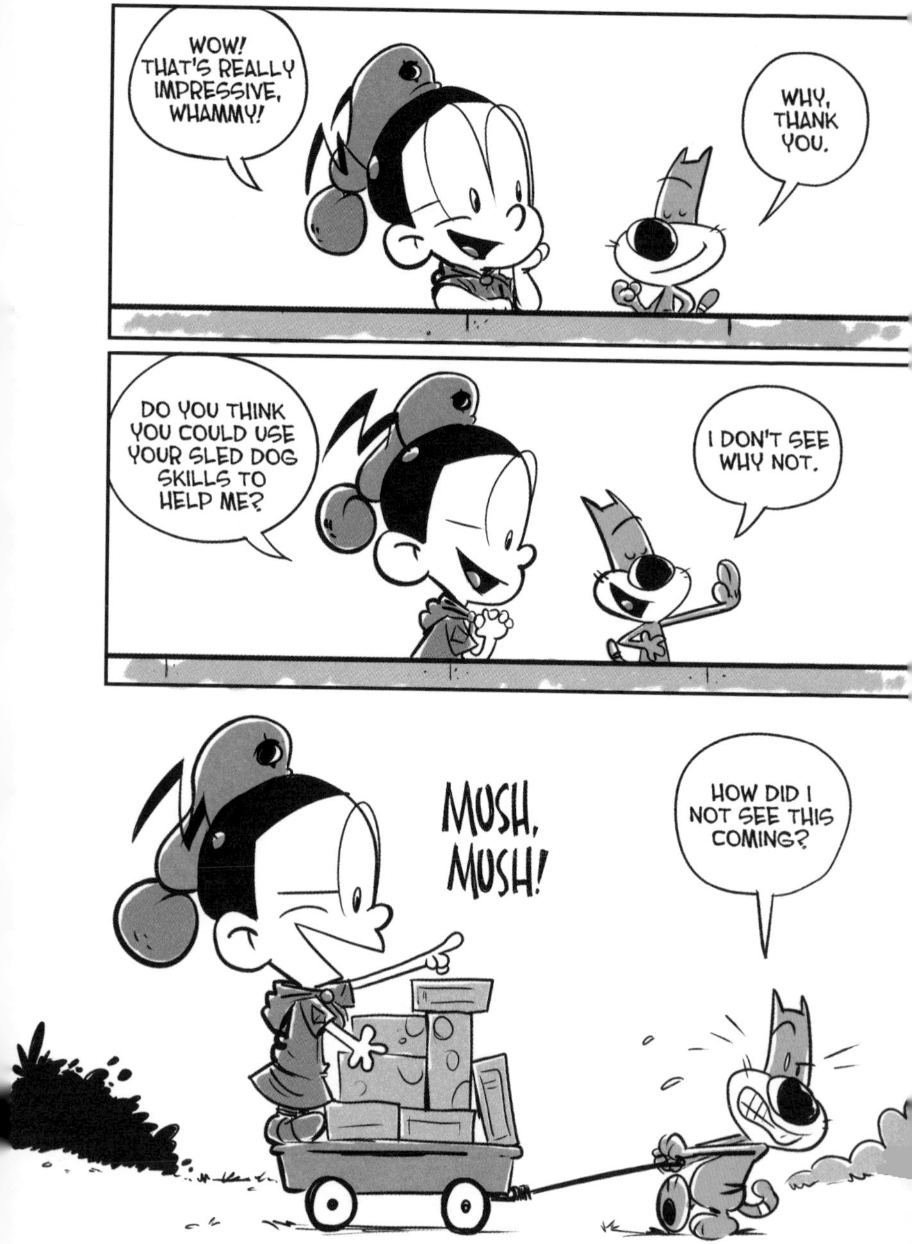
WOW! THAT'S REALLY IMPRESSIVE, WHAMMY!
WHY, THANK YOU.
DO YOU THINK YOU COULD USE YOUR SLED DOG SKILLS TO HELP ME?
I DON'T SEE WHY NOT.
MUSH, MUSH!
HOW DID I NOT SEE THIS COMING?

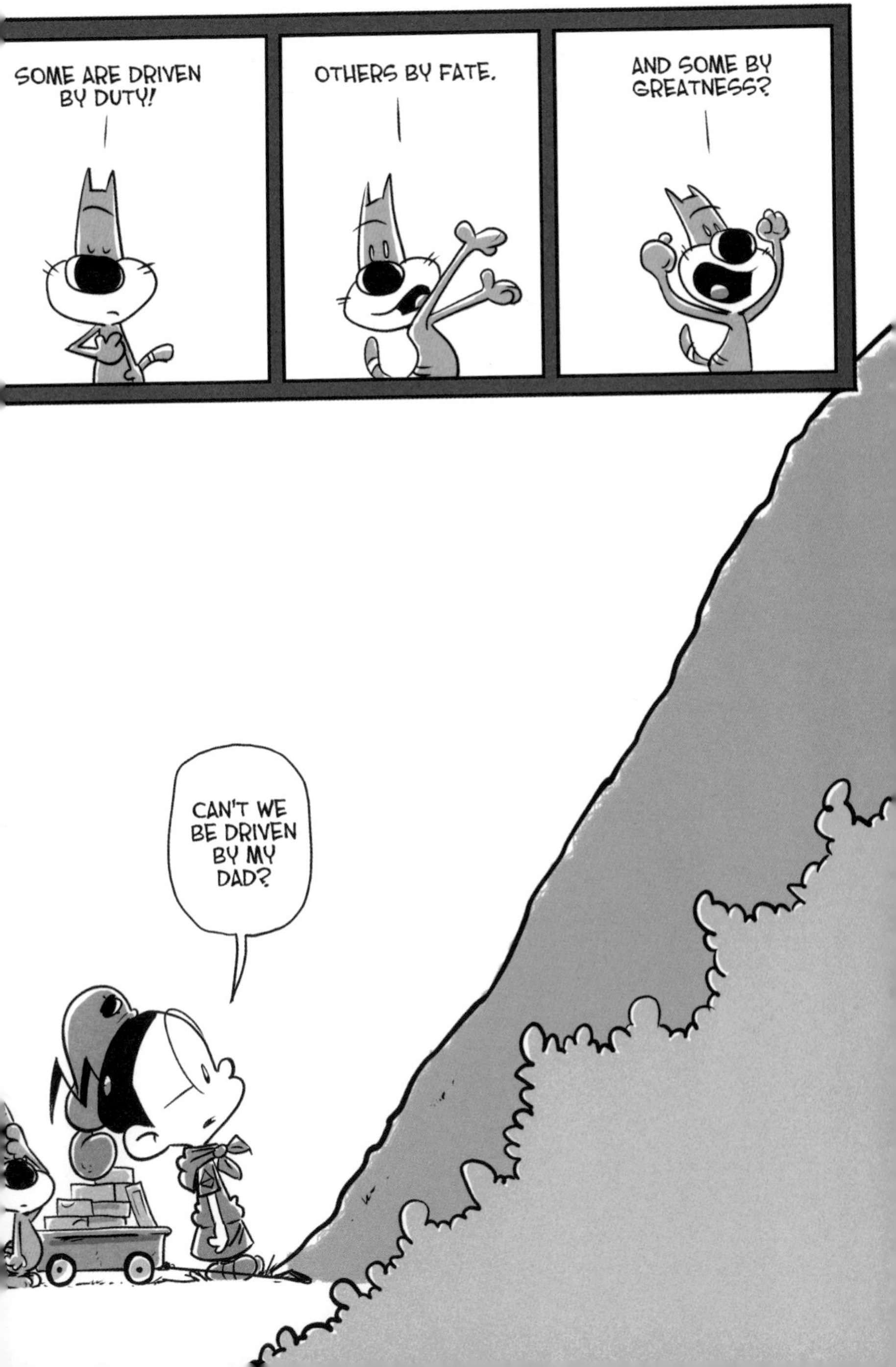
SOME ARE DRIVEN BY DUTY!
OTHERS BY FATE.
AND SOME BY GREATNESS?
CAN'T WE BE DRIVEN BY MY DAD?

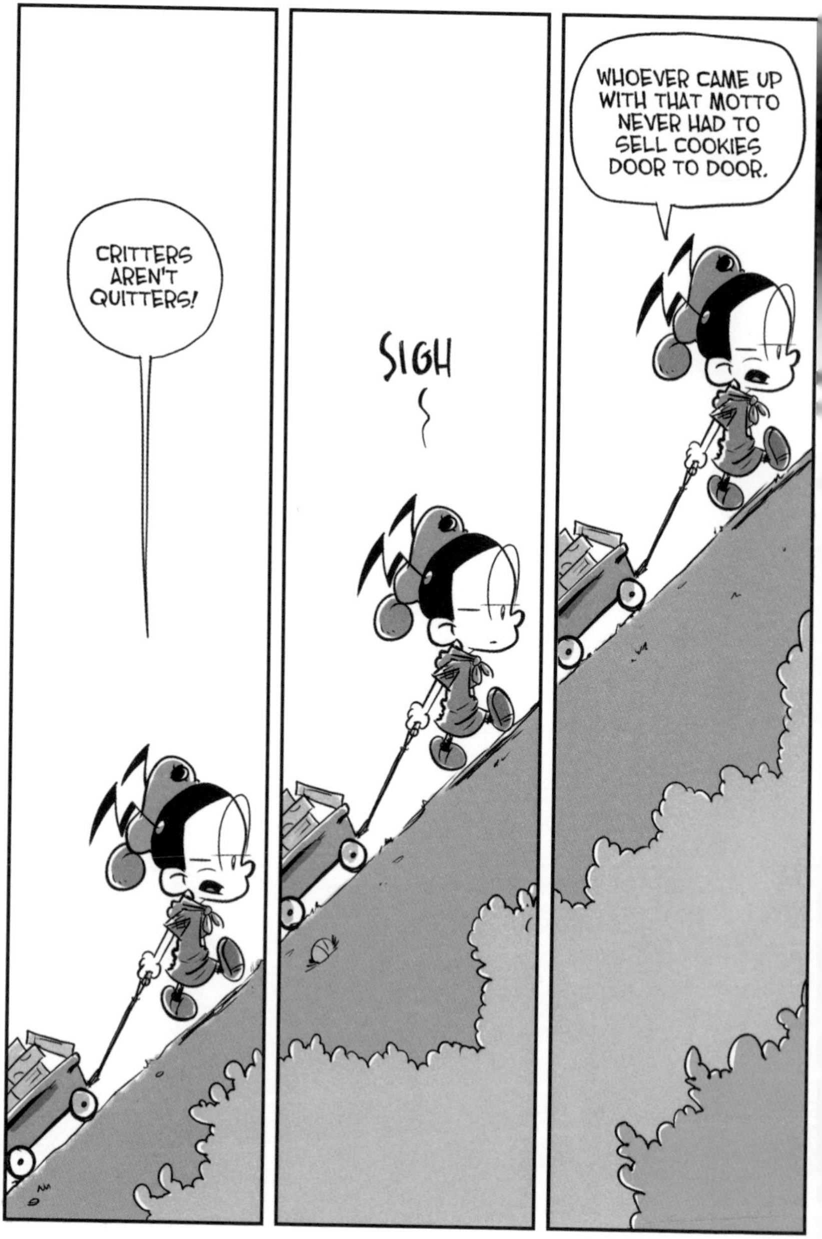
CRITTERS AREN'T QUITTERS!
SIGH
WHOEVER CAME UP WITH THAT MOTTO NEVER HAD TO SELL COOKIES DOOR TO DOOR.

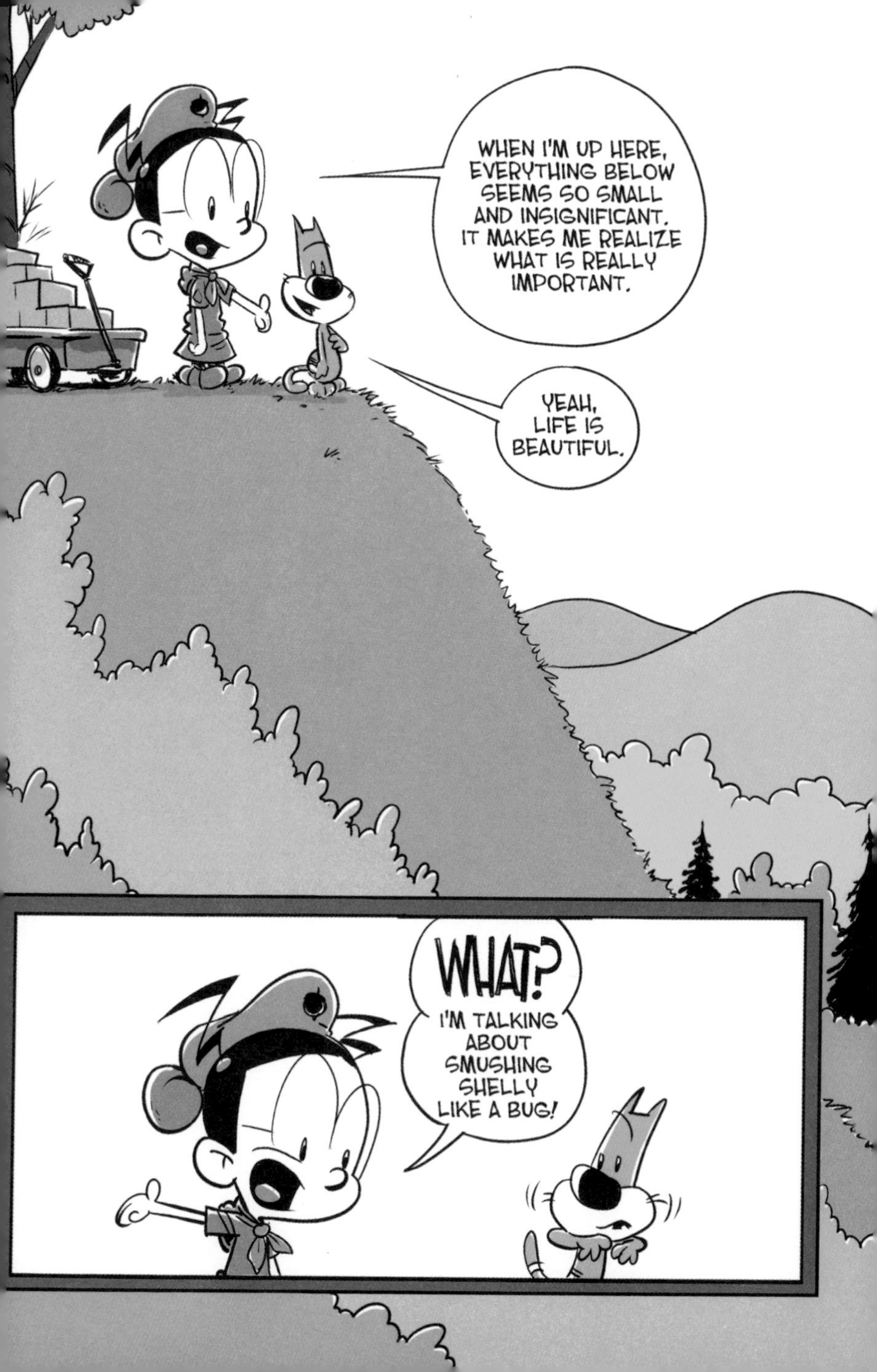
WHEN I'M UP HERE, EVERYTHING BELOW SEEMS SO SMALL AND INSIGNIFICANT. IT MAKES ME REALIZE WHAT IS REALLY IMPORTANT.
YEAH, LIFE IS BEAUTIFUL.
WHAT? I'M TALKING ABOUT SMUSHING SHELLY LIKE A BUG!

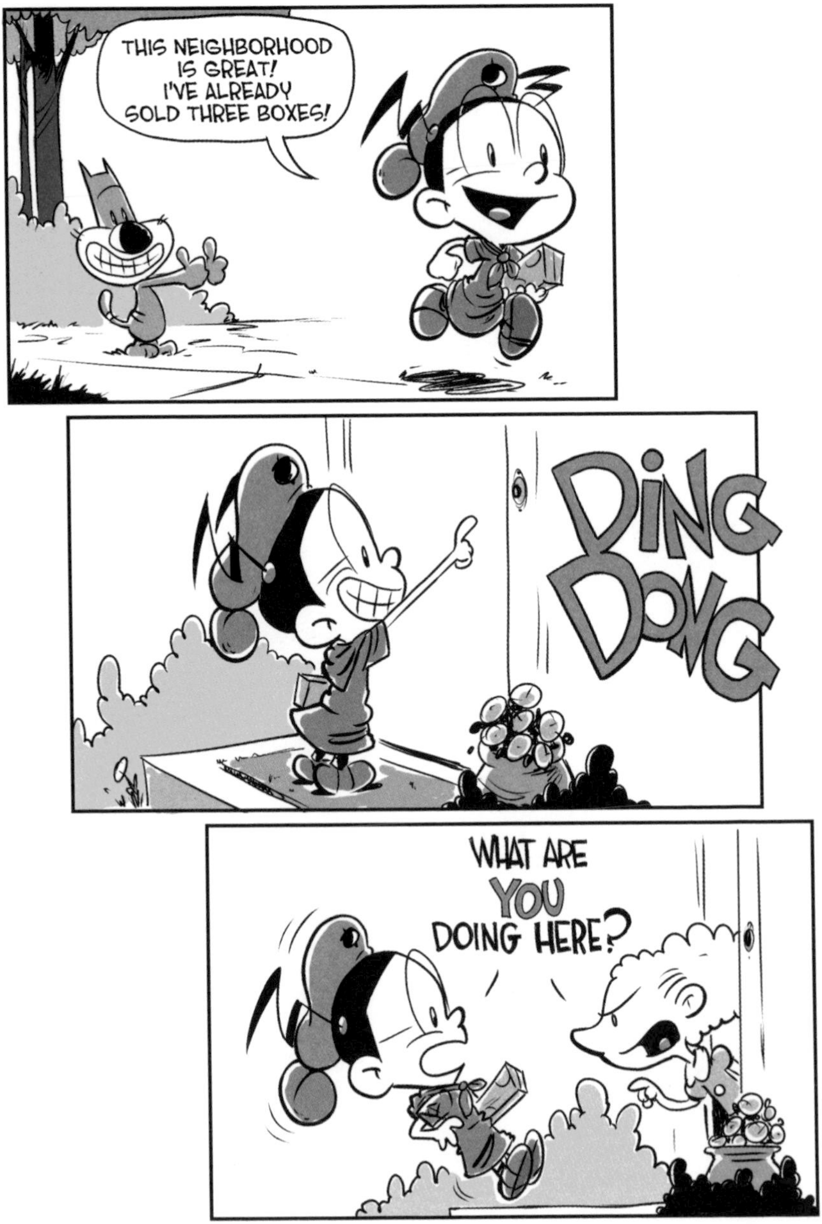
THIS NEIGHBORHOOD IS GREAT! I'VE ALREADY SOLD THREE BOXES!
DING DONG
WHAT ARE YOU DOING HERE?

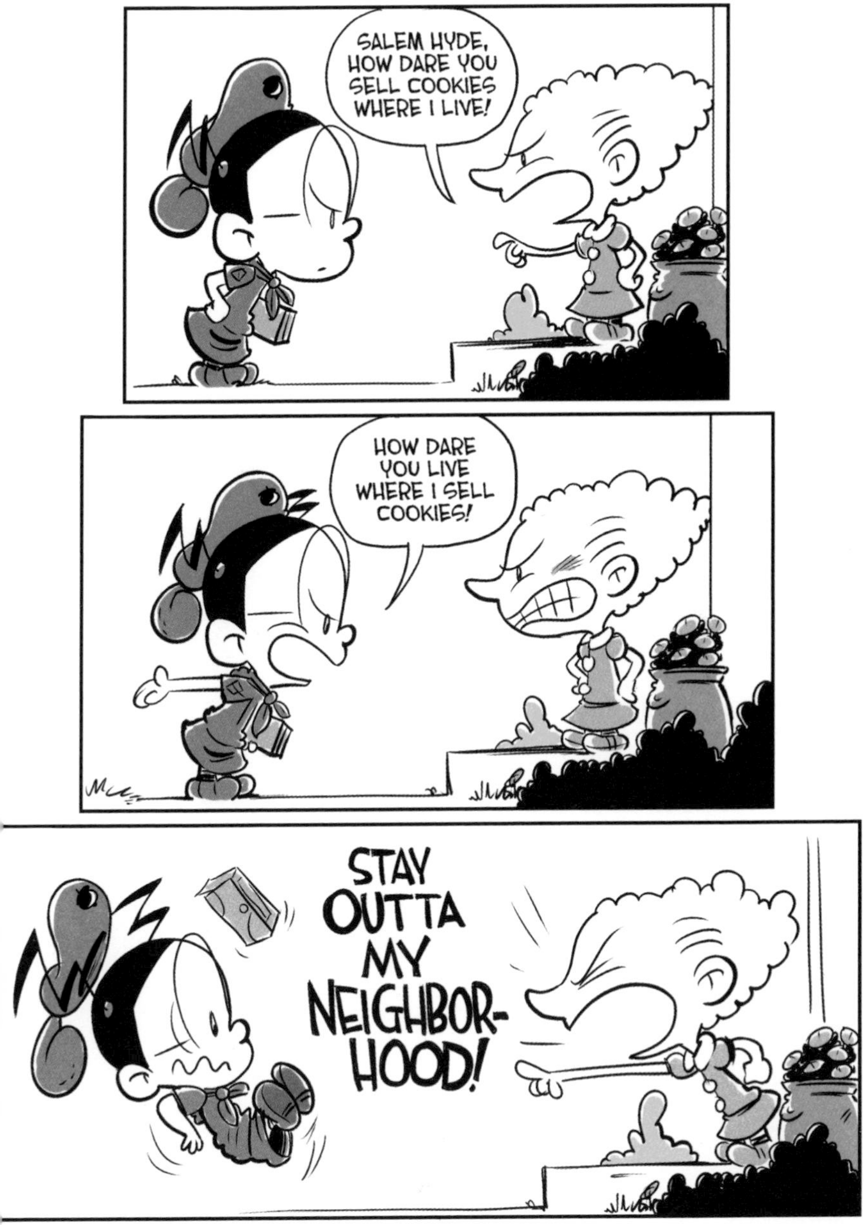
SALEM HYDE, HOW DARE YOU SELL COOKIES WHERE I LIVE!
HOW DARE YOU LIVE WHERE I SELL COOKIES!
STAY OUTTA MY NEIGHBOR-HOOD!

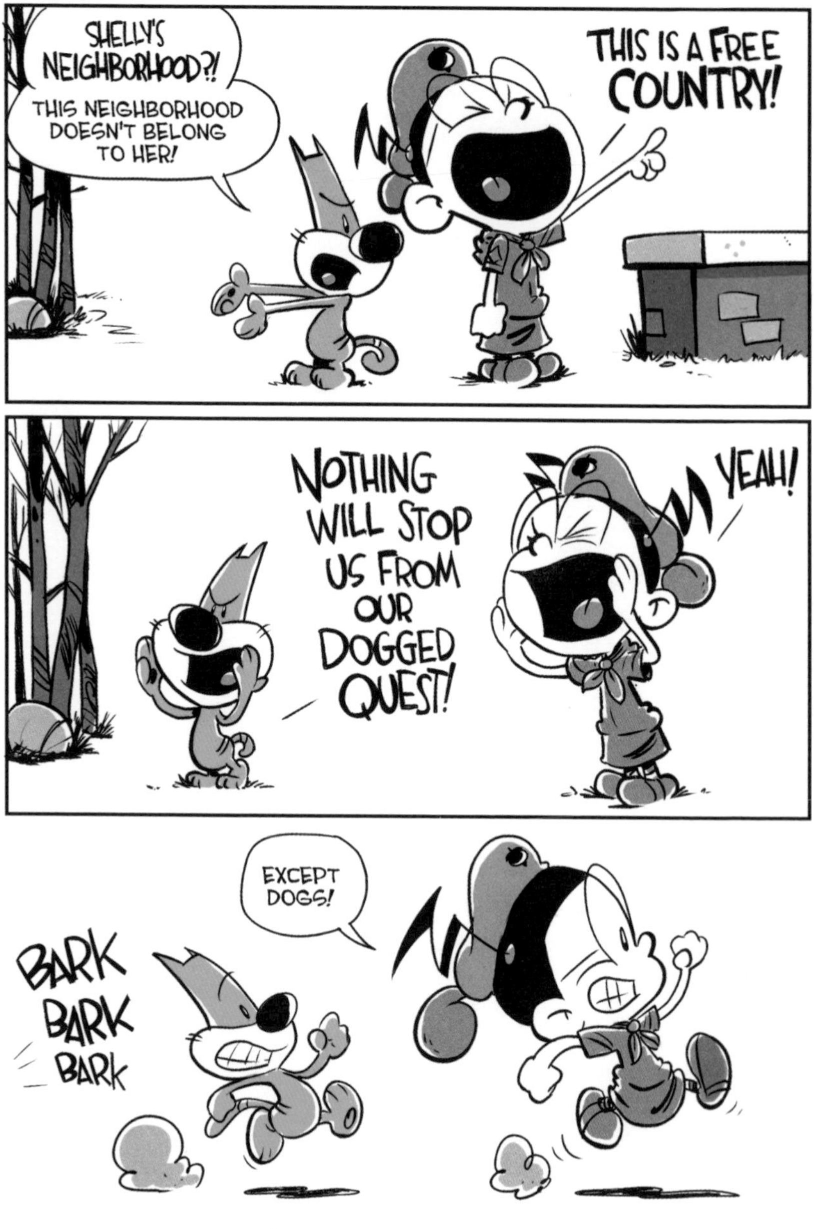
SHELLY'S NEIGHBORHOOD?!
THIS NEIGHBORHOOD DOESN'T BELONG TO HER!
THIS IS A FREE COUNTRY!
NOTHING WILL STOP US FROM OUR DOGGED QUEST!
YEAH!
EXCEPT DOGS!
BARK BARK BARK

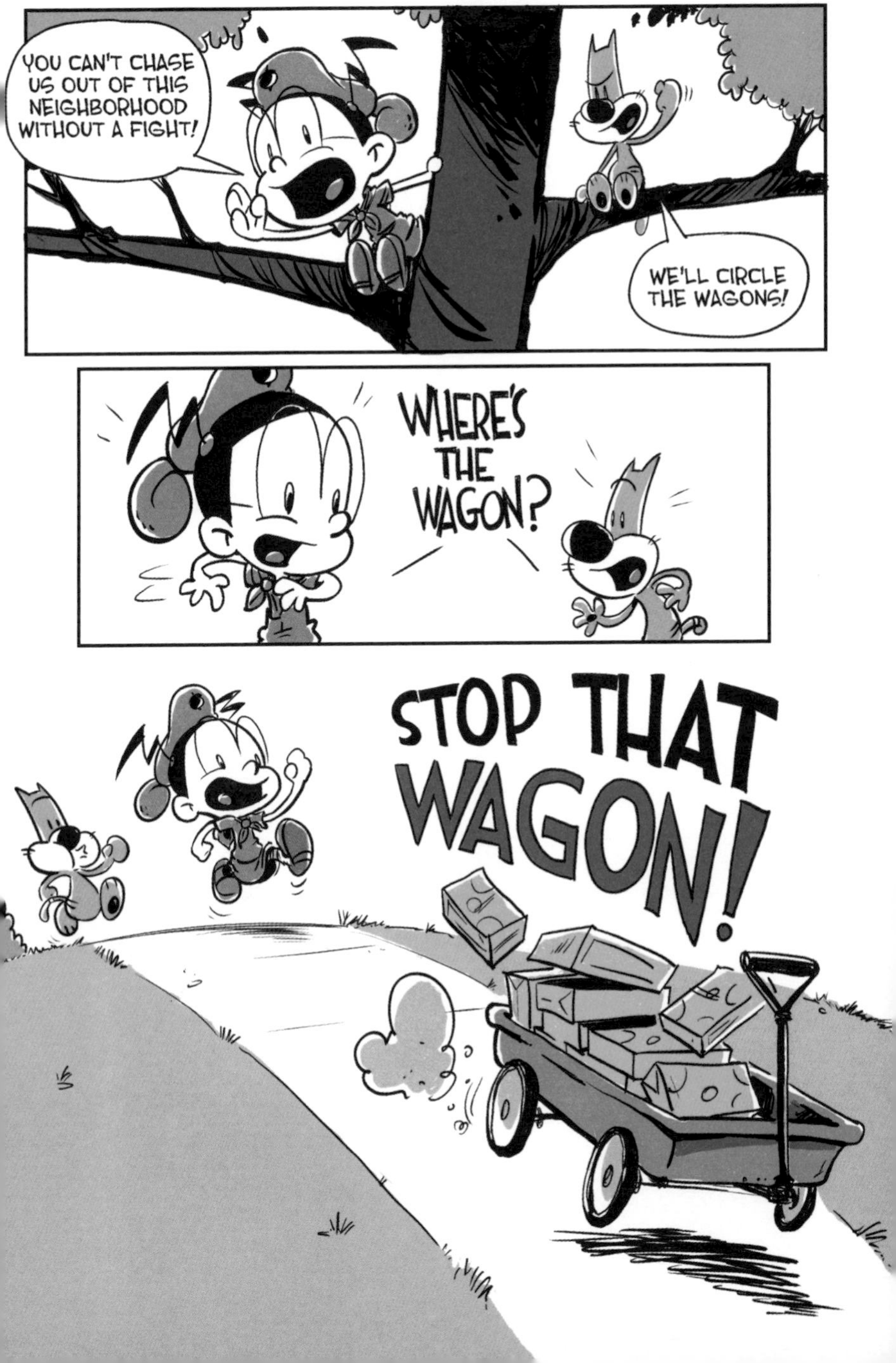

YOU CAN'T CHASE US OUT OF THIS NEIGHBORHOOD WITHOUT A FIGHT!
WE'LL CIRCLE THE WAGONS!
WHERE'S THE WAGON?
STOP THAT WAGON!

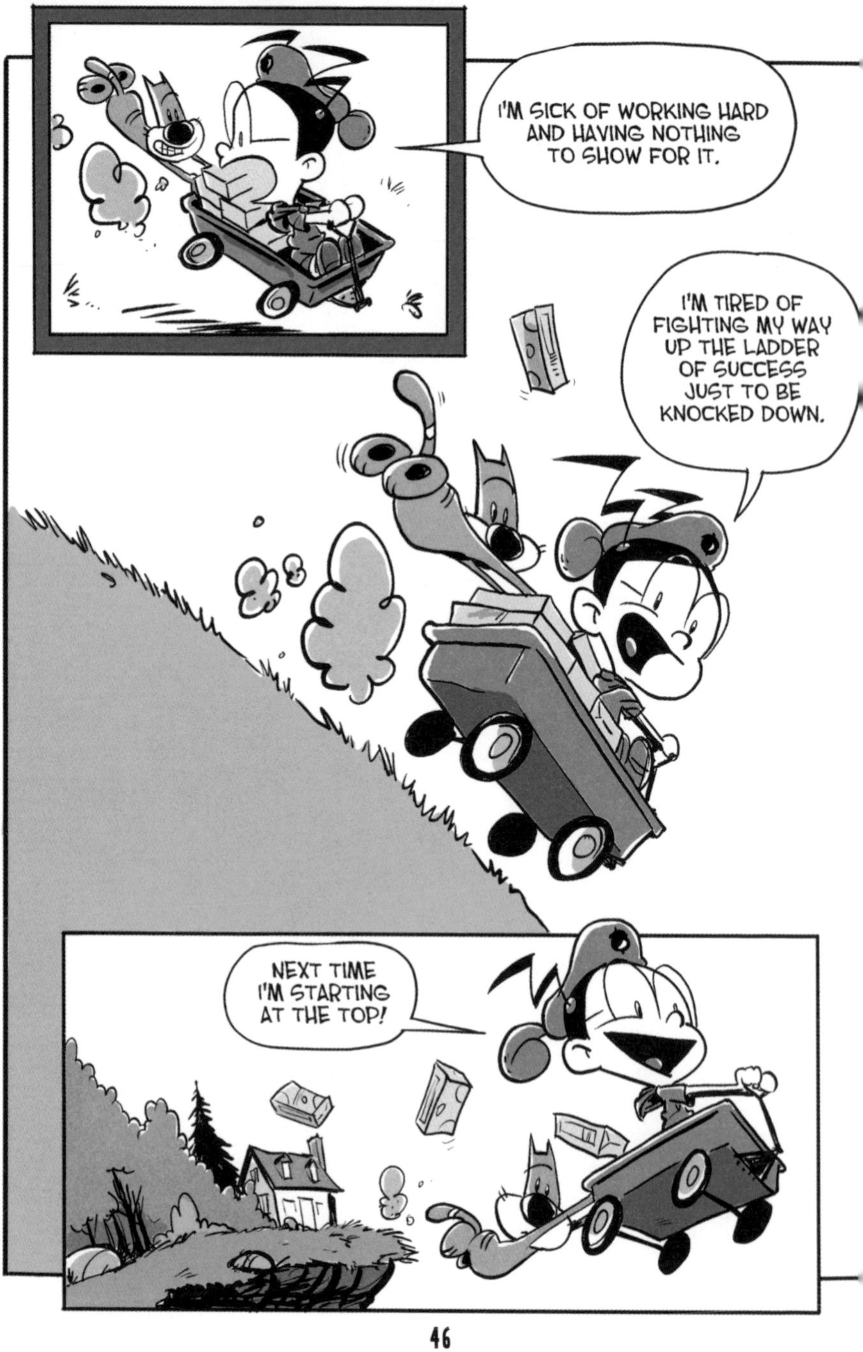
I'M SICK OF WORKING HARD AND HAVING NOTHING TO SHOW FOR IT.
I'M TIRED OF FIGHTING MY WAY UP THE LADDER OF SUCCESS JUST TO BE KNOCKED DOWN.
NEXT TIME I'M STARTING AT THE TOP!

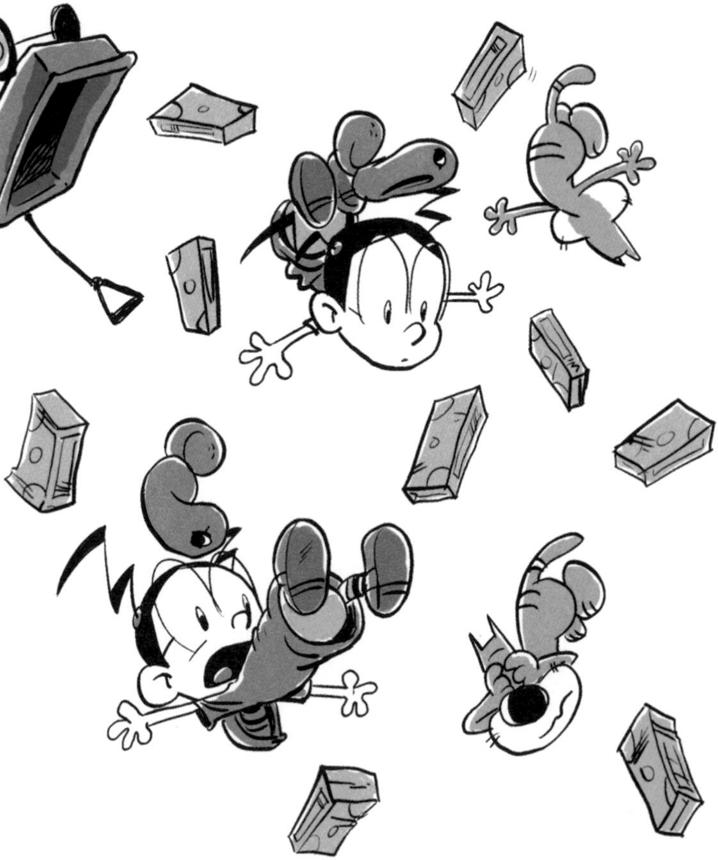

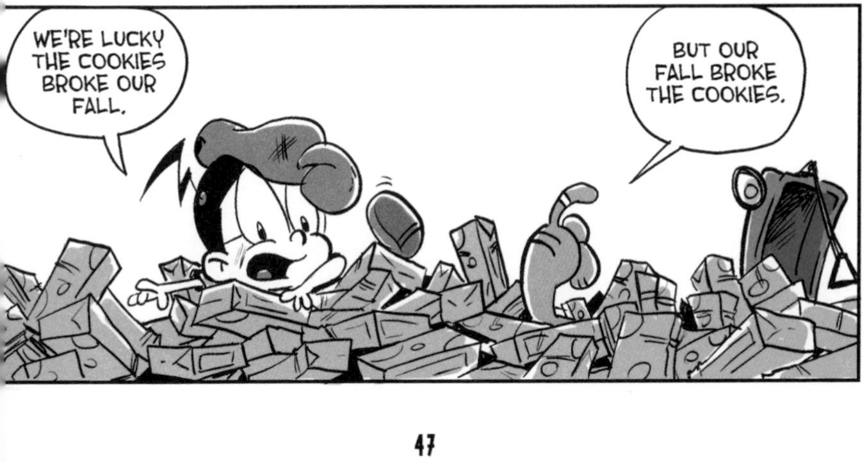
WE'RE LUCKY THE COOKIES BROKE OUR FALL.
BUT OUR FALL BROKE THE COOKIES.

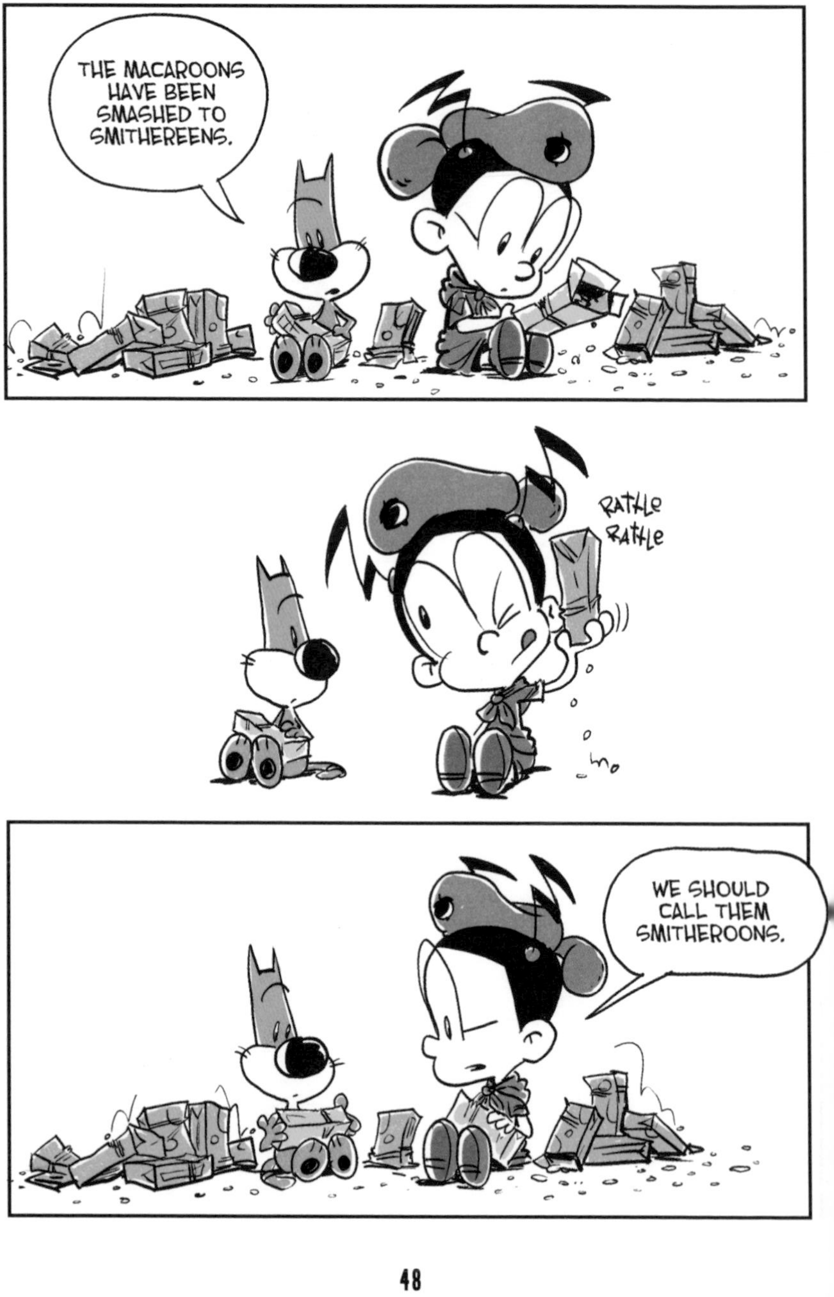
THE MACAROONS HAVE BEEN SMASHED TO SMITHEREENS.
RATTLE RATTLE
WE SHOULD CALL THEM SMITHEROONS.

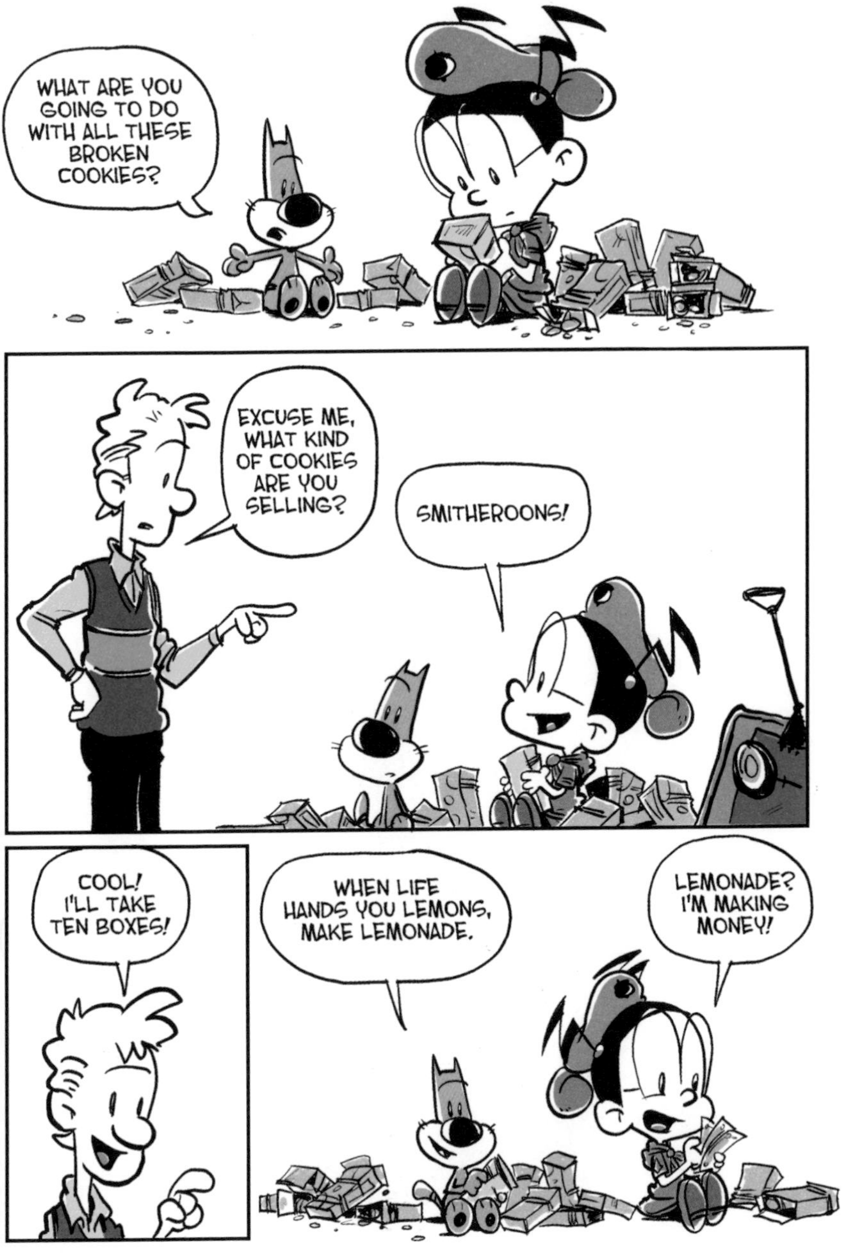
WHAT ARE YOU GOING TO DO WITH ALL THESE BROKEN COOKIES?
EXCUSE ME, WHAT KIND OF COOKIES ARE YOU SELLING?
SMITHEROONS!
COOL! I'LL TAKE TEN BOXES!
WHEN LIFE HANDS YOU LEMONS, MAKE LEMONADE.
LEMONADE? I'M MAKING MONEY!

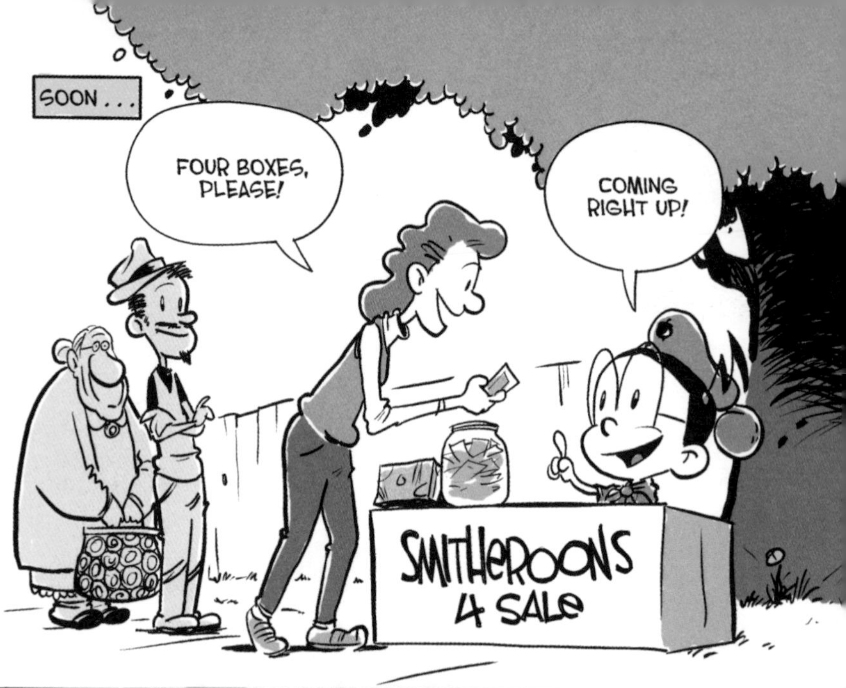
SOON . . .
FOUR BOXES, PLEASE!
COMING RIGHT UP!
SMITHEROONS 4 SALE

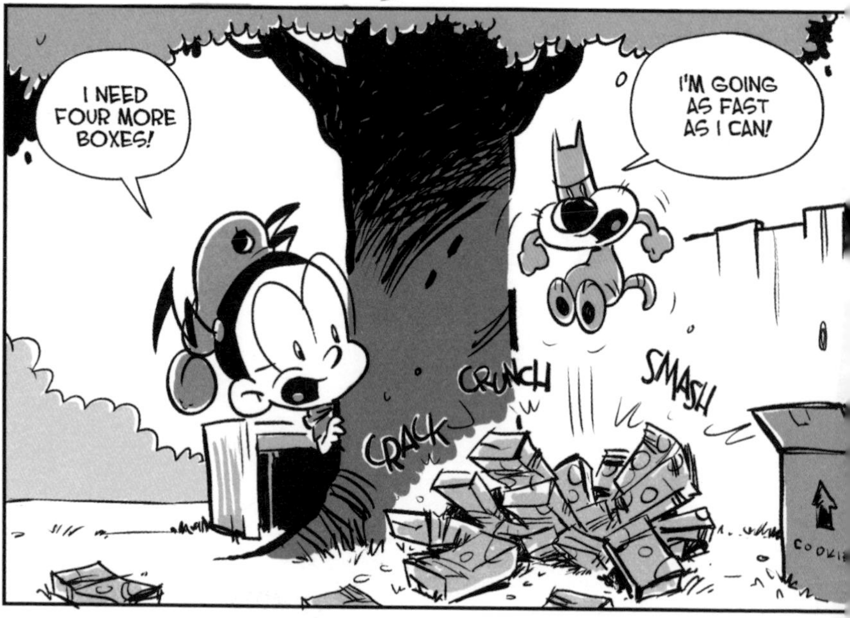
I NEED FOUR MORE BOXES!
I'M GOING AS FAST AS I CAN!
CRUNCH
SMASH
CRACK

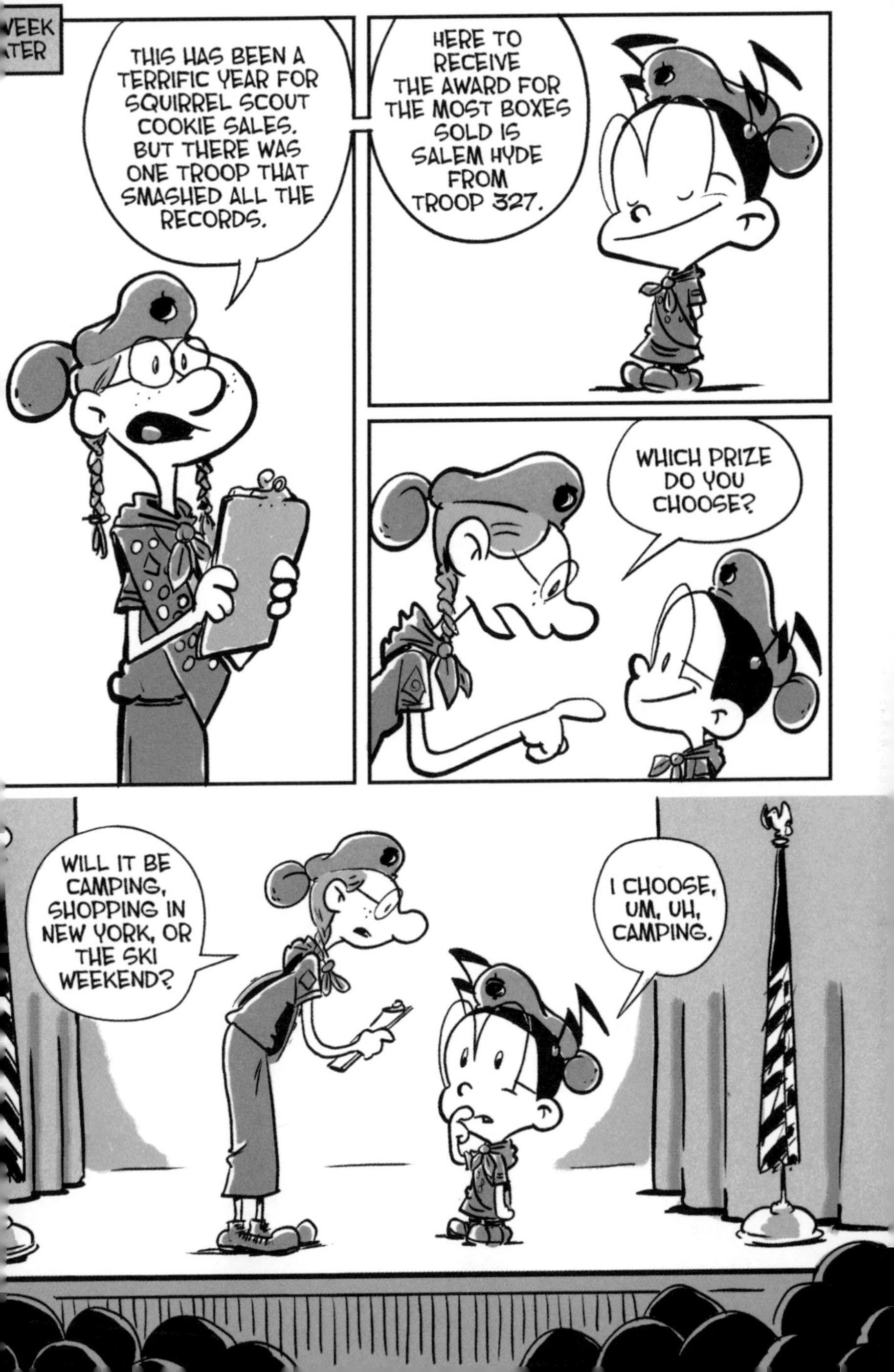
WEEK
TER
THIS HAS BEEN A TERRIFIC YEAR FOR SQUIRREL SCOUT COOKIE SALES. BUT THERE WAS ONE TROOP THAT SMASHED ALL THE RECORDS.
HERE TO RECEIVE THE AWARD FOR THE MOST BOXES SOLD IS SALEM HYDE FROM TROOP 327.
WHICH PRIZE DO YOU CHOOSE?
WILL IT BE CAMPING, SHOPPING IN NEW YORK, OR THE SKI WEEKEND?
I CHOOSE, UM, UH, CAMPING.

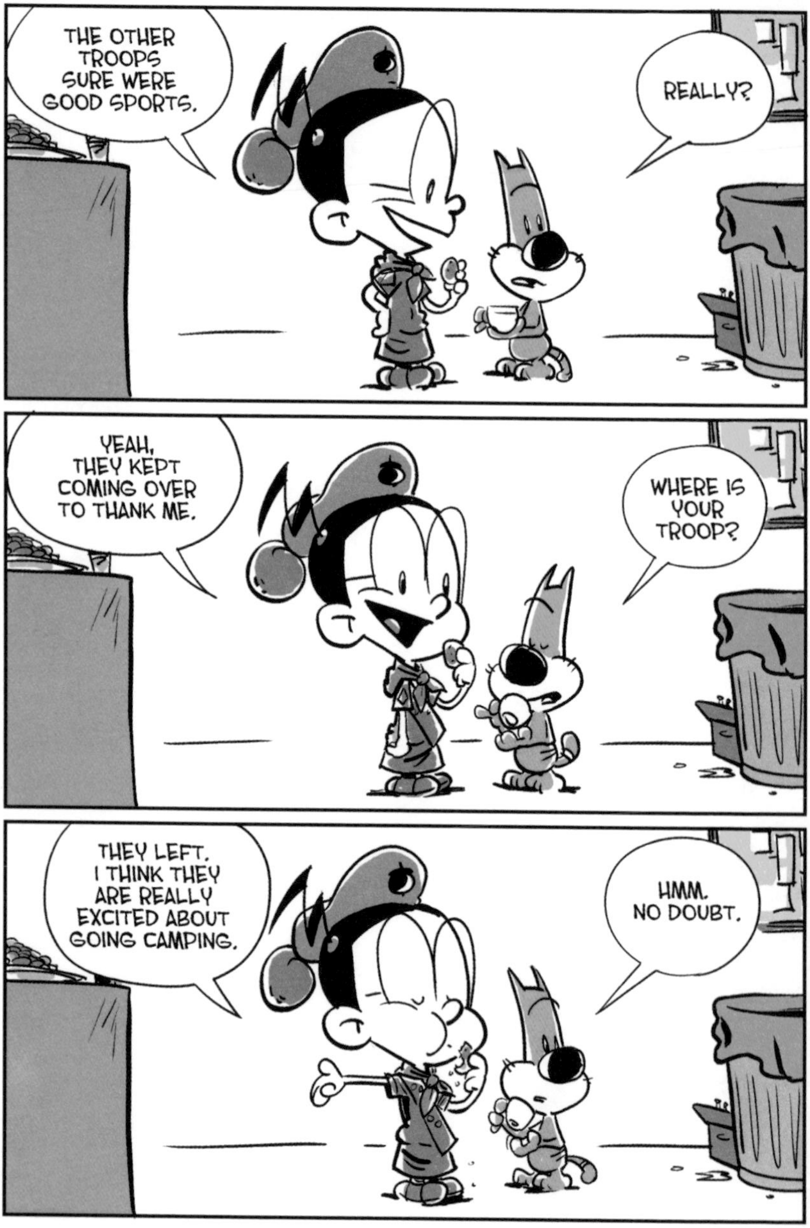
THE OTHER TROOPS SURE WERE GOOD SPORTS.
REALLY?
YEAH, THEY KEPT COMING OVER TO THANK ME.
WHERE IS YOUR TROOP?
THEY LEFT. I THINK THEY ARE REALLY EXCITED ABOUT GOING CAMPING.
HMM. NO DOUBT.

PART 2
Squirrel Scout Guide to Camping

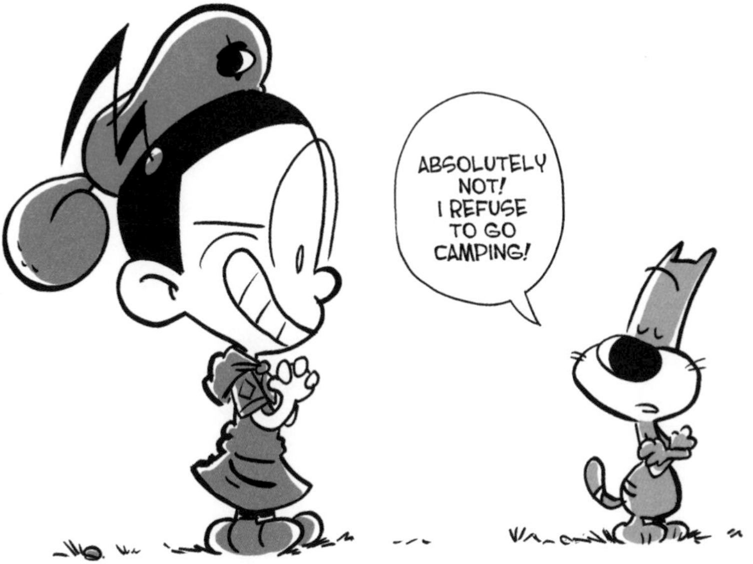
ABSOLUTELY NOT! I REFUSE TO GO CAMPING!

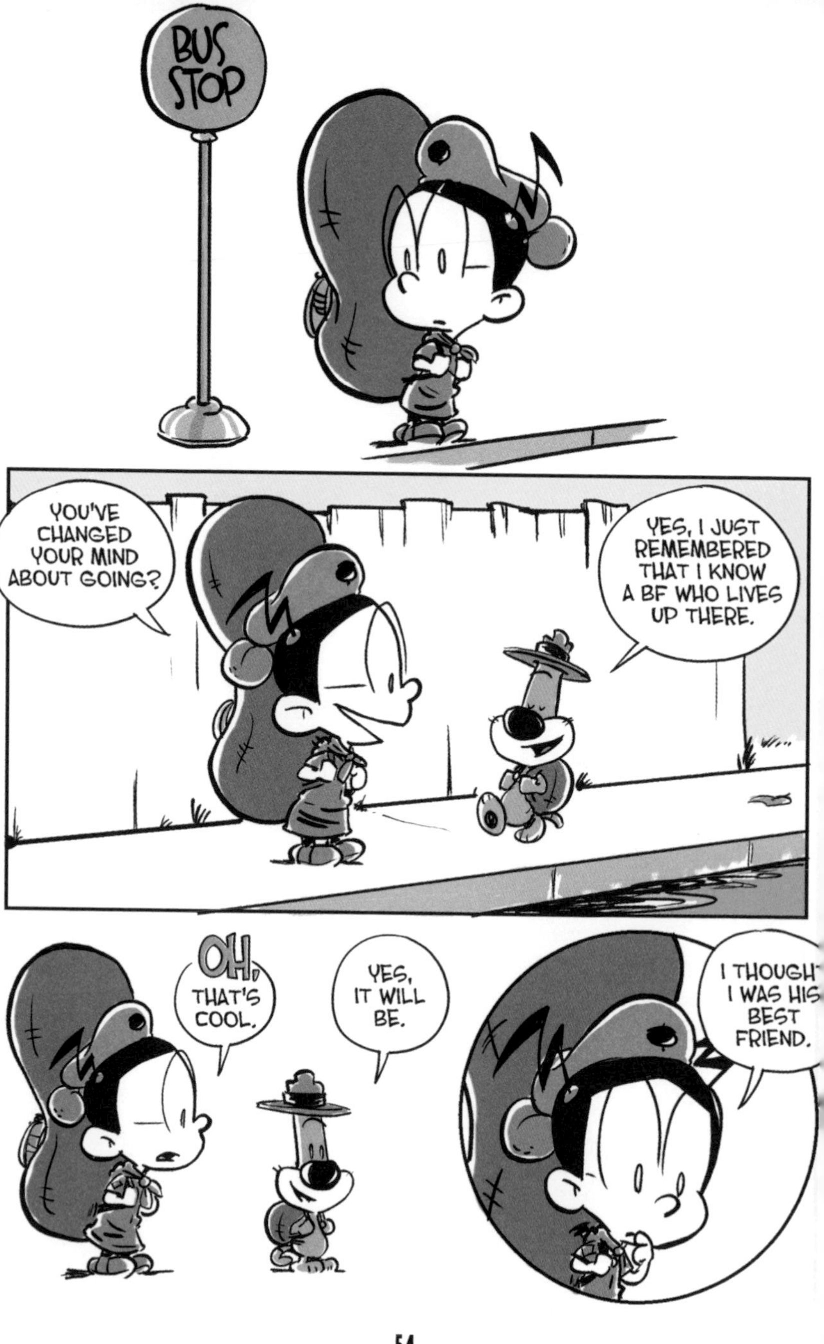
BUS STOP
YOU'VE CHANGED YOUR MIND ABOUT GOING?
YES, I JUST REMEMBERED THAT I KNOW A BF WHO LIVES UP THERE.
OH, THAT'S COOL.
YES, IT WILL BE.
I THOUGHT I WAS HIS BEST FRIEND.

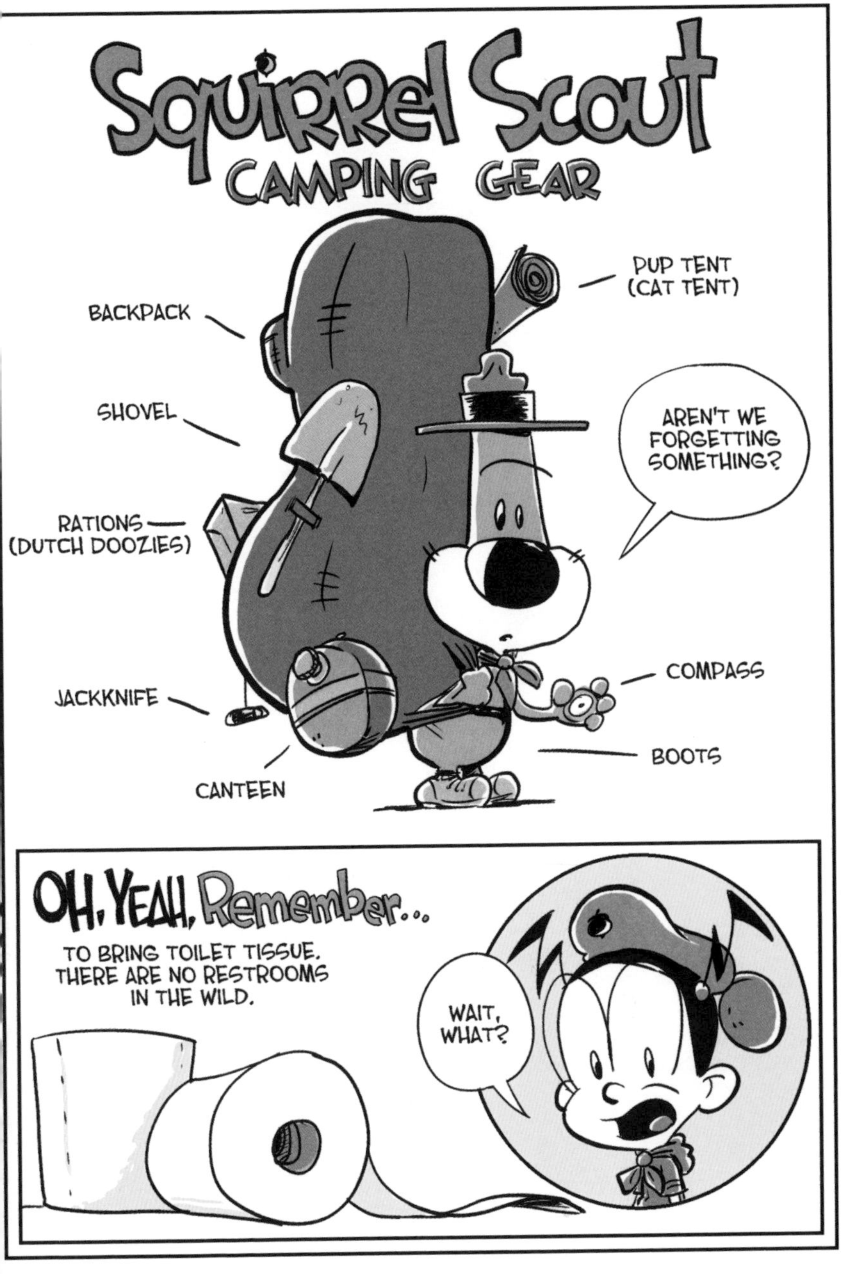
Squirrel Scout
CAMPING GEAR
PUP TENT
(CAT TENT)
BACKPACK
SHOVEL
ARE'NT WE FORGETTING SOMETHING?
RATIONS
(DUTCH DOOZIES)
COMPASS
JACKKNIFE
BOOTS
CANTEEN
OH, YEAH, Remember...
TO BRING TOILET TISSUE. THERE ARE NO RESTROOMS IN THE WILD.
WAIT, WHAT?

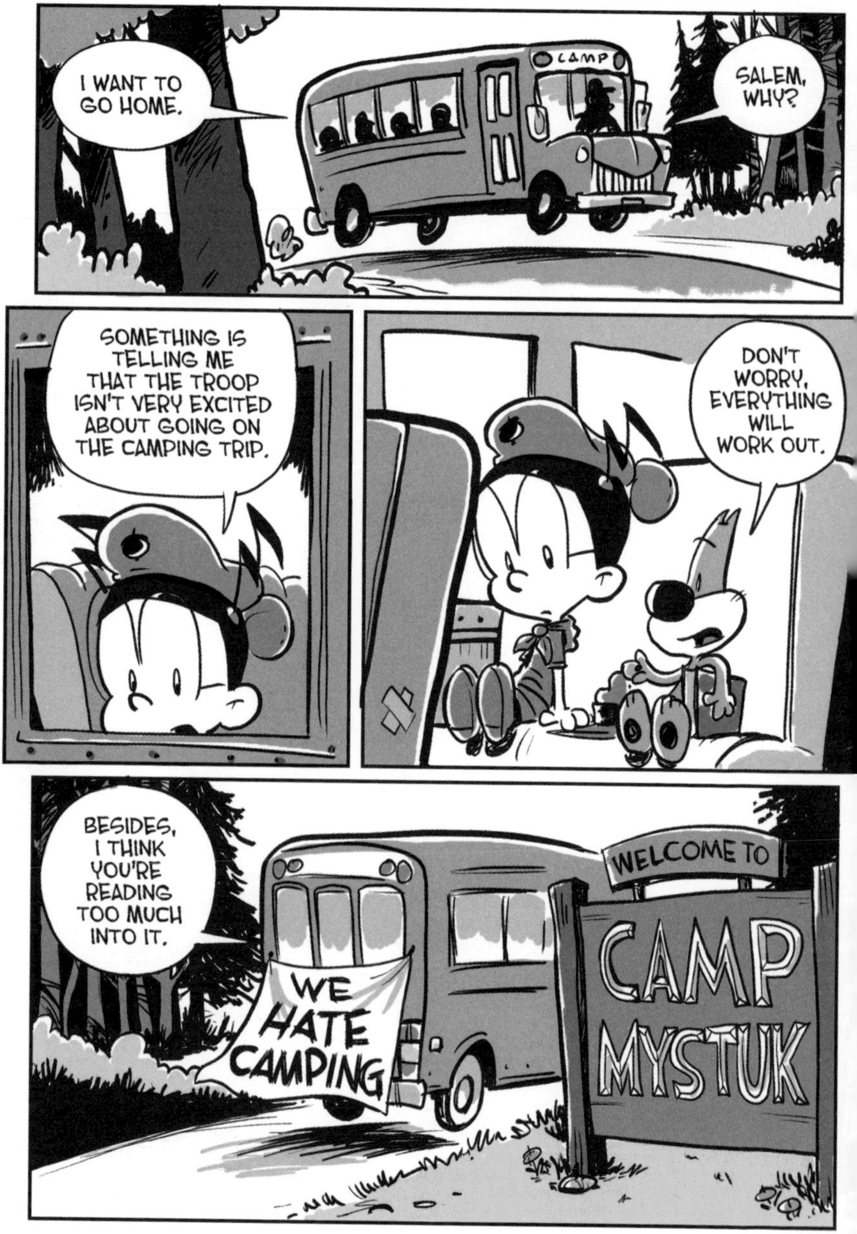
CAMP
I WANT TO GO HOME.
SALEM, WHY?
SOMETHING IS TELLING ME THAT THE TROOP ISN'T VERY EXCITED ABOUT GOING ON THE CAMPING TRIP.
DON'T WORRY. EVERYTHING WILL WORK OUT.
BESIDES, I THINK YOU'RE READING TOO MUCH INTO IT.
WE HATE CAMPING
WELCOME TO
CAMP MYSTUK

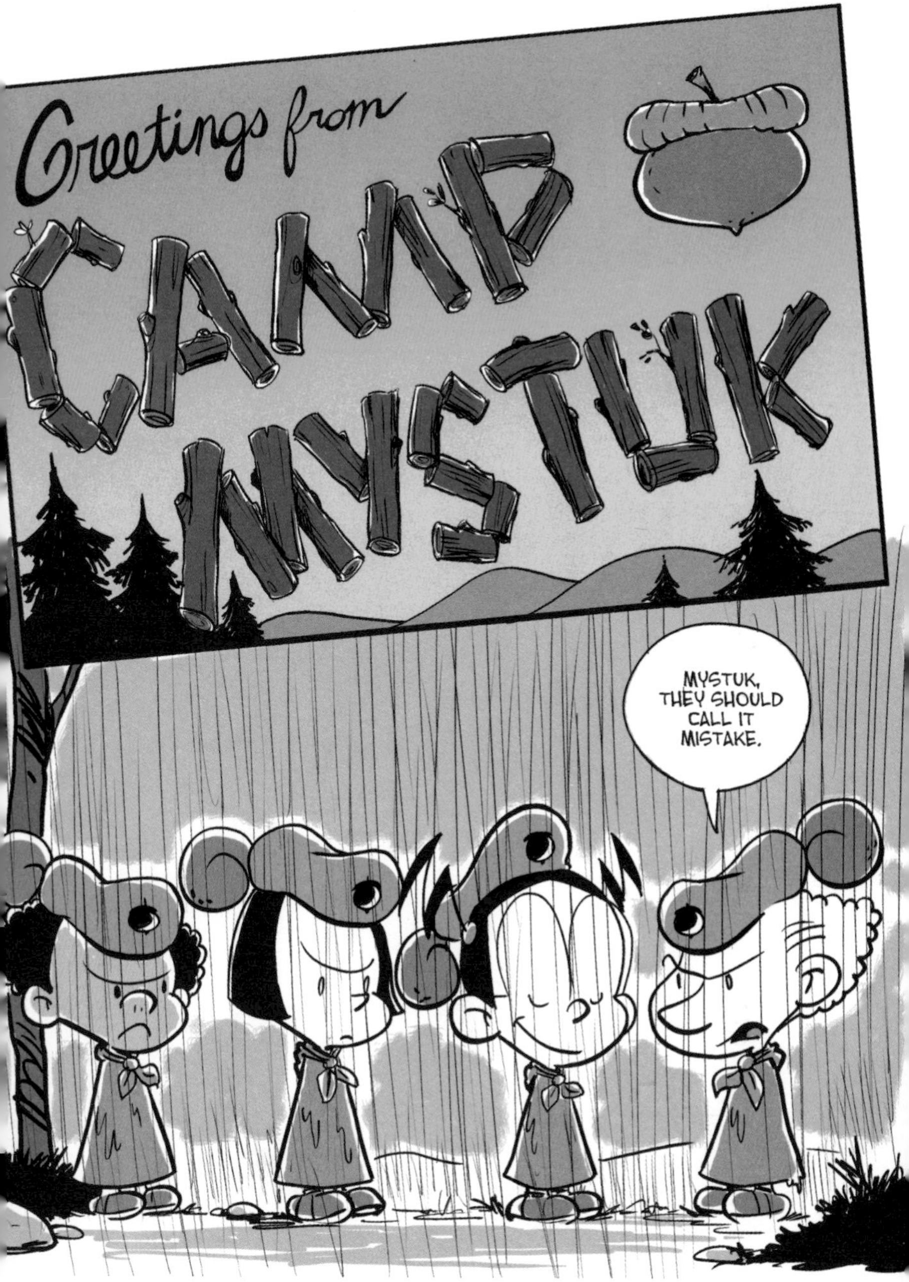
Greetings from
CAMP MYSTUK
MYSTUK, THEY SHOULD CALL IT MISTAKE.

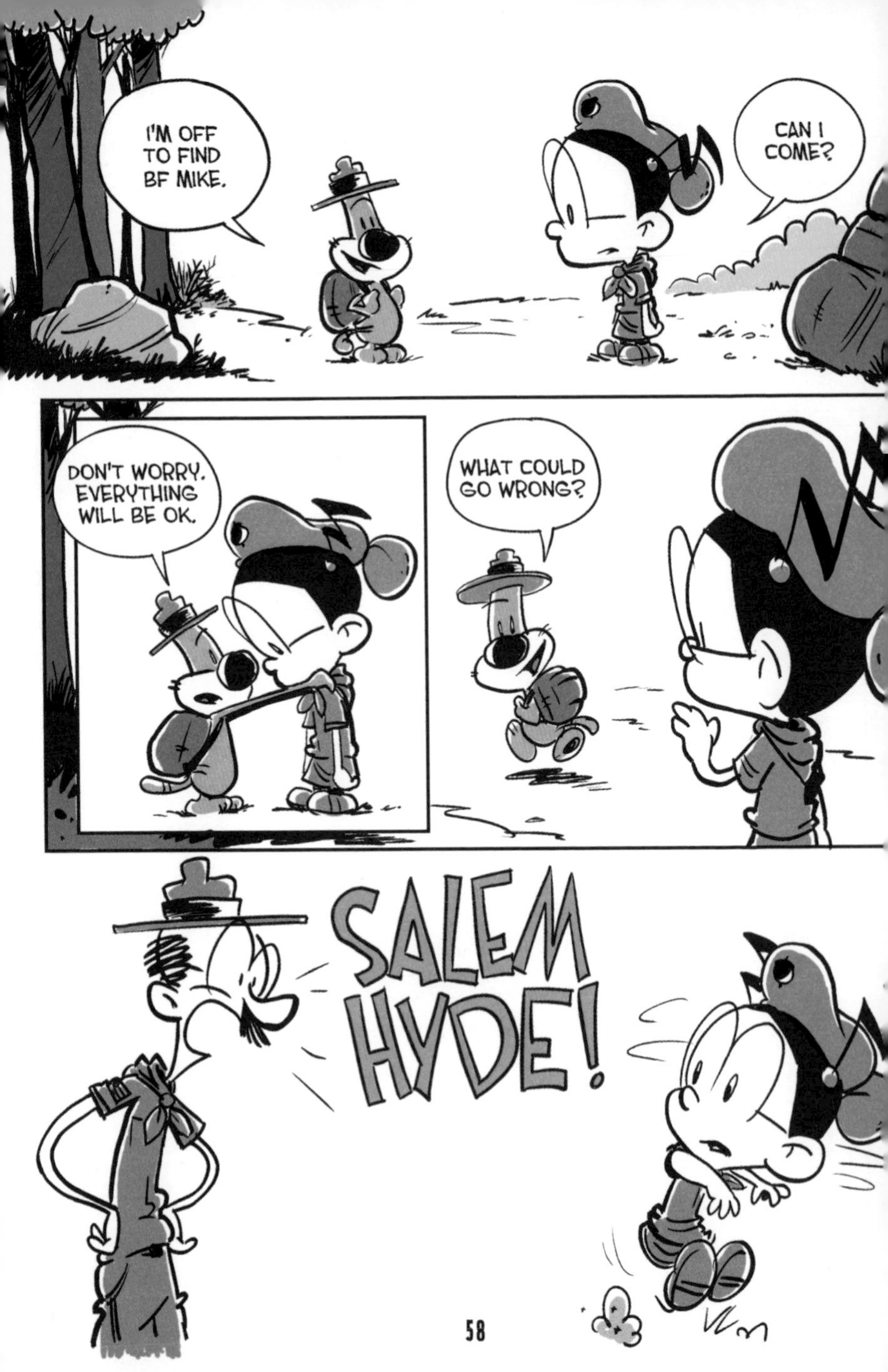
I'M OFF TO FIND BF MIKE.
CAN I COME?
DON'T WORRY. EVERYTHING WILL BE OK.
WHAT COULD GO WRONG?
SALEM HYDE!

Getting to Know... MR. FINK

TEACHER, STORE MANAGER, SCOUTMASTER, AND LITTLE LEAGUE UMPIRE

LIKES
ORDER
QUIET
PEACE

DISLIKES
FUN (IN GENERAL)
PUPPIES
GUPPIES
BIKES
TRIKES
TYKES
CANDY
TOYS
PARTIES
VIDEO GAMES
PIZZA
CARTOONS
BALLOONS
MACAROONS
BASSOONS
LEGUMES
CATS
CHAOS
KIDS
(ALL KINDS, BUT
ESPECIALLY SALEM HYDE)

DID YOU KNOW...
MR. FINK CANNOT SEE
WITHOUT HIS
GLASSES.

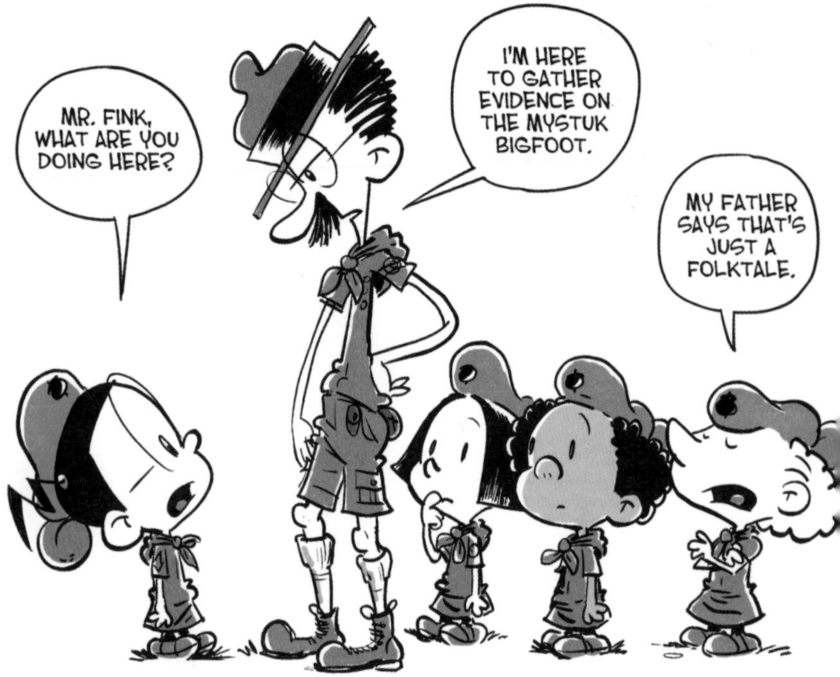
MR. FINK, WHAT ARE YOU DOING HERE?
I'M HERE TO GATHER EVIDENCE ON THE MYSTUK BIGFOOT.
MY FATHER SAYS THAT'S JUST A FOLKTALE.

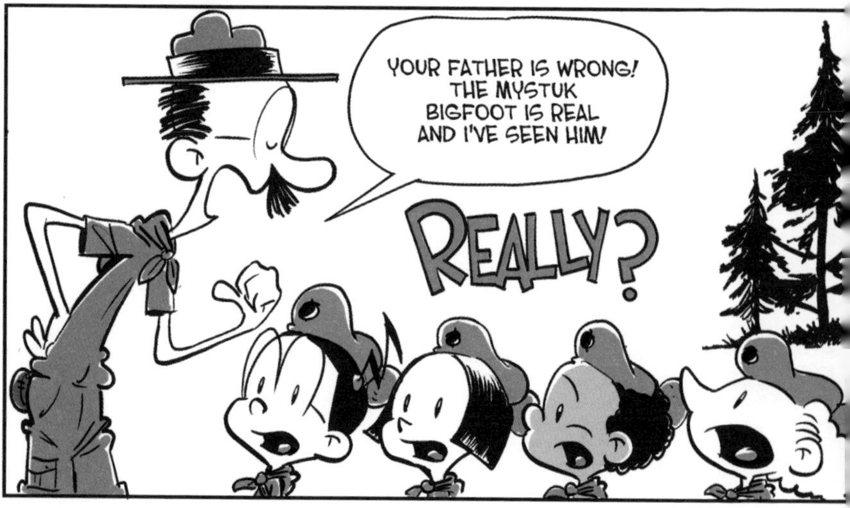
YOUR FATHER IS WRONG! THE MYSTUK BIGFOOT IS REAL AND I'VE SEEN HIM!
REALLY?

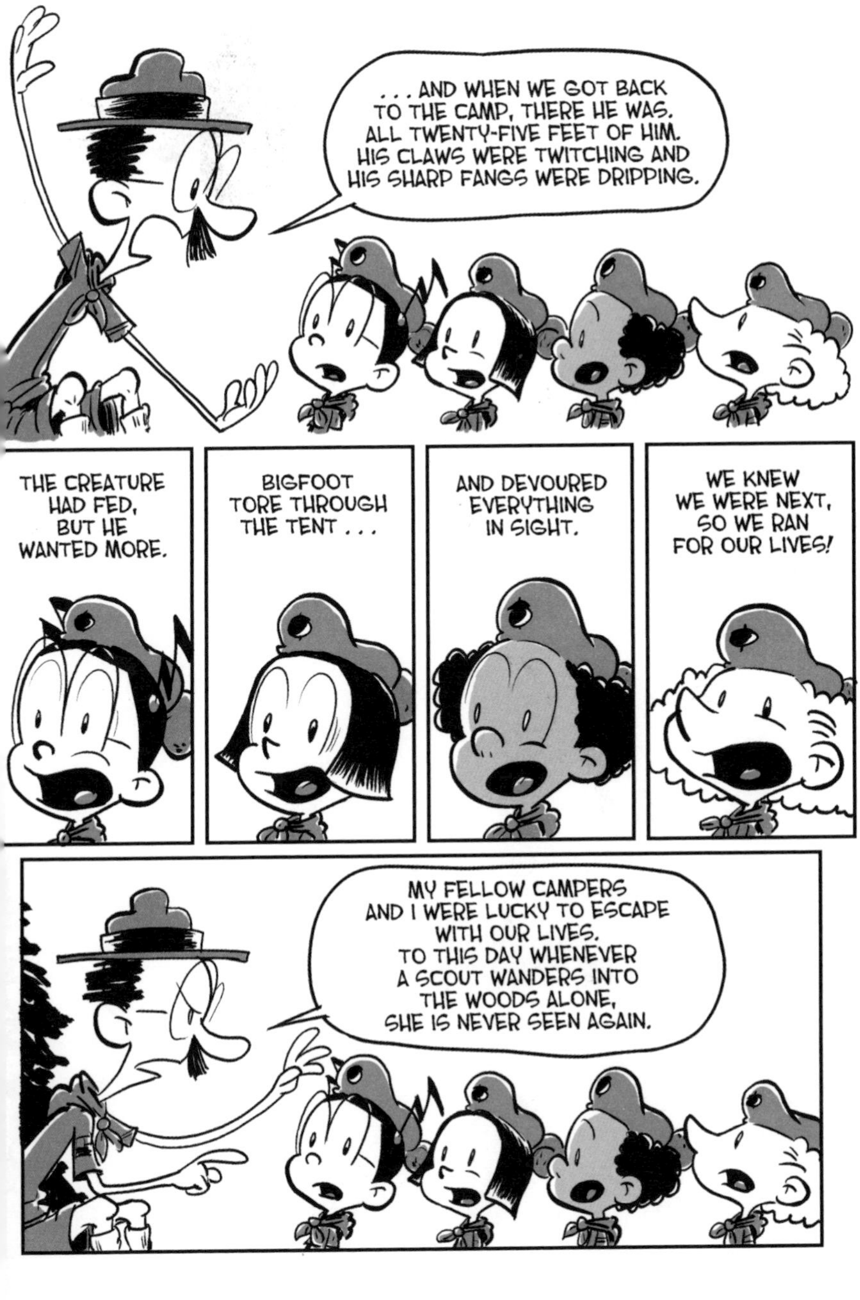
. . . AND WHEN WE GOT BACK TO THE CAMP, THERE HE WAS. ALL TWENTY-FIVE FEET OF HIM. HIS CLAWS WERE TWITCHING AND HIS SHARP FANGS WERE DRIPPING.
THE CREATURE HAD FED, BUT HE WANTED MORE.
BIGFOOT TORE THROUGH THE TENT . . .
AND DEVOURED EVERYTHING IN SIGHT.
WE KNEW WE WERE NEXT, SO WE RAN FOR OUR LIVES!
MY FELLOW CAMPERS AND I WERE LUCKY TO ESCAPE WITH OUR LIVES. TO THIS DAY WHENEVER A SCOUT WANDERS INTO THE WOODS ALONE, SHE IS NEVER SEEN AGAIN.

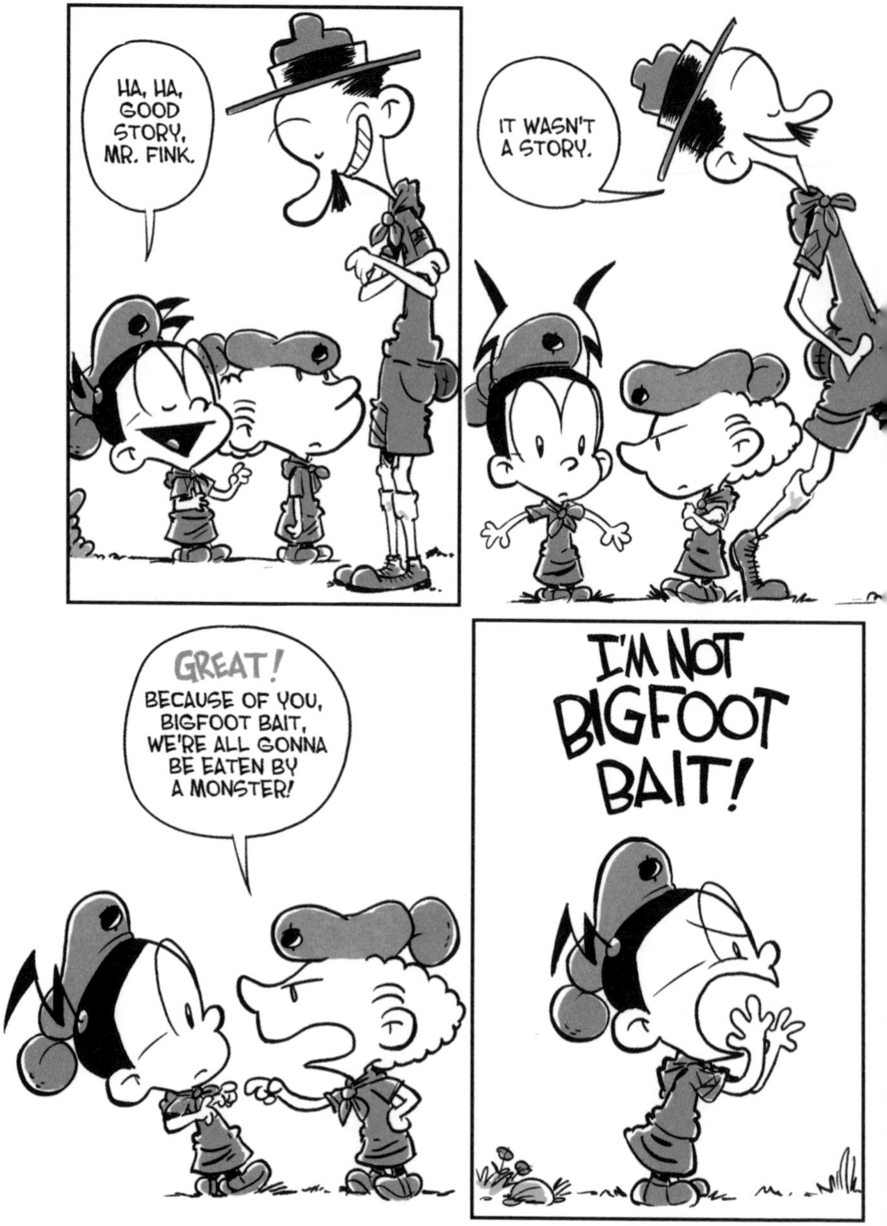
HA, HA, GOOD STORY, MR. FINK.
IT WASN'T A STORY.
GREAT! BECAUSE OF YOU, BIGFOOT BAIT, WE'RE ALL GONNA BE EATEN BY A MONSTER!
I'M NOT BIGFOOT BAIT!

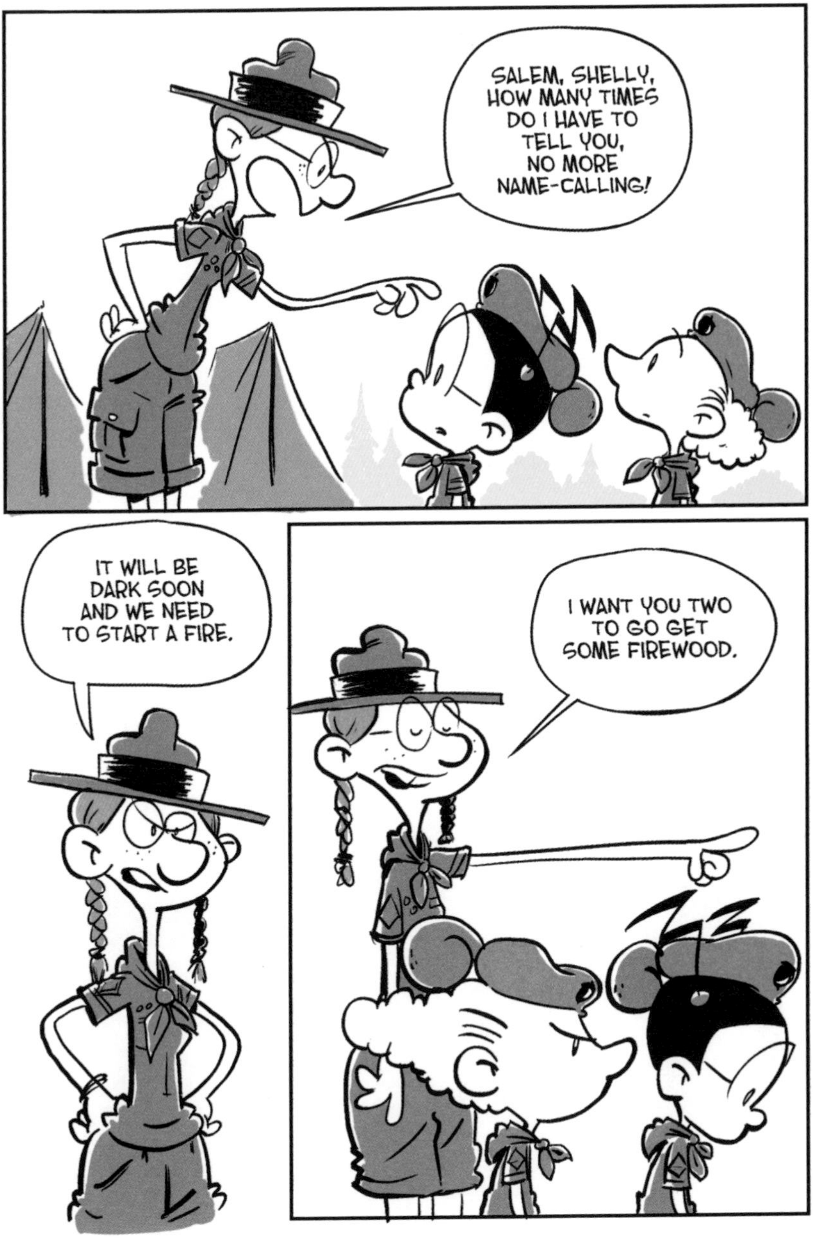
SALEM, SHELLY, HOW MANY TIMES DO I HAVE TO TELL YOU, NO MORE NAME-CALLING!
IT WILL BE DARK SOON AND WE NEED TO START A FIRE.
I WANT YOU TWO TO GO GET SOME FIREWOOD.

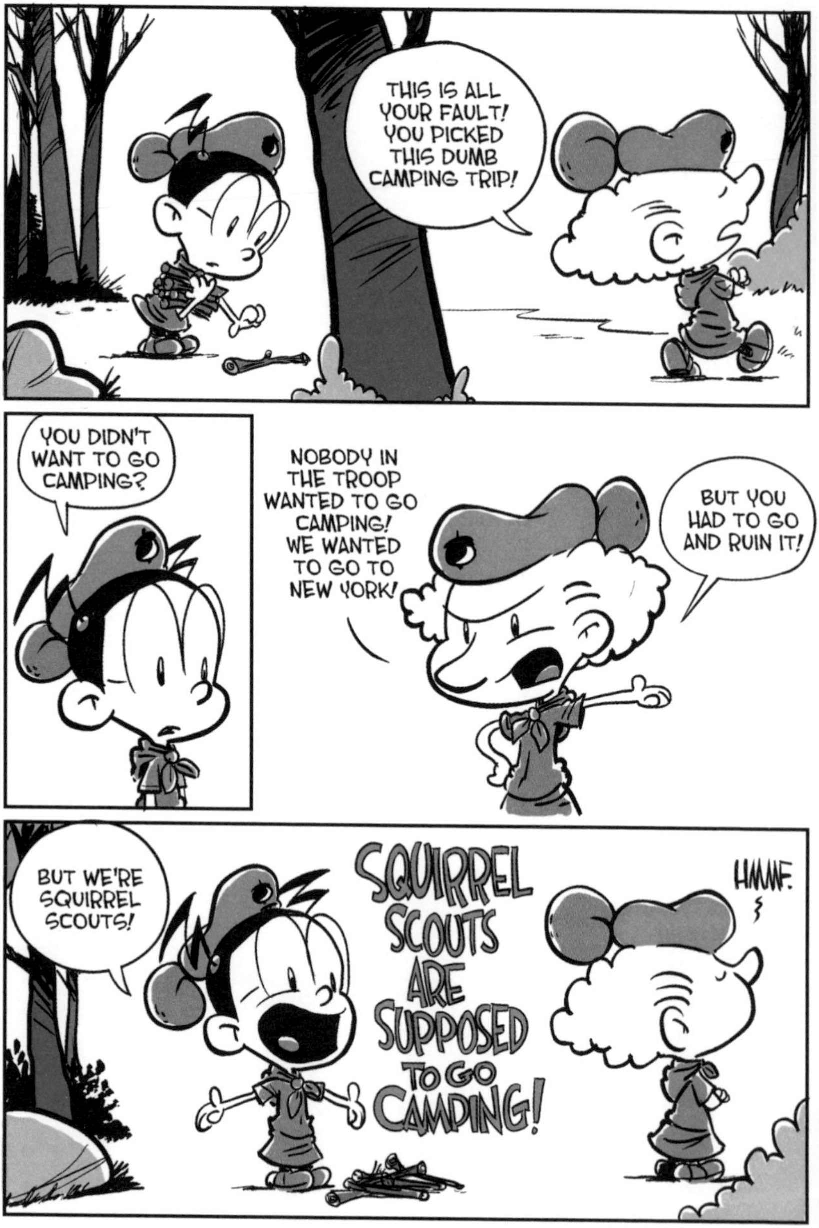
THIS IS ALL YOUR FAULT! YOU PICKED THIS DUMB CAMPING TRIP!
YOU DIDN'T WANT TO GO CAMPING?
NOBODY IN THE TROOP WANTED TO GO CAMPING! WE WANTED TO GO TO NEW YORK!
BUT YOU HAD TO GO AND RUIN IT!
BUT WE'RE SQUIRREL SCOUTS!
SQUIRREL SCOUTS ARE SUPPOSED TO GO CAMPING!
HMMF.

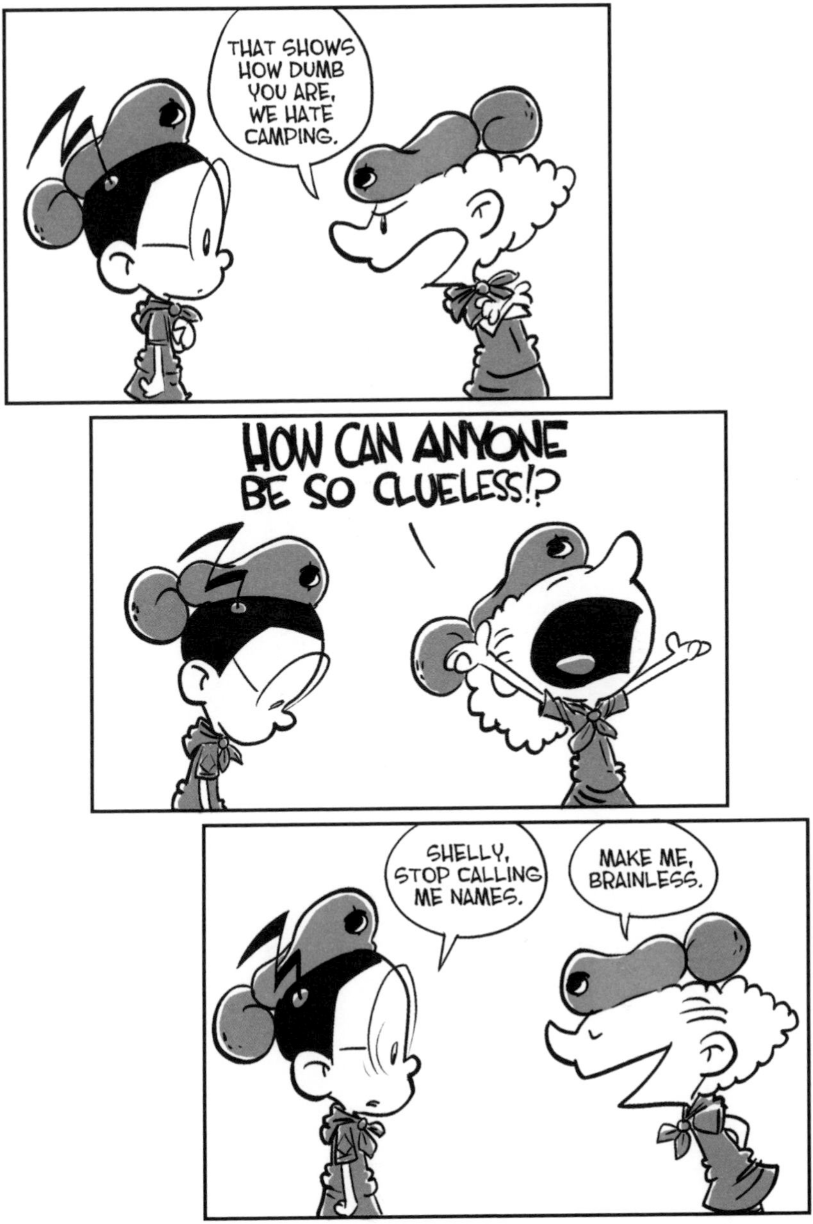
THAT SHOWS HOW DUMB YOU ARE, WE HATE CAMPING.
HOW CAN ANYONE BE SO CLUELESS!?
SHELLY, STOP CALLING ME NAMES.
MAKE ME, BRAINLESS.

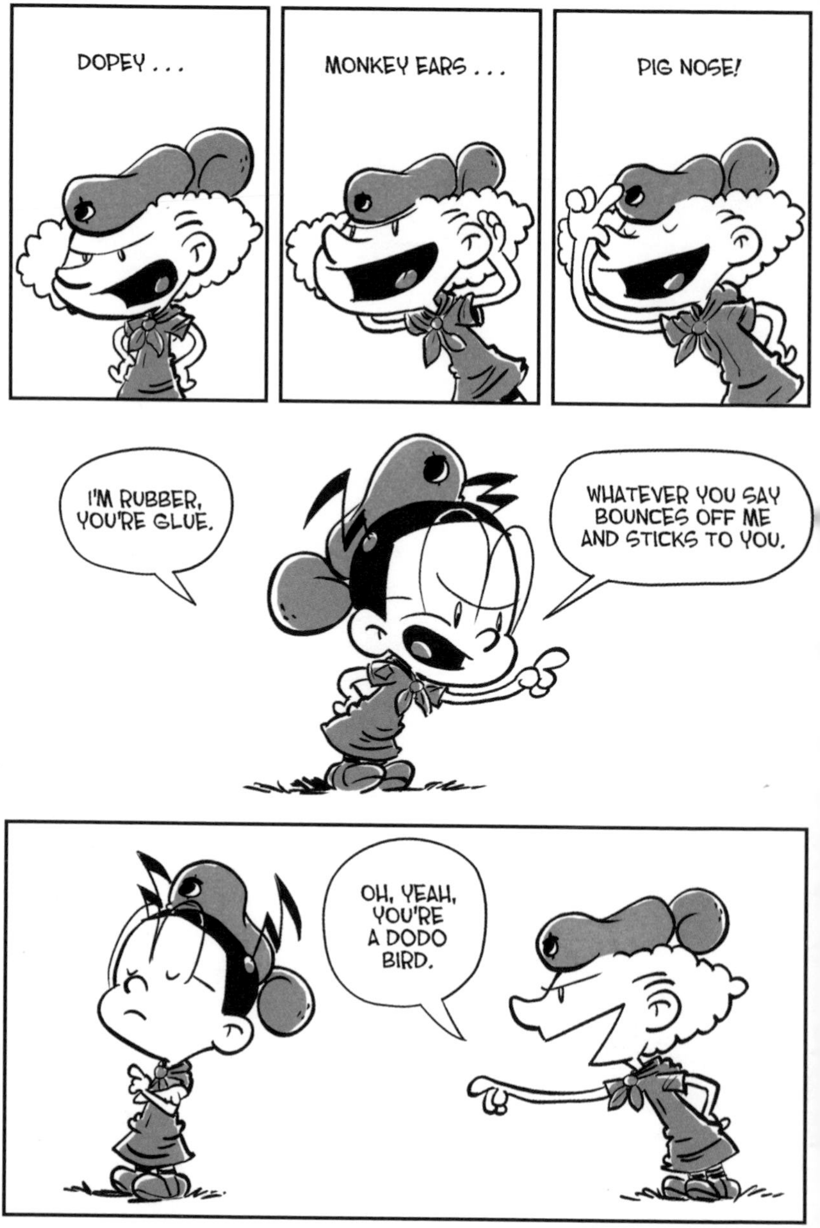

DOPEY . . .
MONKEY EARS . . .
PIG NOSE!
I'M RUBBER, YOU'RE GLUE.
WHATEVER YOU SAY BOUNCES OFF ME AND STICKS TO YOU.
OH, YEAH, YOU'RE A DODO BIRD.

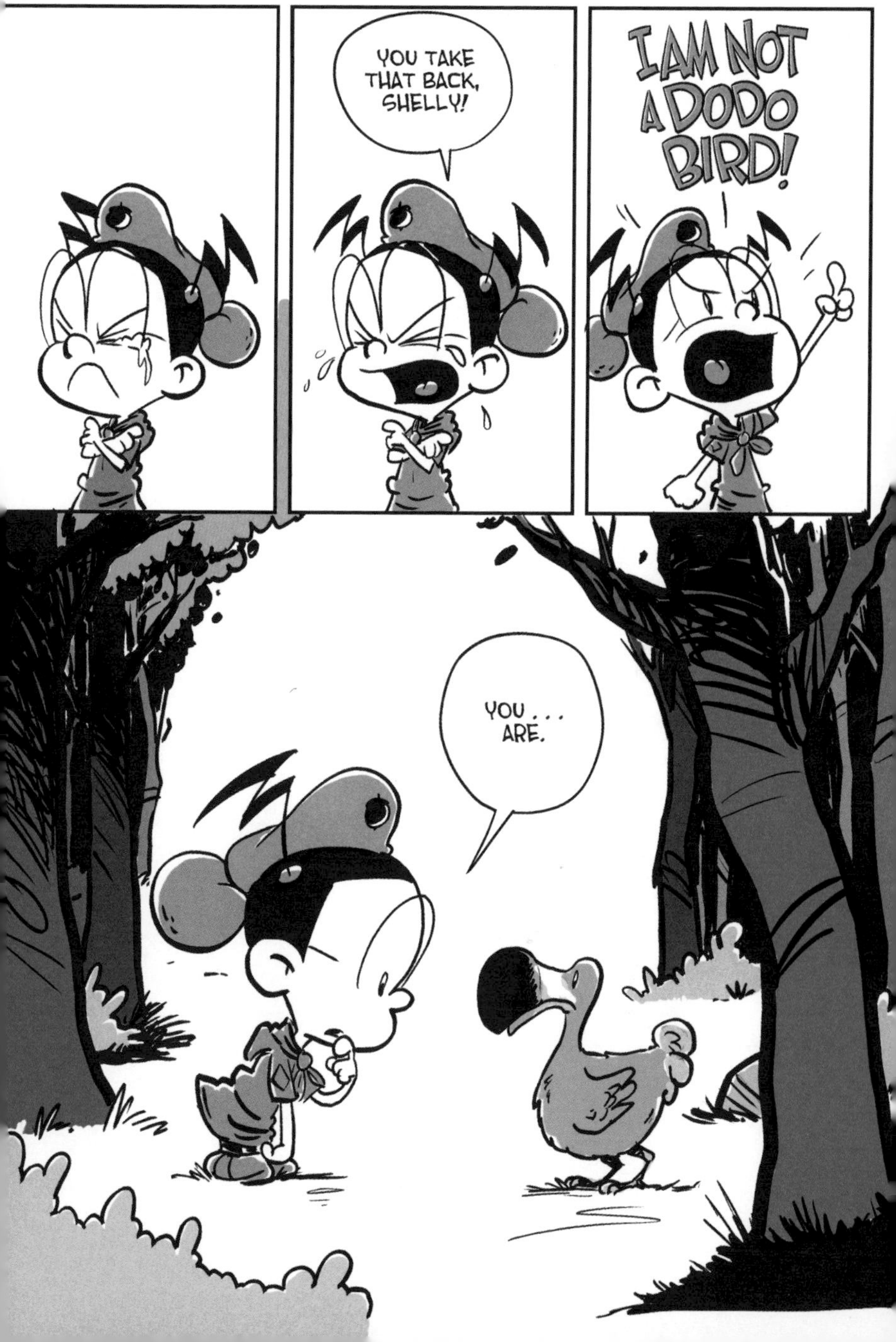
YOU TAKE THAT BACK, SHELLY!
I AM NOT A DODO BIRD!
YOU . . . ARE.

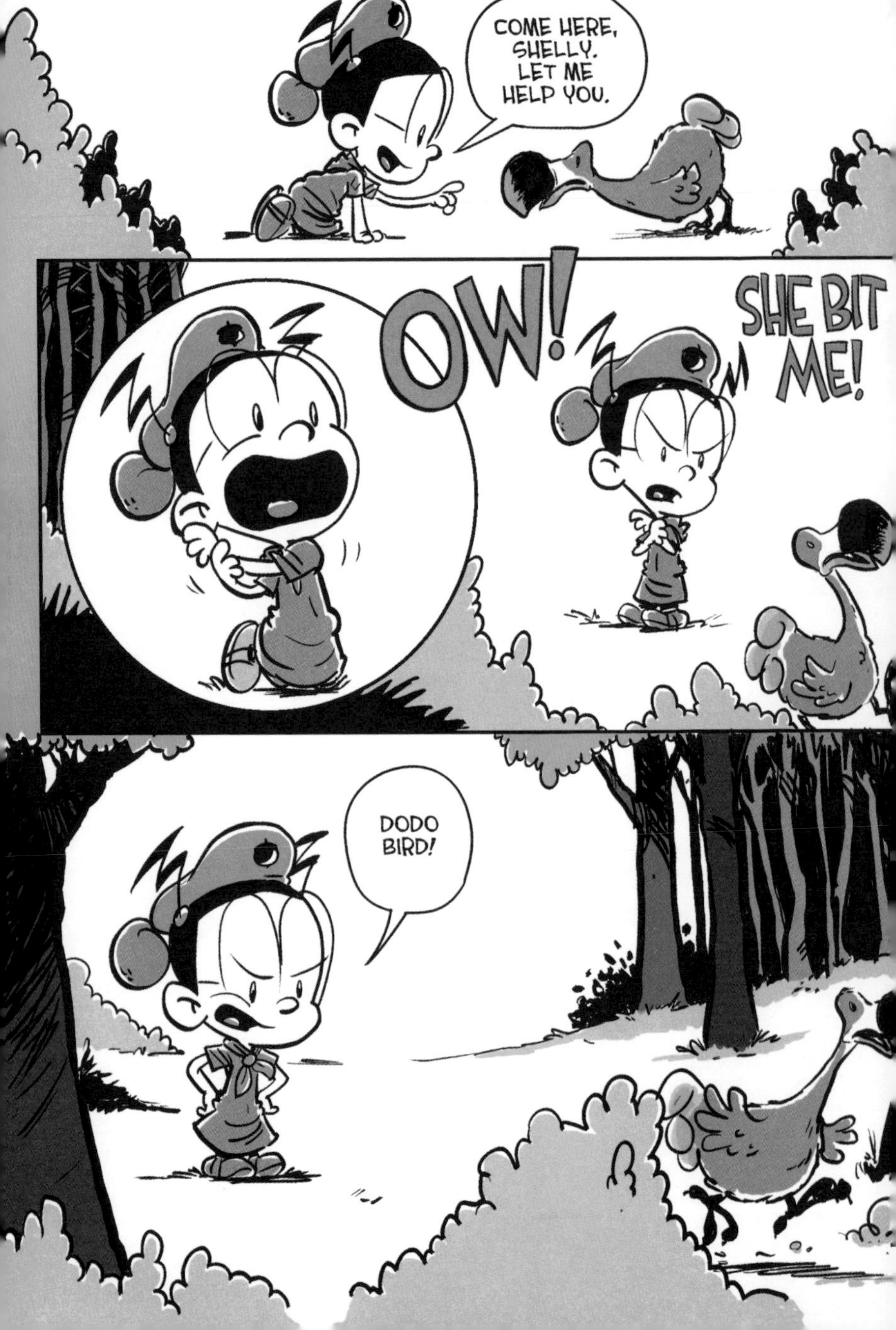
COME HERE, SHELLY. LET ME HELP YOU.
OW!
SHE BIT ME!
DODO BIRD!

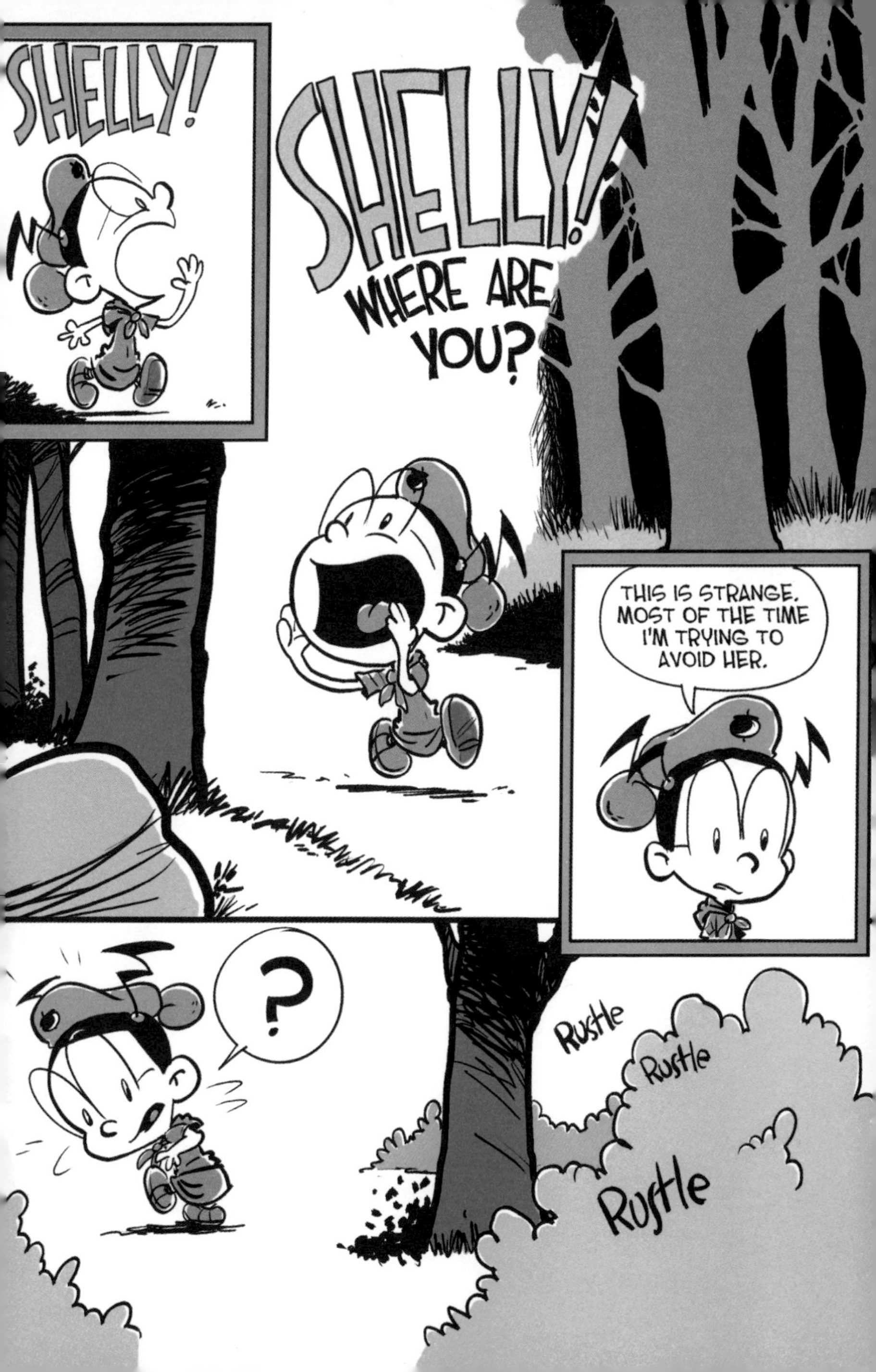
SHELLY!
SHELLY! WHERE ARE YOU?
THIS IS STRANGE. MOST OF THE TIME I'M TRYING TO AVOID HER.
?
Rustle
Rustle
Rustle

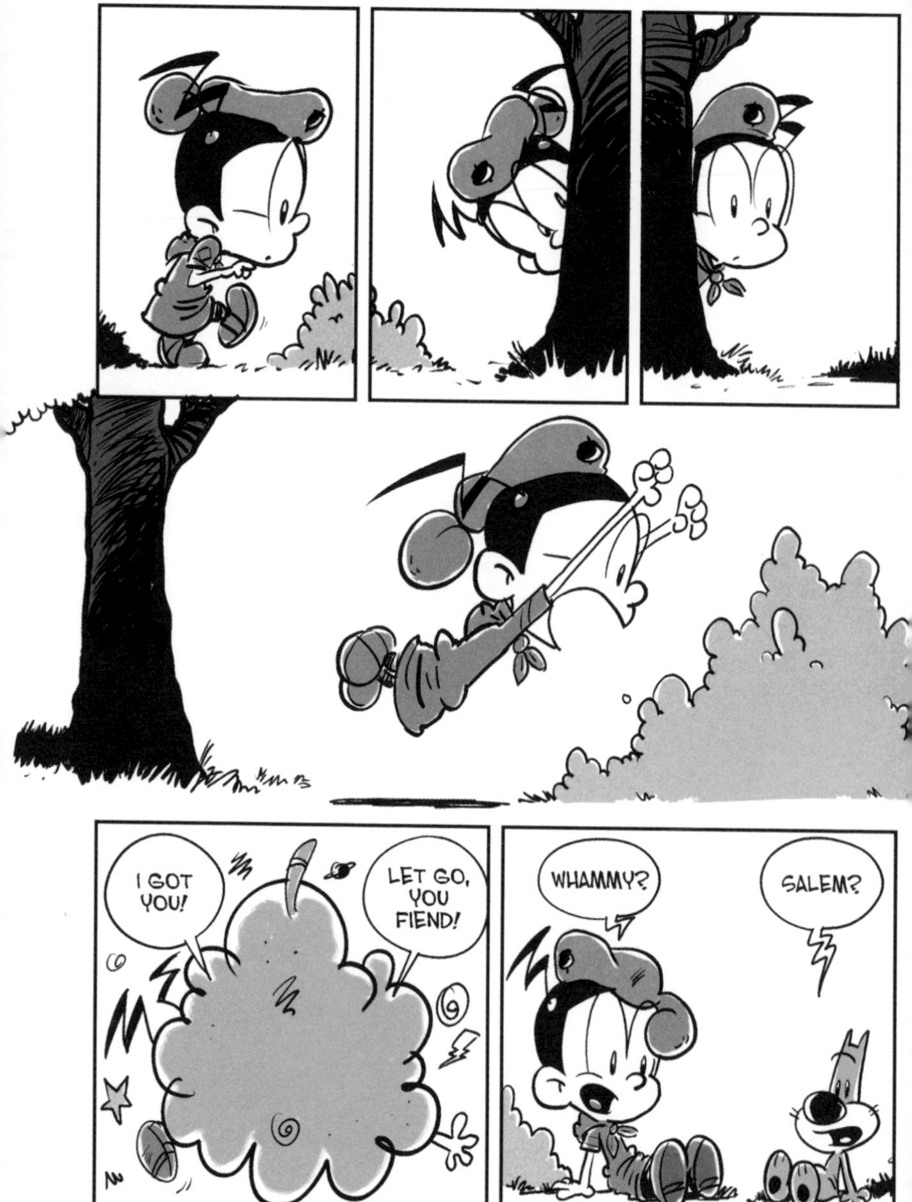
I GOT YOU!
LET GO, YOU FIEND!
WHAMMY?
SALEM?

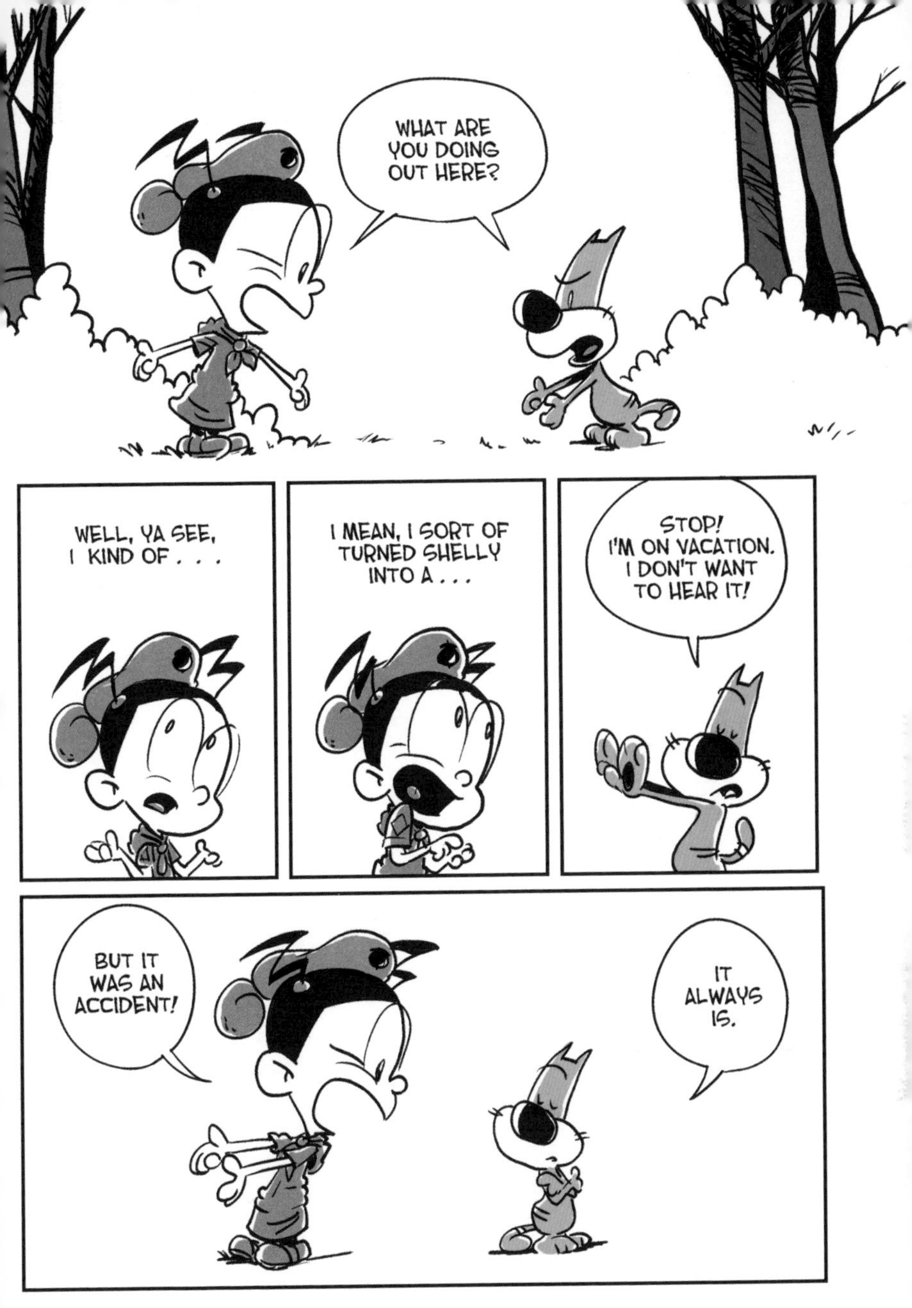
WHAT ARE YOU DOING OUT HERE?
WELL, YA SEE, I KIND OF . . .
I MEAN, I SORT OF TURNED SHELLY INTO A . . .
STOP! I'M ON VACATION. I DON'T WANT TO HEAR IT!
BUT IT WAS AN ACCIDENT!
IT ALWAYS IS.

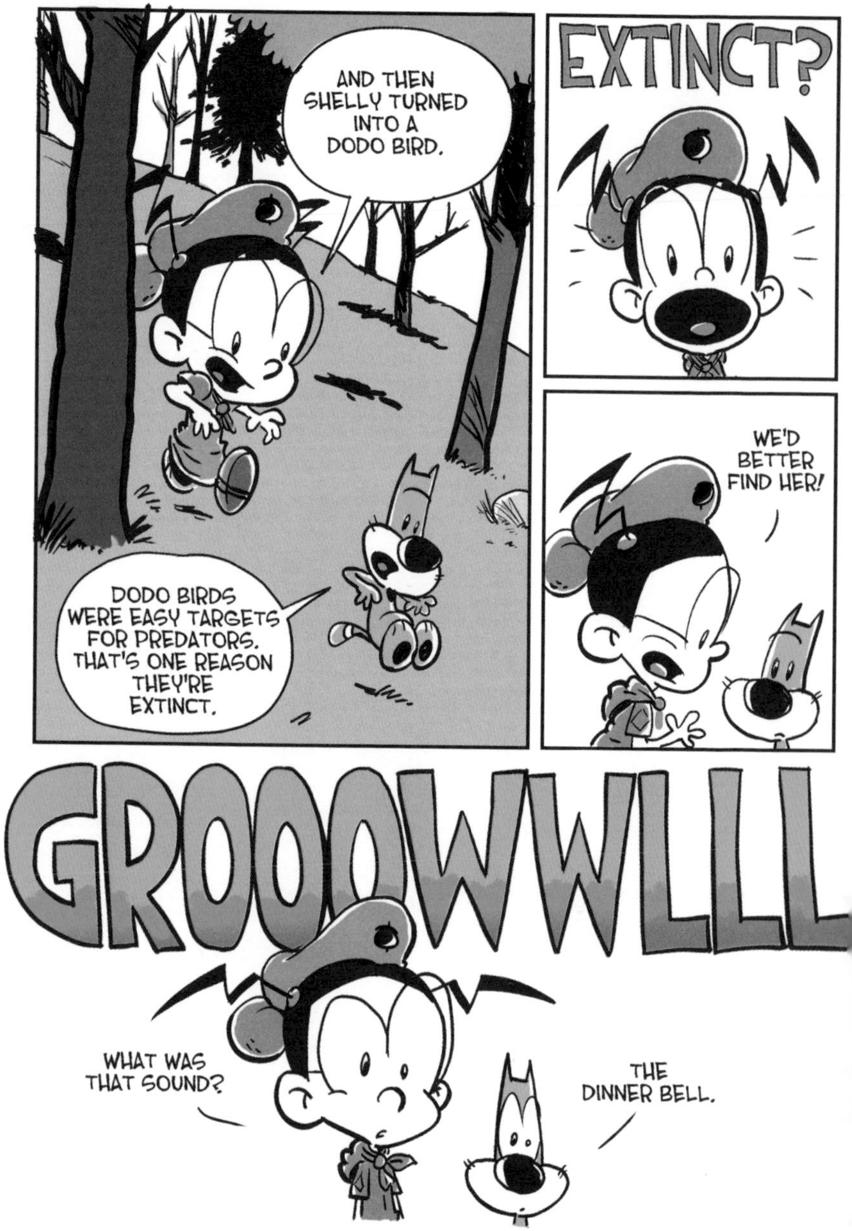
AND THEN SHELLY TURNED INTO A DODO BIRD.
DODO BIRDS WERE EASY TARGETS FOR PREDATORS. THAT'S ONE REASON THEY'RE EXTINCT.
EXTINCT?
WE'D BETTER FIND HER!
GROOOWWLLL
WHAT WAS THAT SOUND?
THE DINNER BELL.

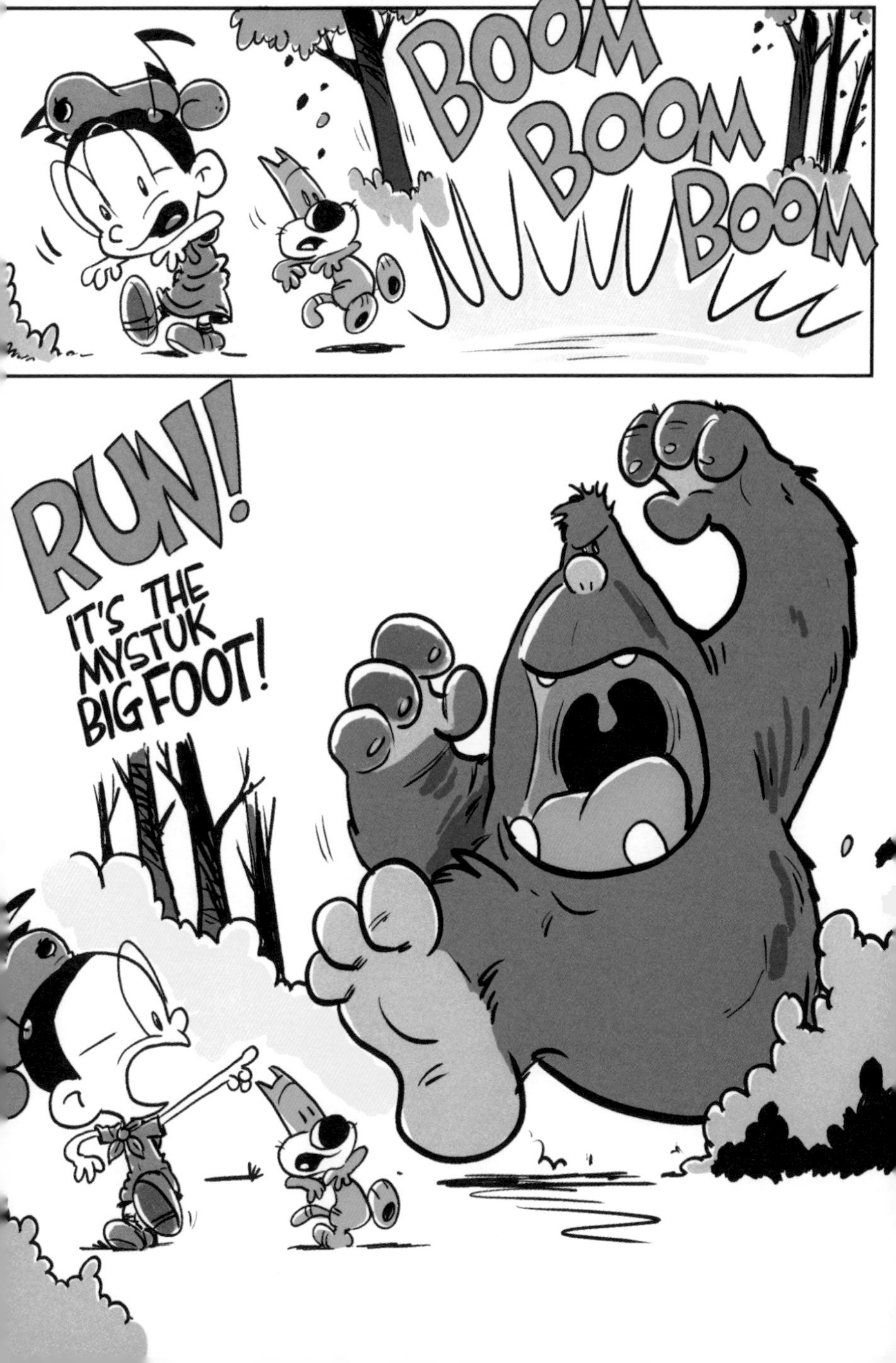
BOOM
BOOM
BOOM
RUN!
IT'S THE MYSTUK BIGFOOT!

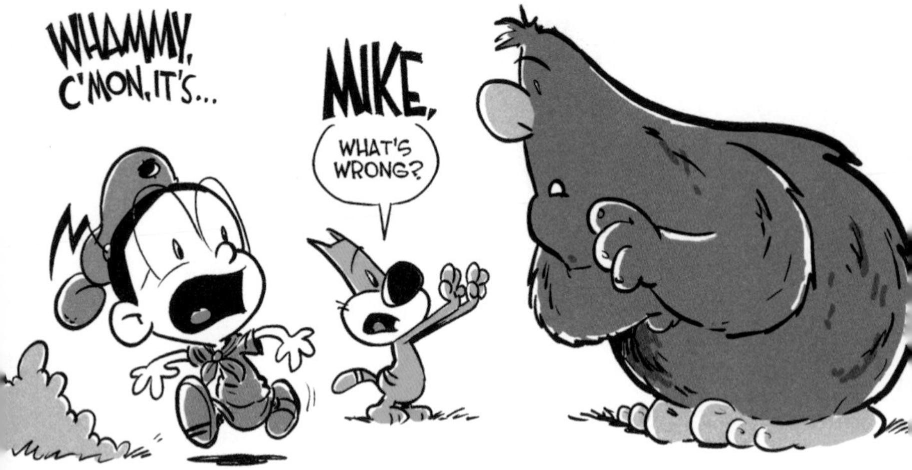
WHAMMY, C'MON, IT'S...
MIKE,
WHAT'S WRONG?

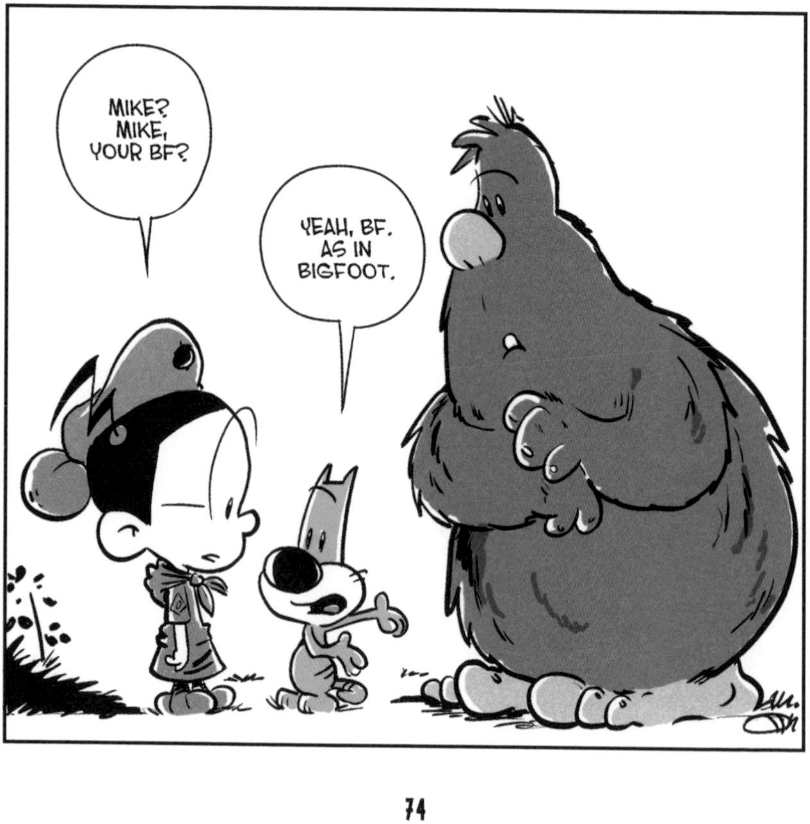
MIKE? MIKE, YOUR BF?
YEAH, BF. AS IN BIGFOOT.

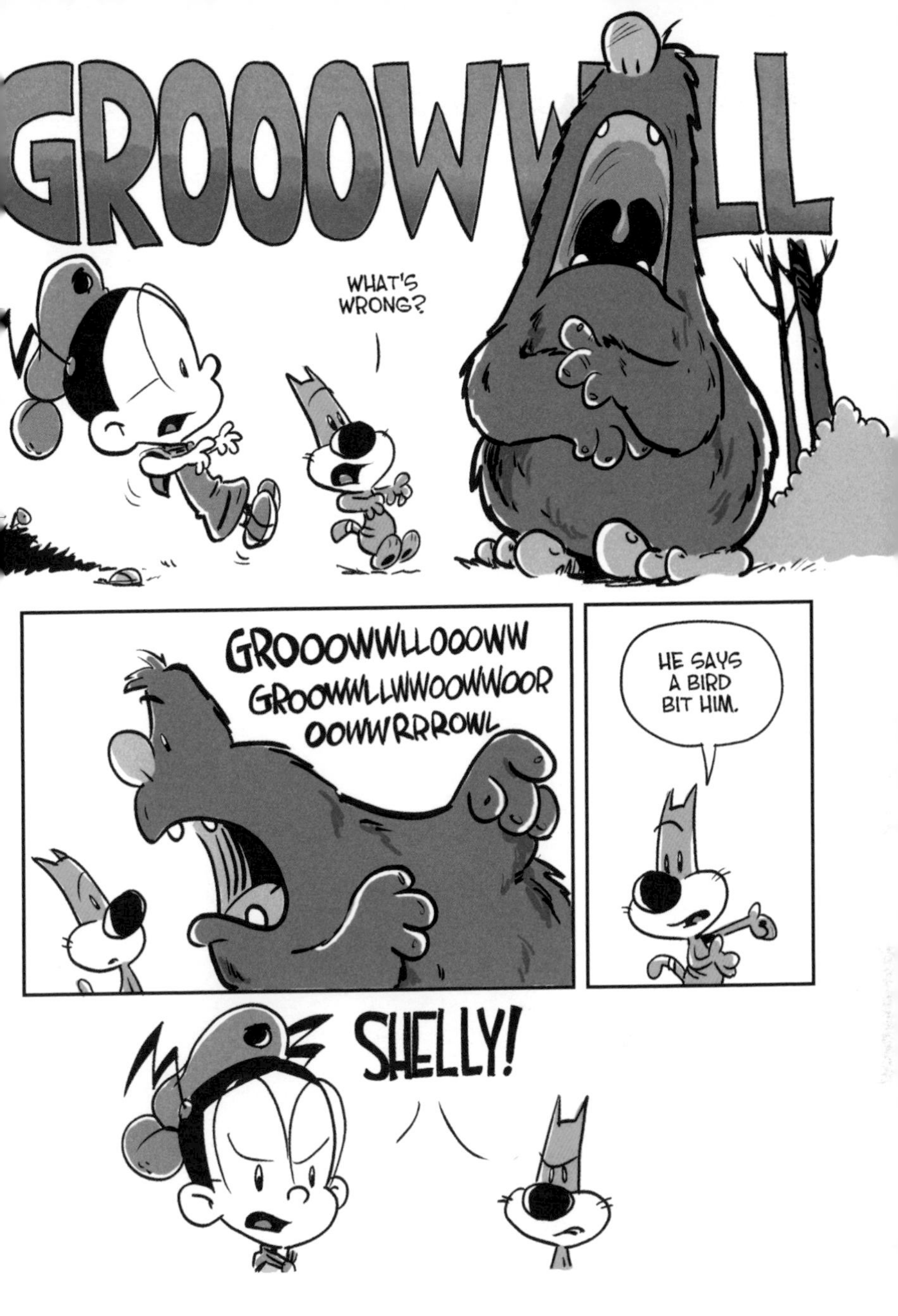
GROOOWWLL
WHAT'S WRONG?
GROOOWWLLOOOWW GROOWWLLWWOOWWOOR OOWWRRROWL
HE SAYS A BIRD BIT HIM.
SHELLY!

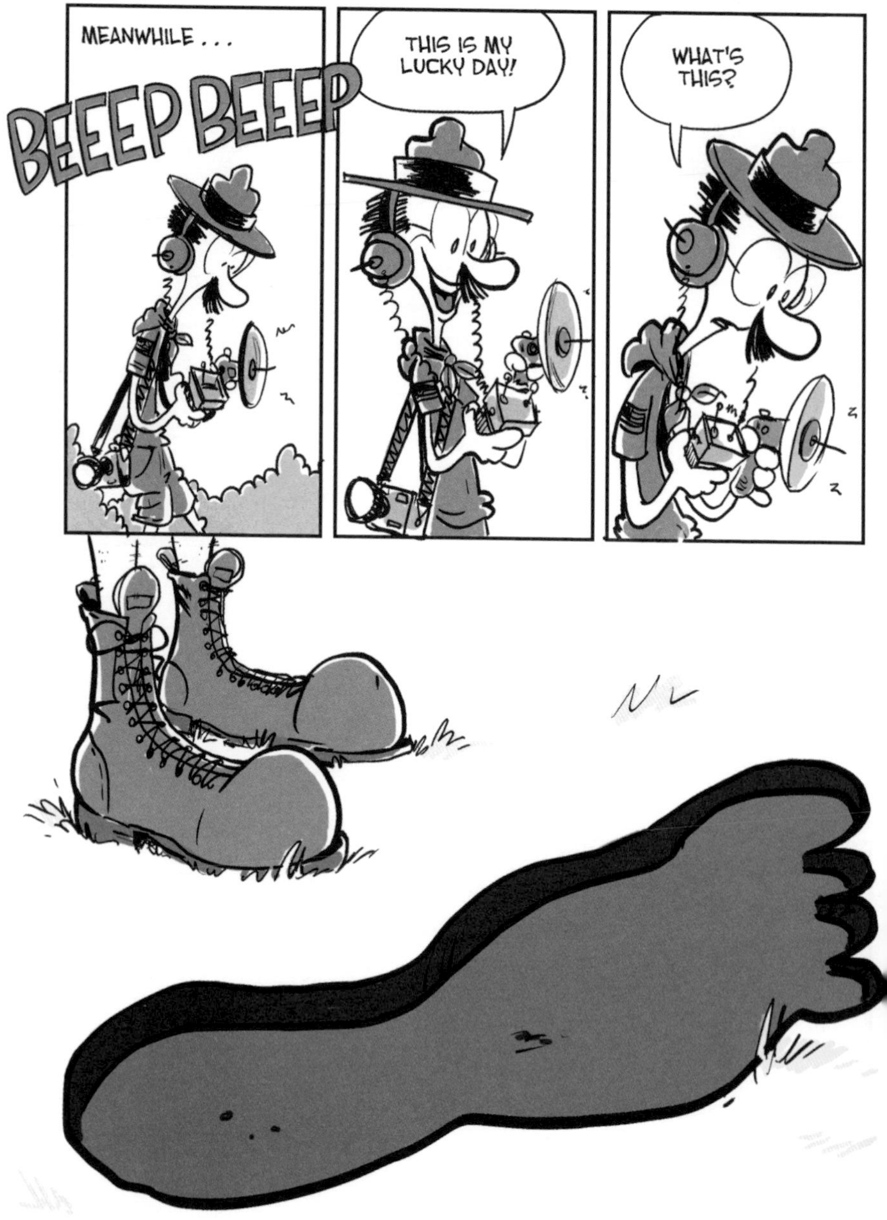
MEANWHILE . . .
BEEEP BEEEP
THIS IS MY LUCKY DAY!
WHAT'S THIS?

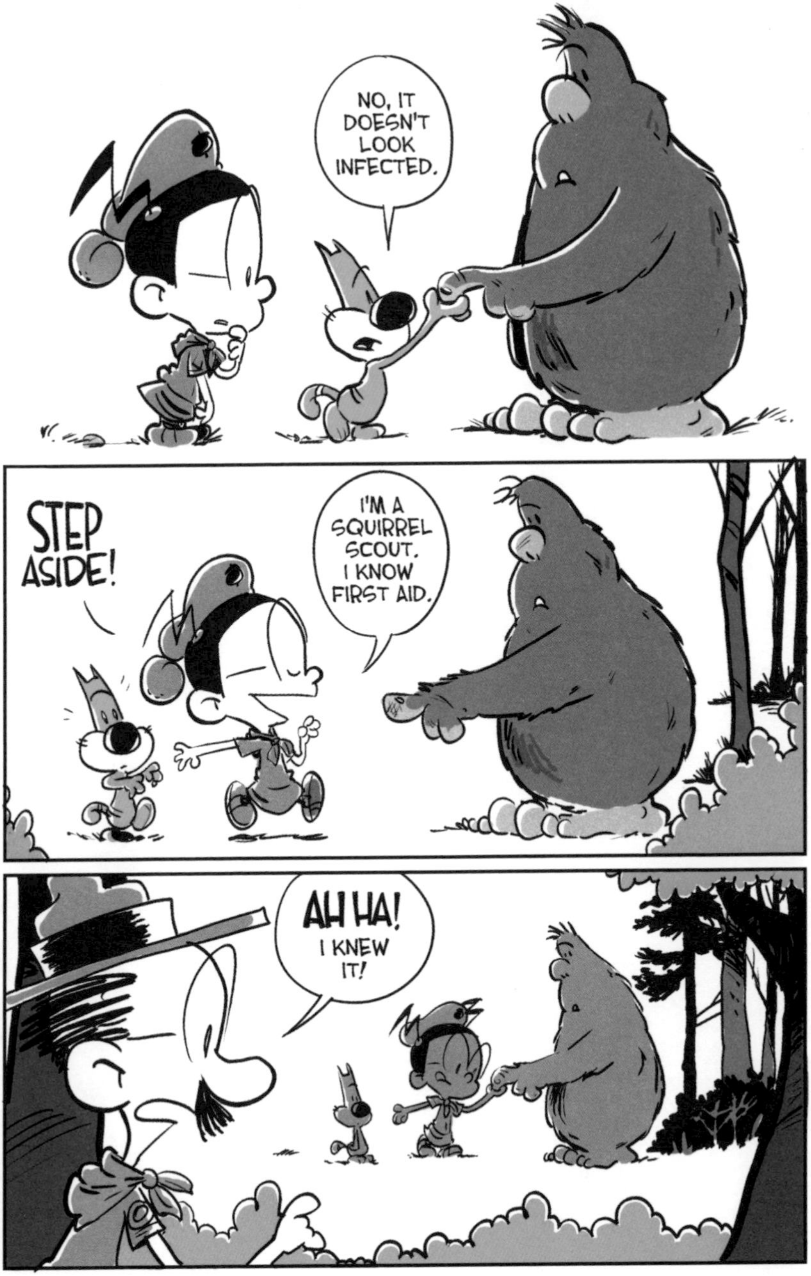
NO, IT DOESN'T LOOK INFECTED.
STEP ASIDE!
I'M A SQUIRREL SCOUT. I KNOW FIRST AID.
AH HA! I KNEW IT!

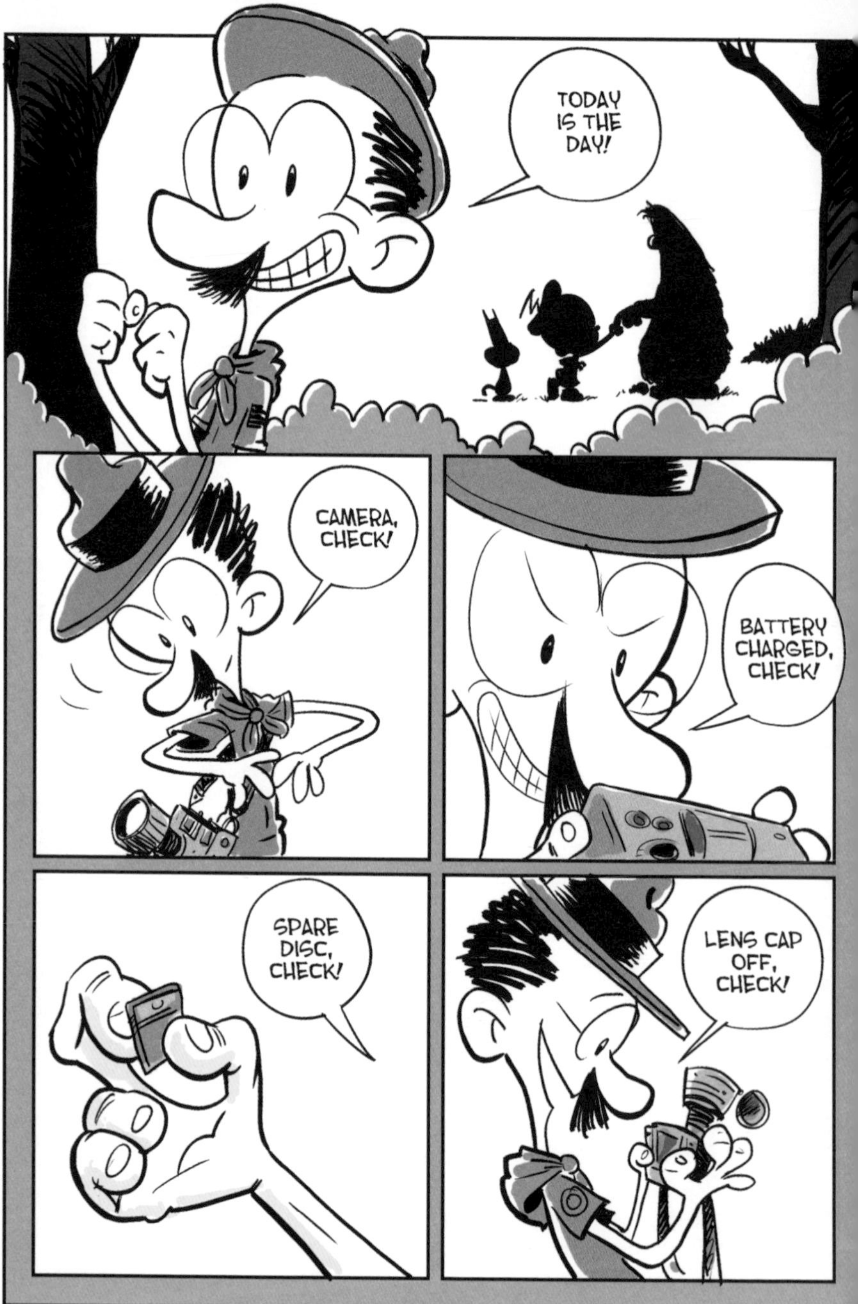
TODAY IS THE DAY!
CAMERA, CHECK!
BATTERY CHARGED, CHECK!
SPARE DISC, CHECK!
LENS CAP OFF, CHECK!

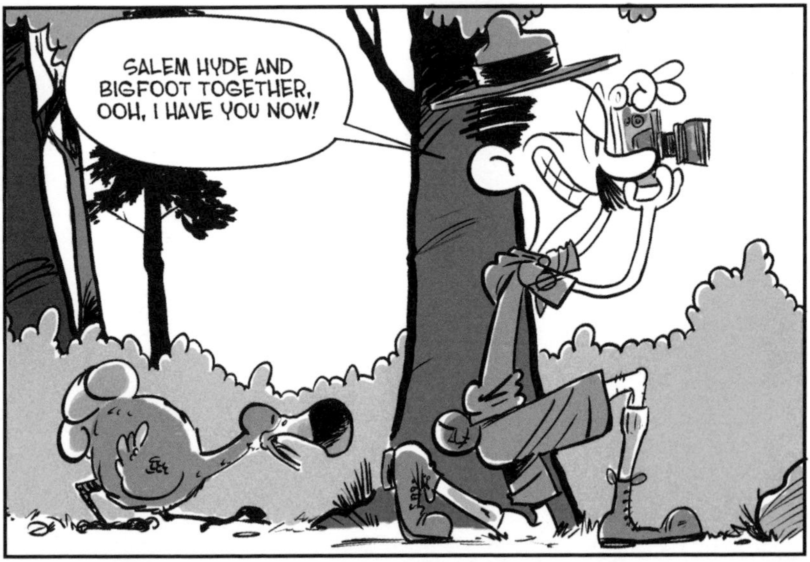
SALEM HYDE AND BIGFOOT TOGETHER, OOH, I HAVE YOU NOW!

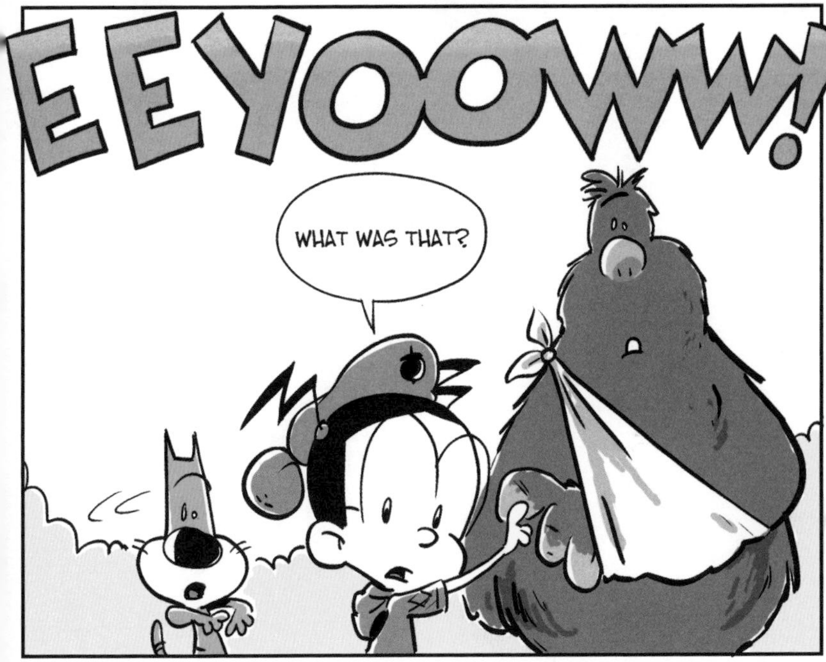
EEYOOWW!
WHAT WAS THAT?

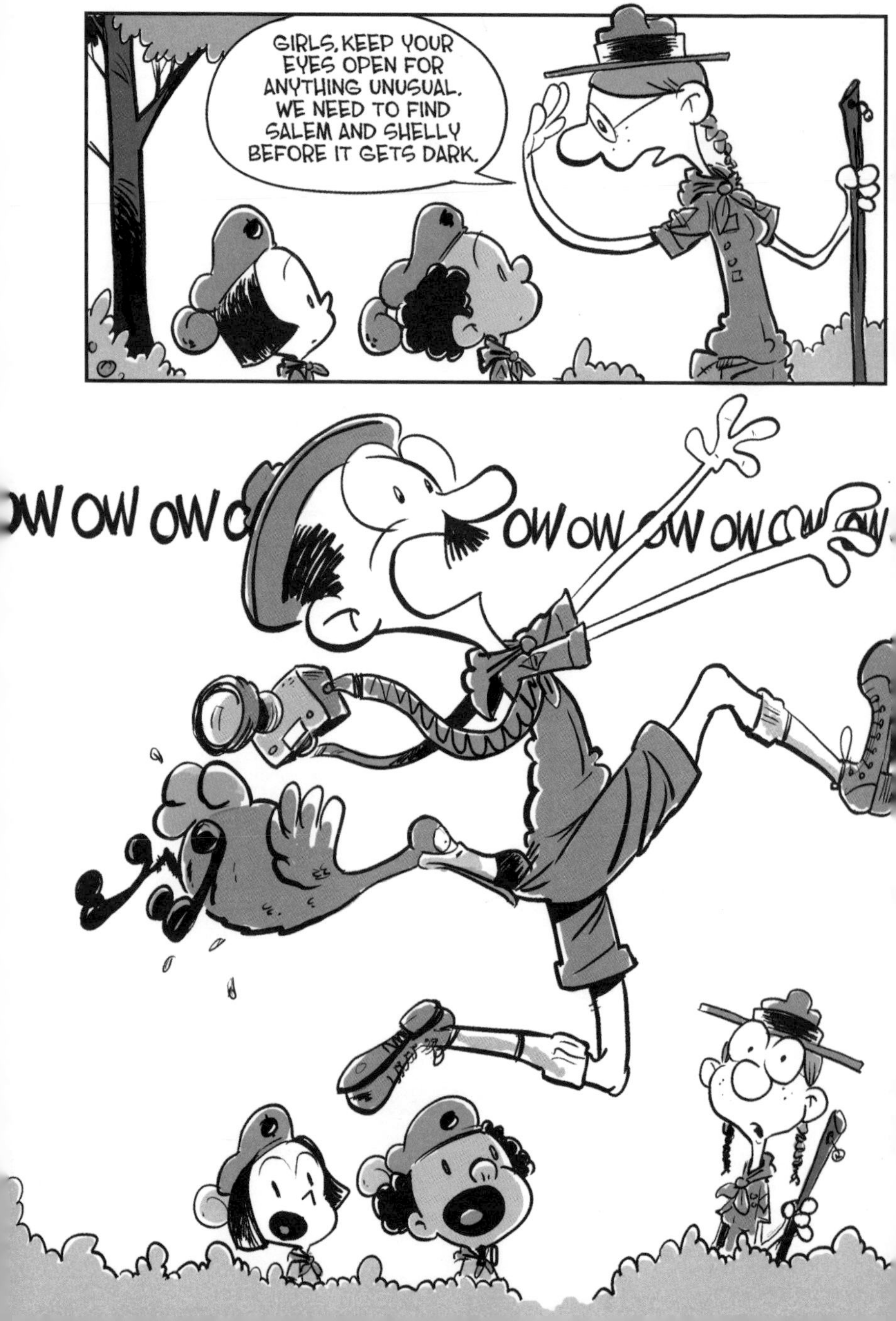
GIRLS, KEEP YOUR EYES OPEN FOR ANYTHING UNUSUAL. WE NEED TO FIND SALEM AND SHELLY BEFORE IT GETS DARK.
OW OW OW
OW OW OW OW

GET OFF...
OF ME...
YOU...
DODO BIRD!

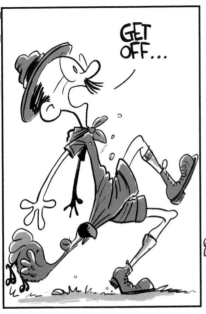

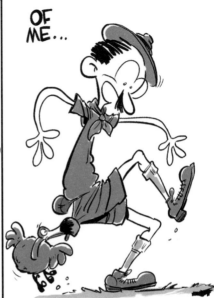

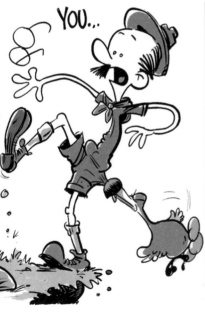

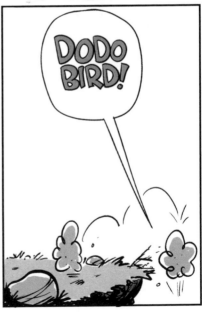

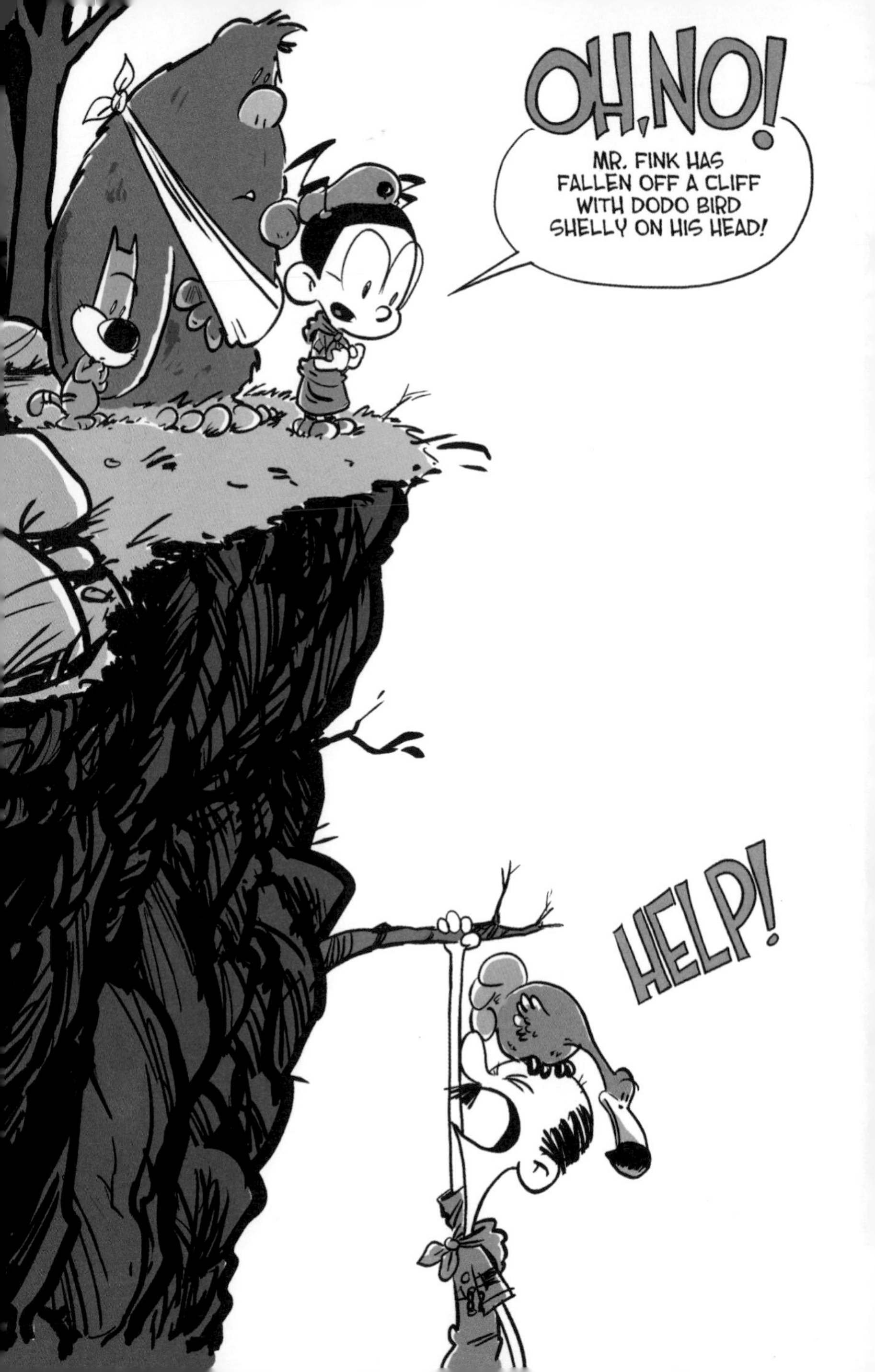

OH, NO!
MR. FINK HAS FALLEN OFF A CLIFF WITH DODO BIRD SHELLY ON HIS HEAD!
HELP!

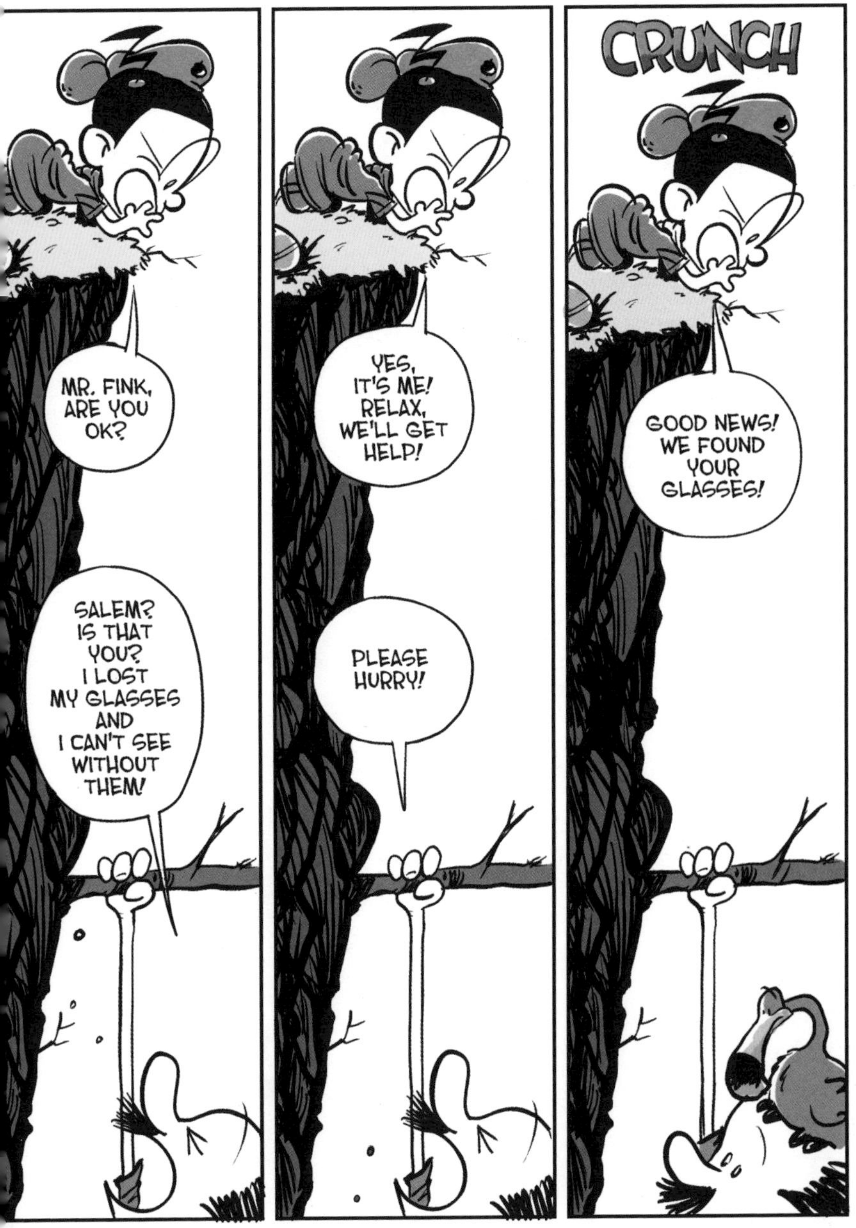
MR. FINK, ARE YOU OK?
SALEM? IS THAT YOU? I LOST MY GLASSES AND I CAN'T SEE WITHOUT THEM!
YES, IT'S ME! RELAX, WE'LL GET HELP!
PLEASE HURRY!
CRUNCH
GOOD NEWS! WE FOUND YOUR GLASSES!

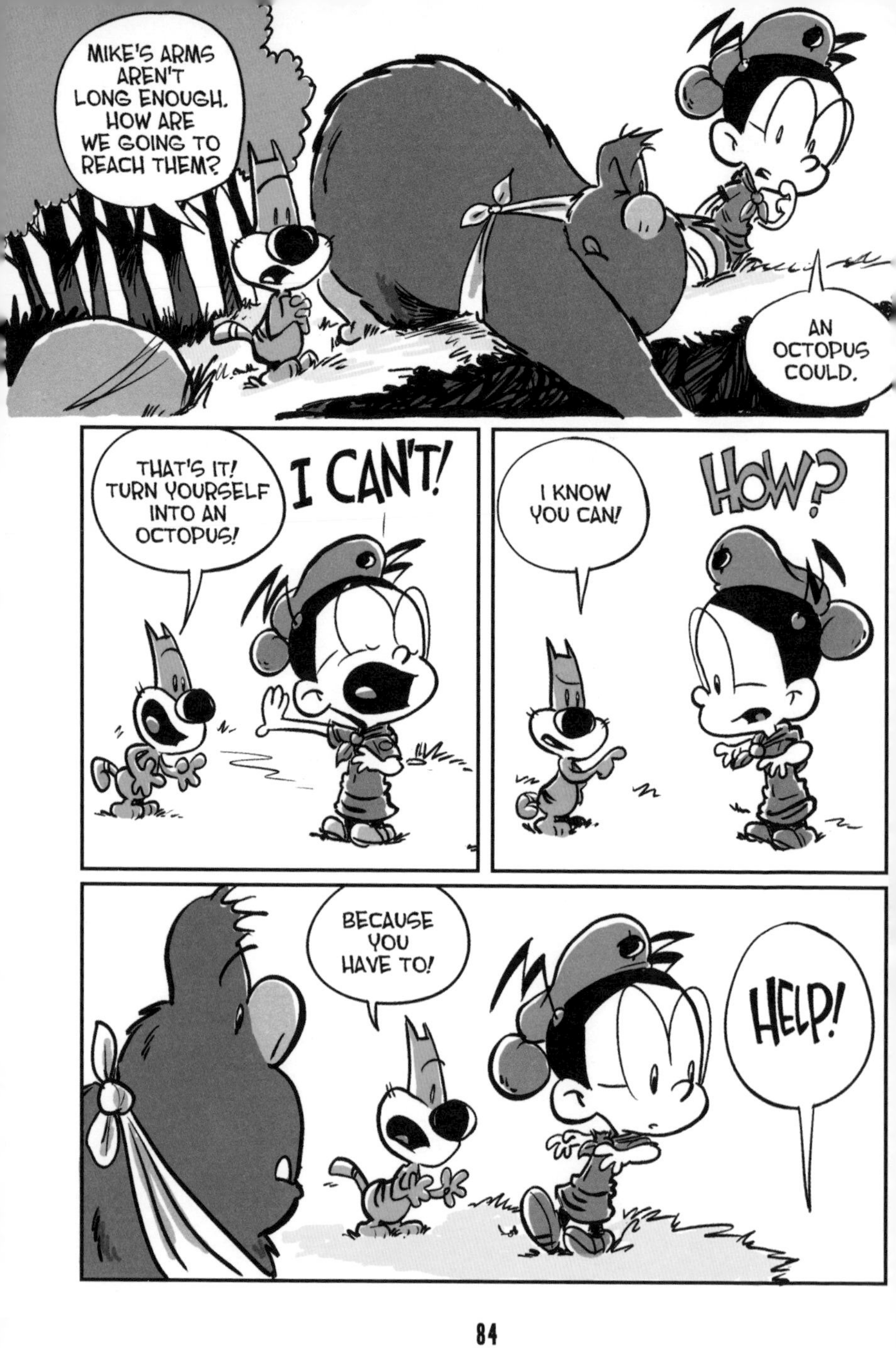
MIKE'S ARMS AREN'T LONG ENOUGH. HOW ARE WE GOING TO REACH THEM?
AN OCTOPUS COULD.
THAT'S IT! TURN YOURSELF INTO AN OCTOPUS!
I CAN'T!
I KNOW YOU CAN!
HOW?
BECAUSE YOU HAVE TO!
HELP!

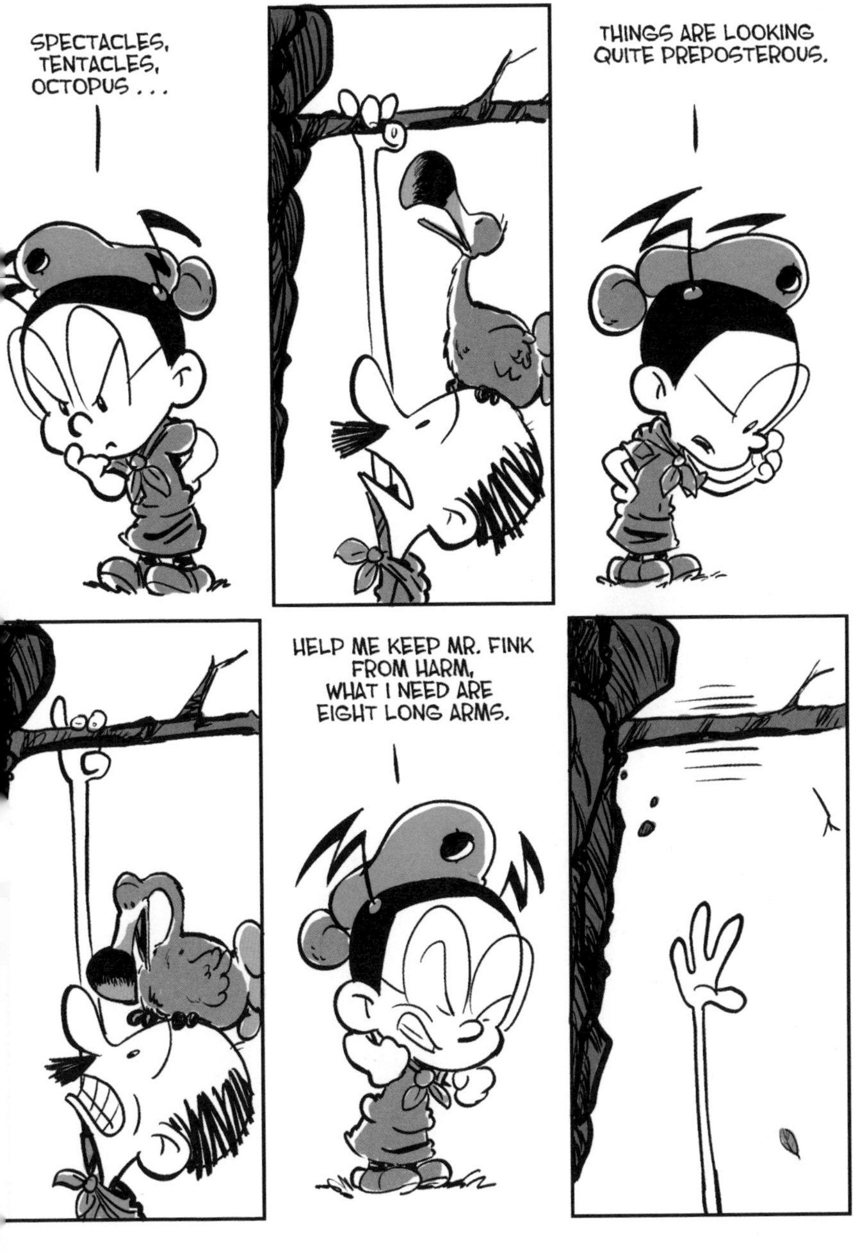
SPECTACLES, TENTACLES, OCTOPUS . . .
THINGS ARE LOOKING QUITE PREPOSTEROUS.
HELP ME KEEP MR. FINK FROM HARM, WHAT I NEED ARE EIGHT LONG ARMS.

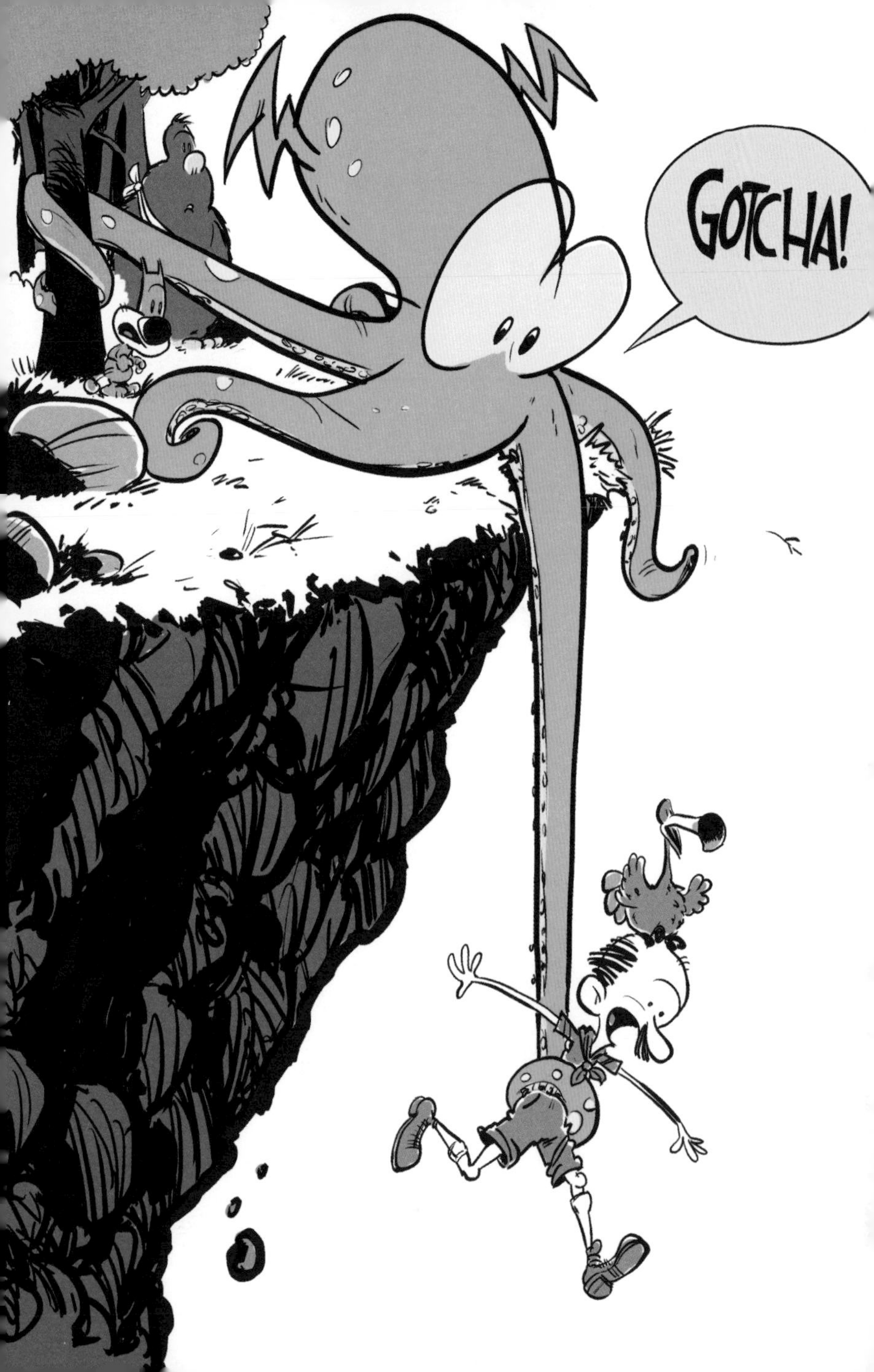
GOTCHA!

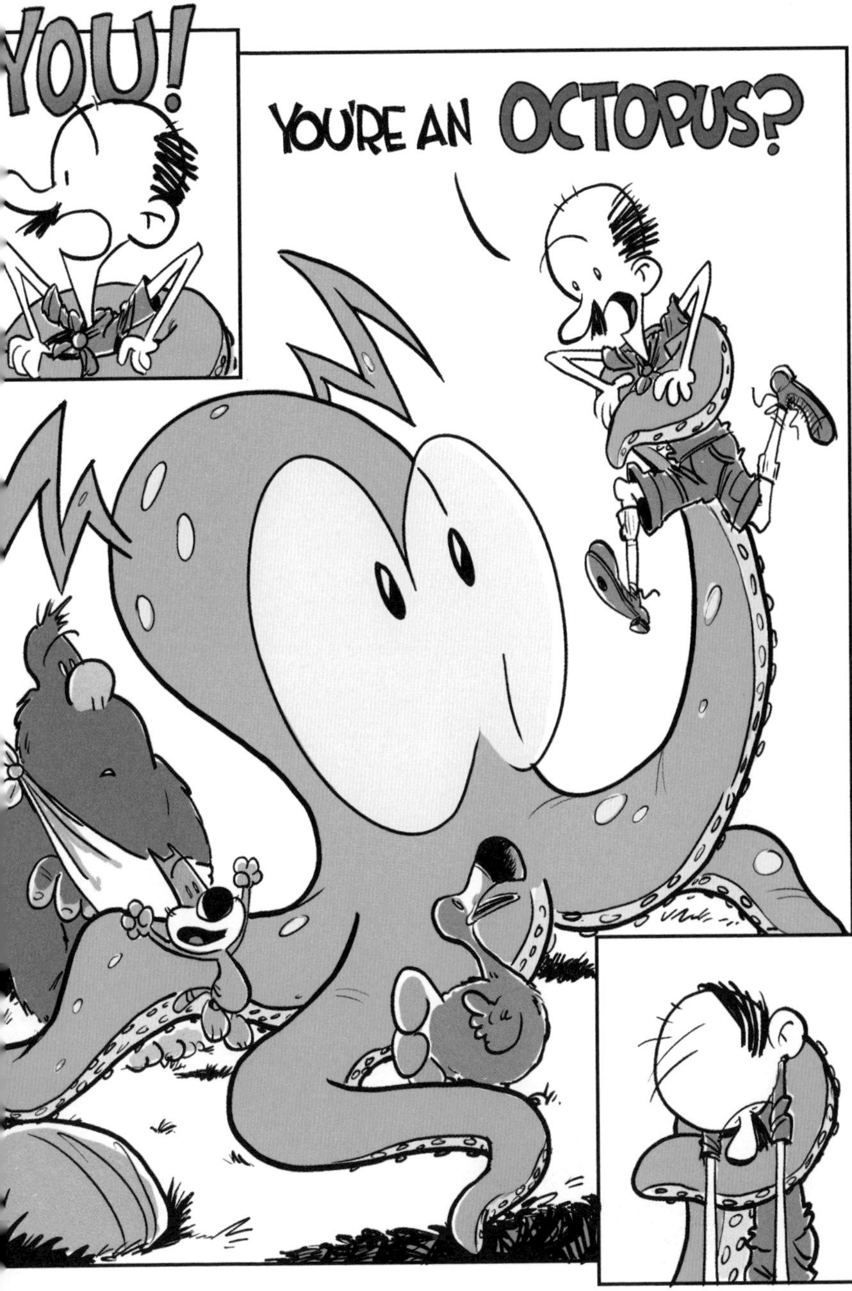
YOU!
YOU'RE AN OCTOPUS?

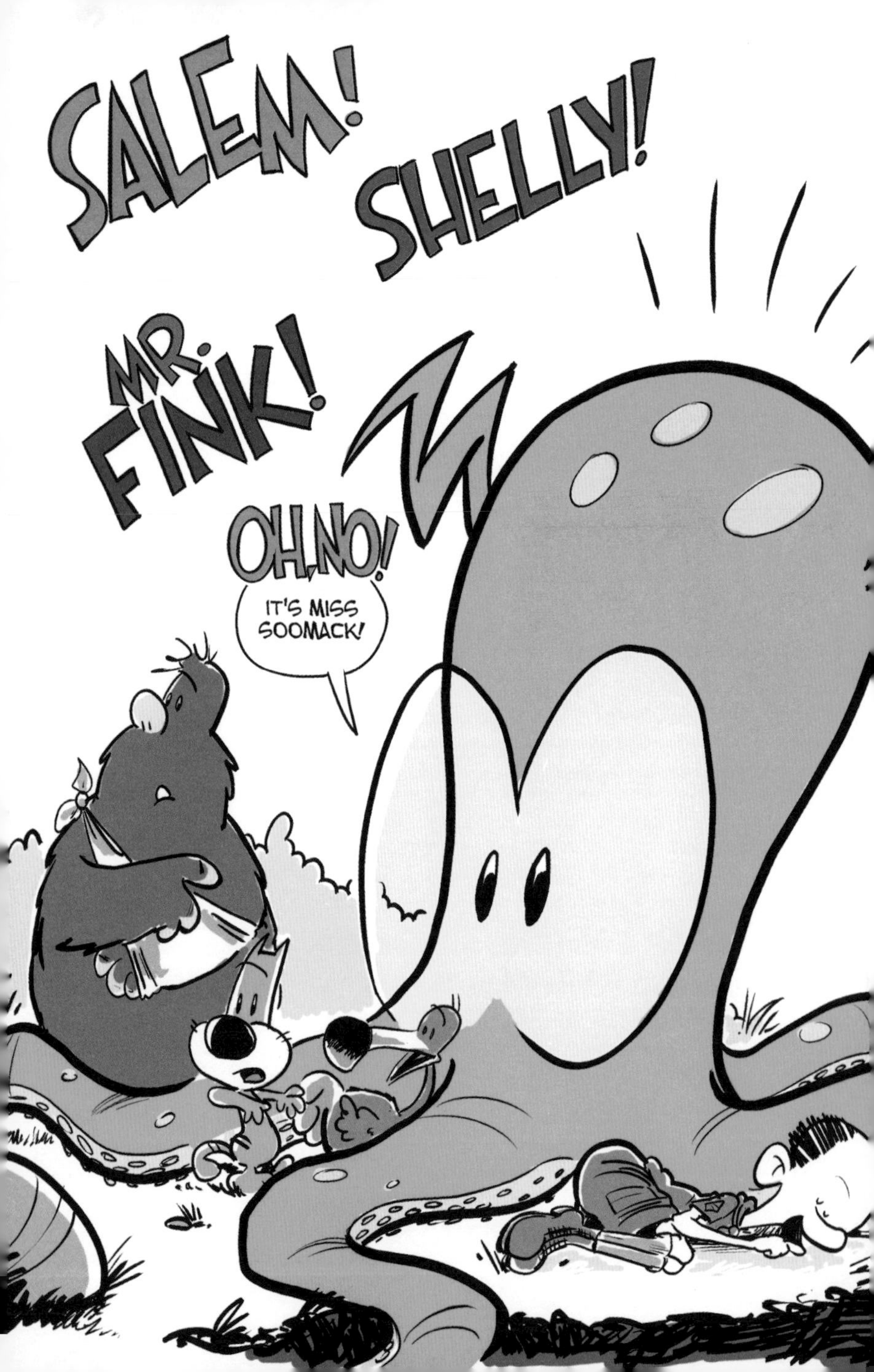
SALEM!
SHELLY!
MR. FINK!
OH, NO!
IT'S MISS SOOMACK!

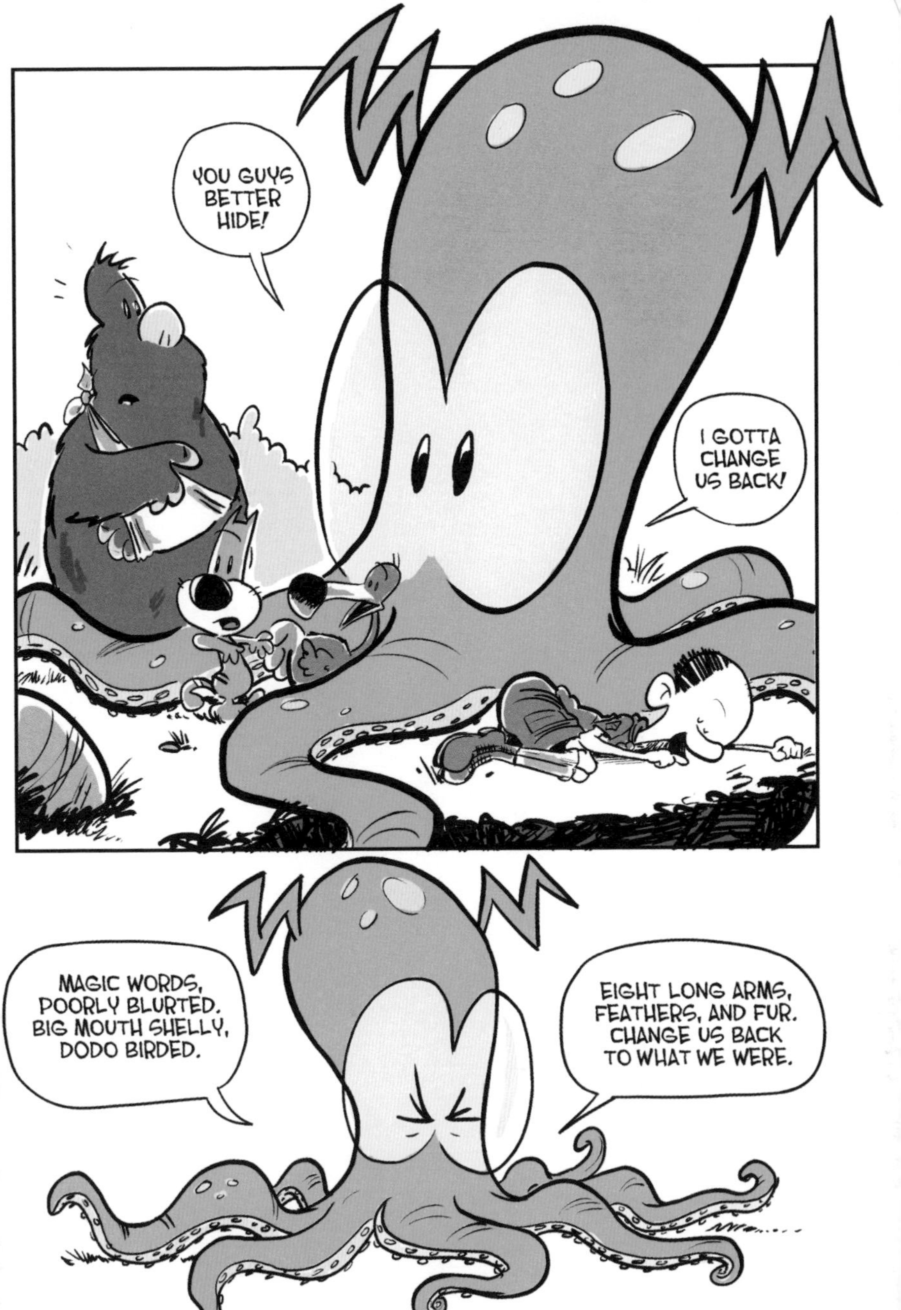
YOU GUYS BETTER HIDE!
I GOTTA CHANGE US BACK!
MAGIC WORDS, POORLY BLURTED. BIG MOUTH SHELLY, DODO BIRDED.
EIGHT LONG ARMS, FEATHERS, AND FUR. CHANGE US BACK TO WHAT WE WERE.

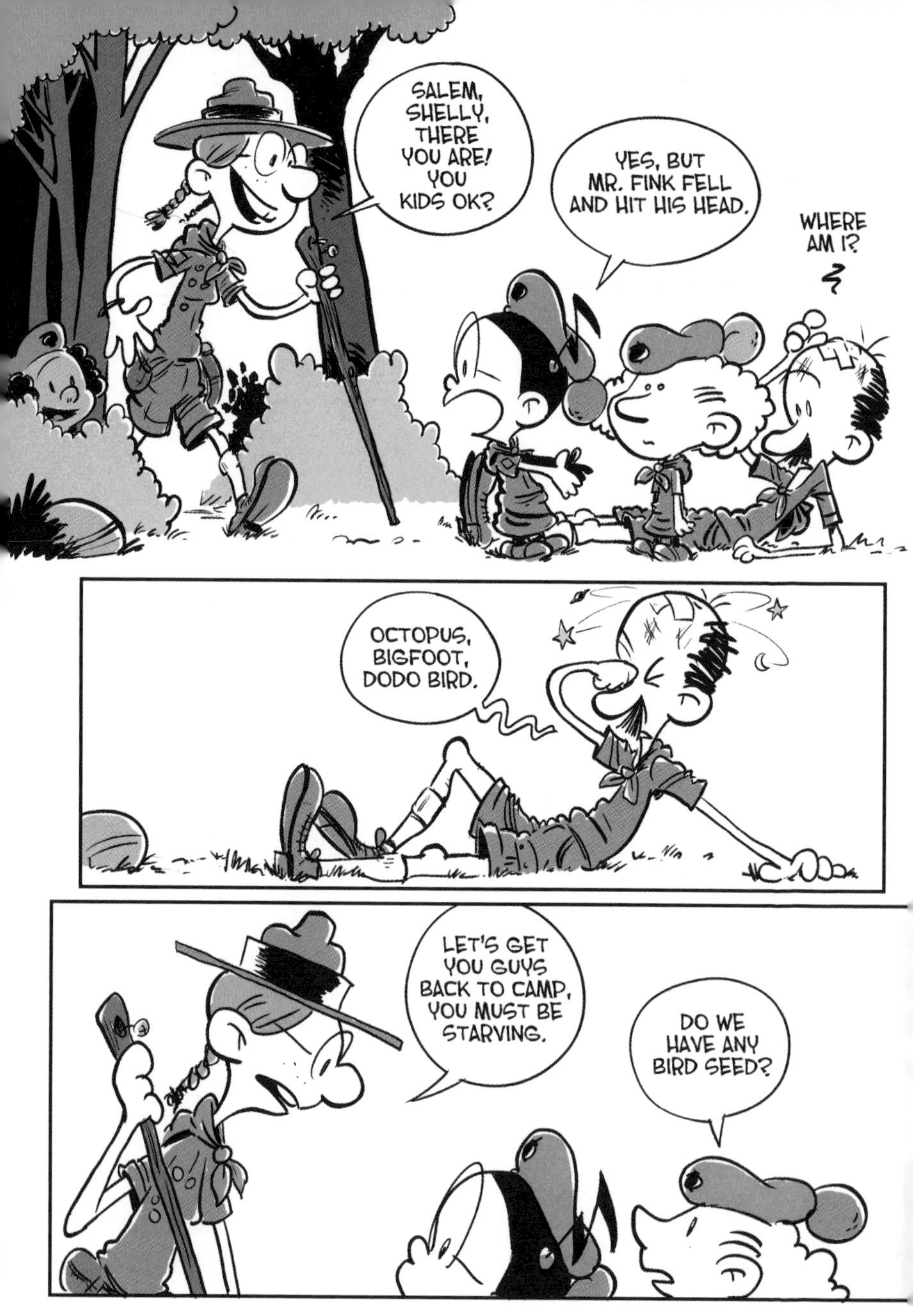
SALEM, SHELLY, THERE YOU ARE! YOU KIDS OK?
YES, BUT MR. FINK FELL AND HIT HIS HEAD.
WHERE AM I?
OCTOPUS, BIGFOOT, DODO BIRD.
LET'S GET YOU GUYS BACK TO CAMP. YOU MUST BE STARVING.
DO WE HAVE ANY BIRD SEED?

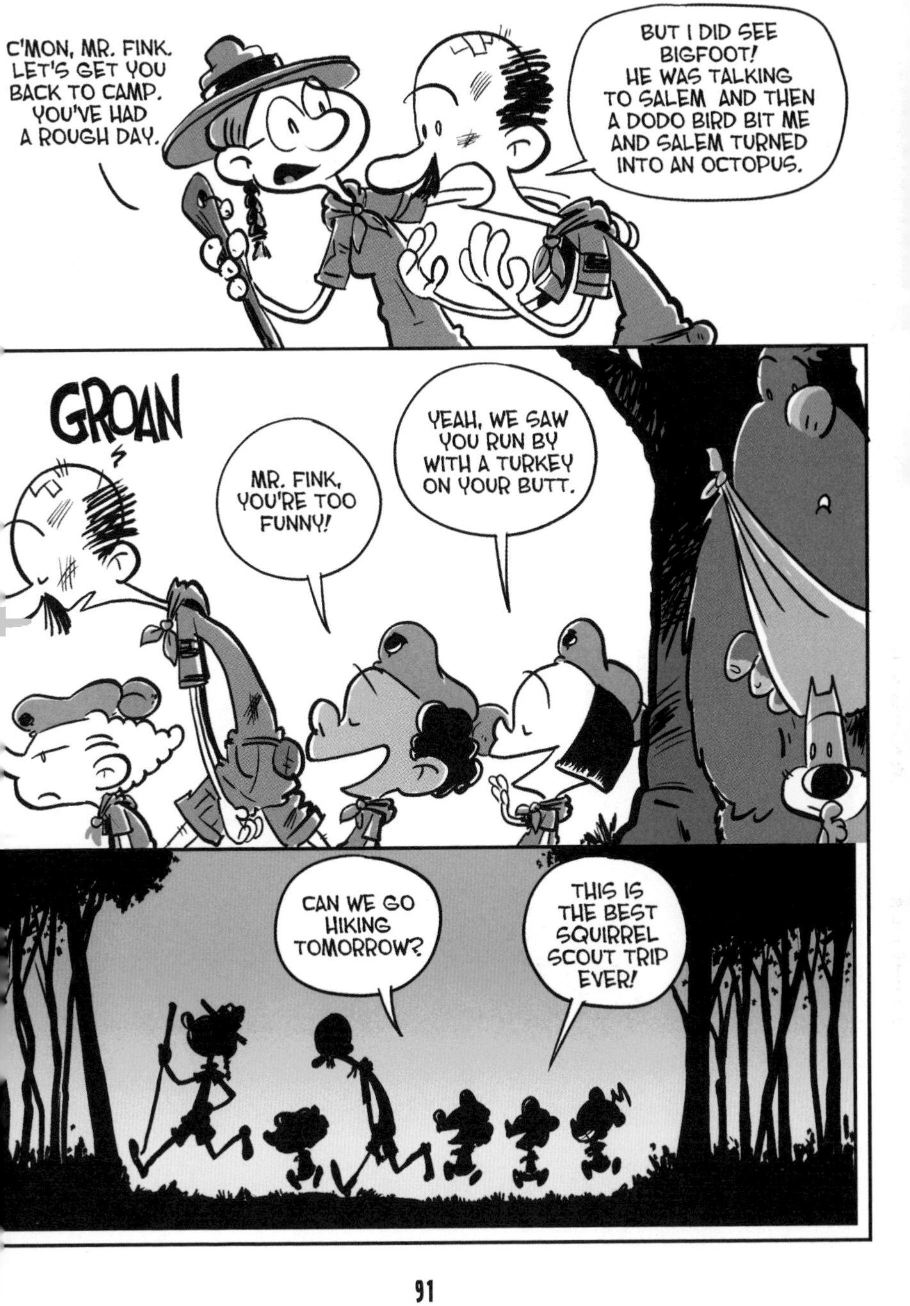
C'MON, MR. FINK. LET'S GET YOU BACK TO CAMP. YOU'VE HAD A ROUGH DAY.
BUT I DID SEE BIGFOOT! HE WAS TALKING TO SALEM AND THEN A DODO BIRD BIT ME AND SALEM TURNED INTO AN OCTOPUS.
GROAN
MR. FINK, YOU'RE TOO FUNNY!
YEAH, WE SAW YOU RUN BY WITH A TURKEY ON YOUR BUTT.
CAN WE GO HIKING TOMORROW?
THIS IS THE BEST SQUIRREL SCOUT TRIP EVER!

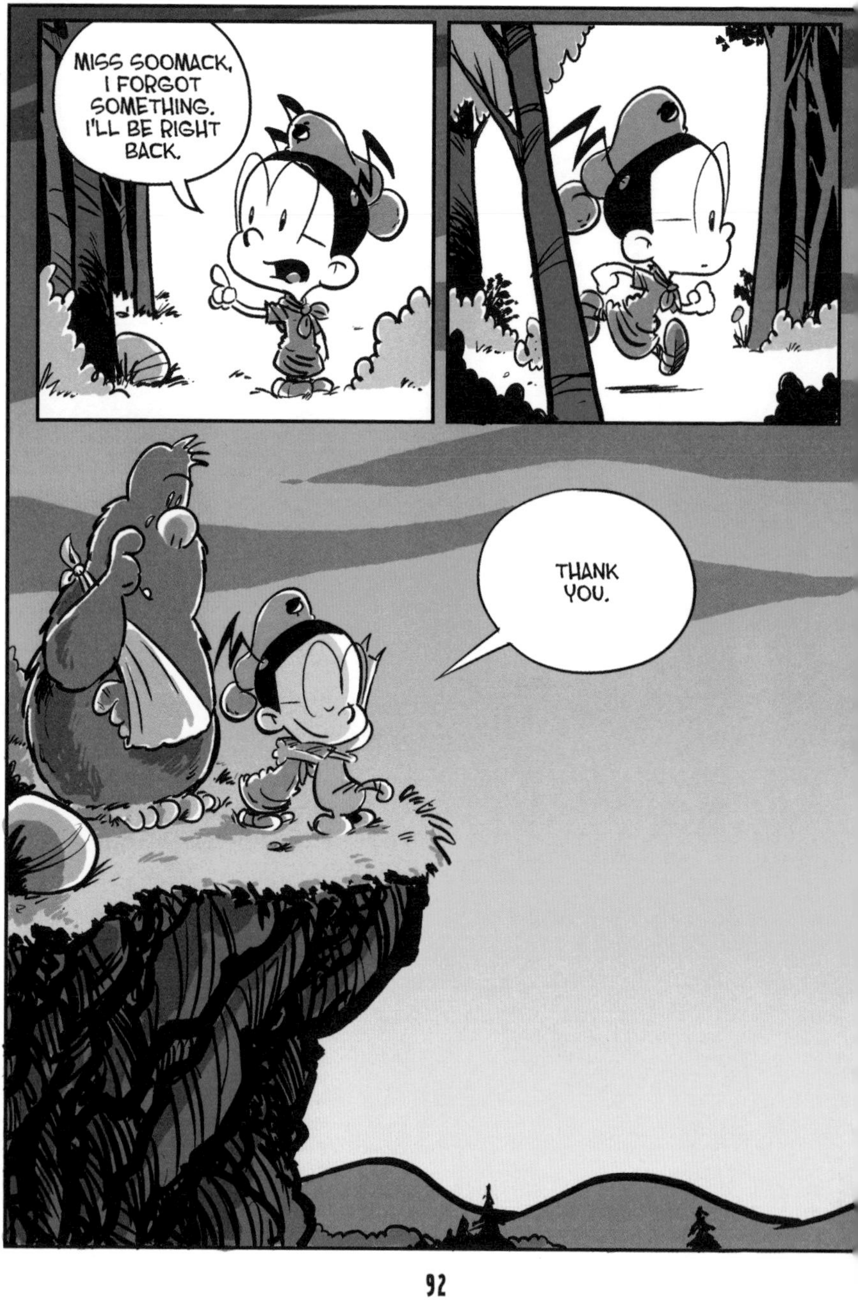
MISS SOOMACK, I FORGOT SOMETHING. I'LL BE RIGHT BACK.
THANK YOU.

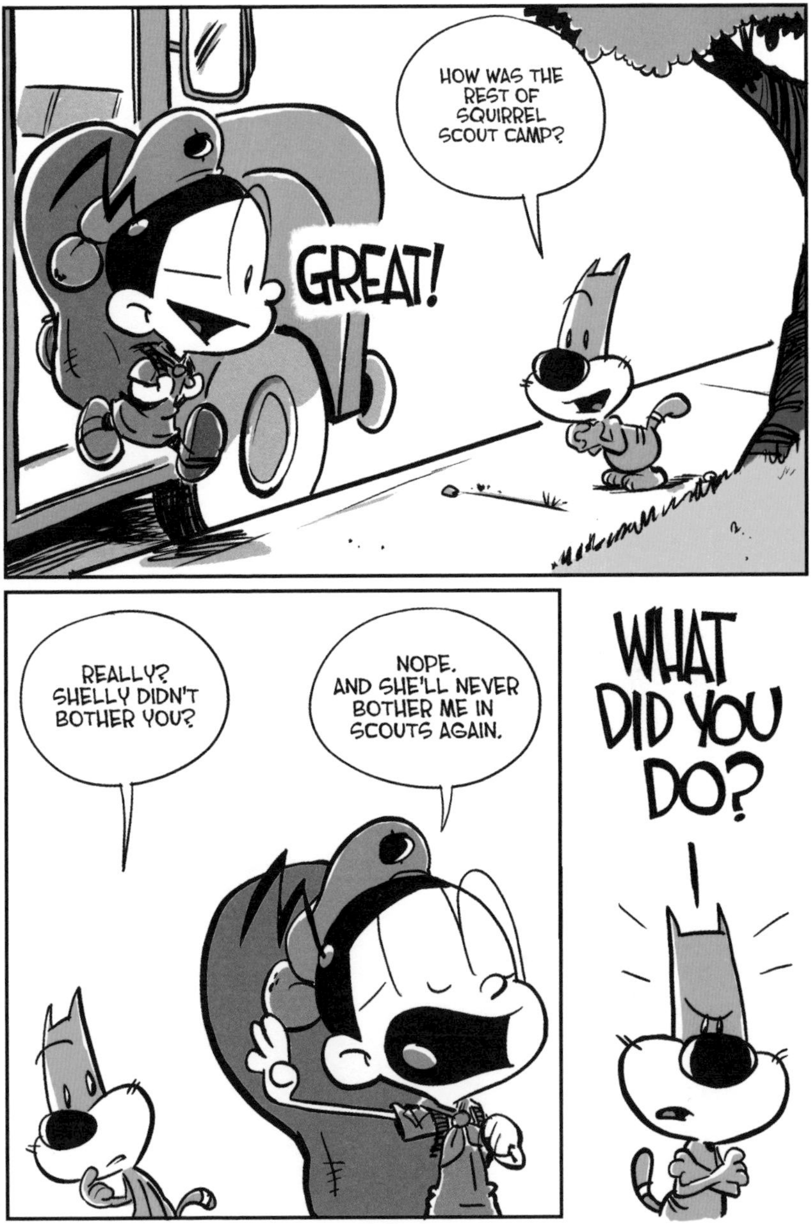
HOW WAS THE REST OF SQUIRREL SCOUT CAMP?
GREAT!
REALLY? SHELLY DIDN'T BOTHER YOU?
NOPE. AND SHE'LL NEVER BOTHER ME IN SCOUTS AGAIN.
WHAT DID YOU DO?

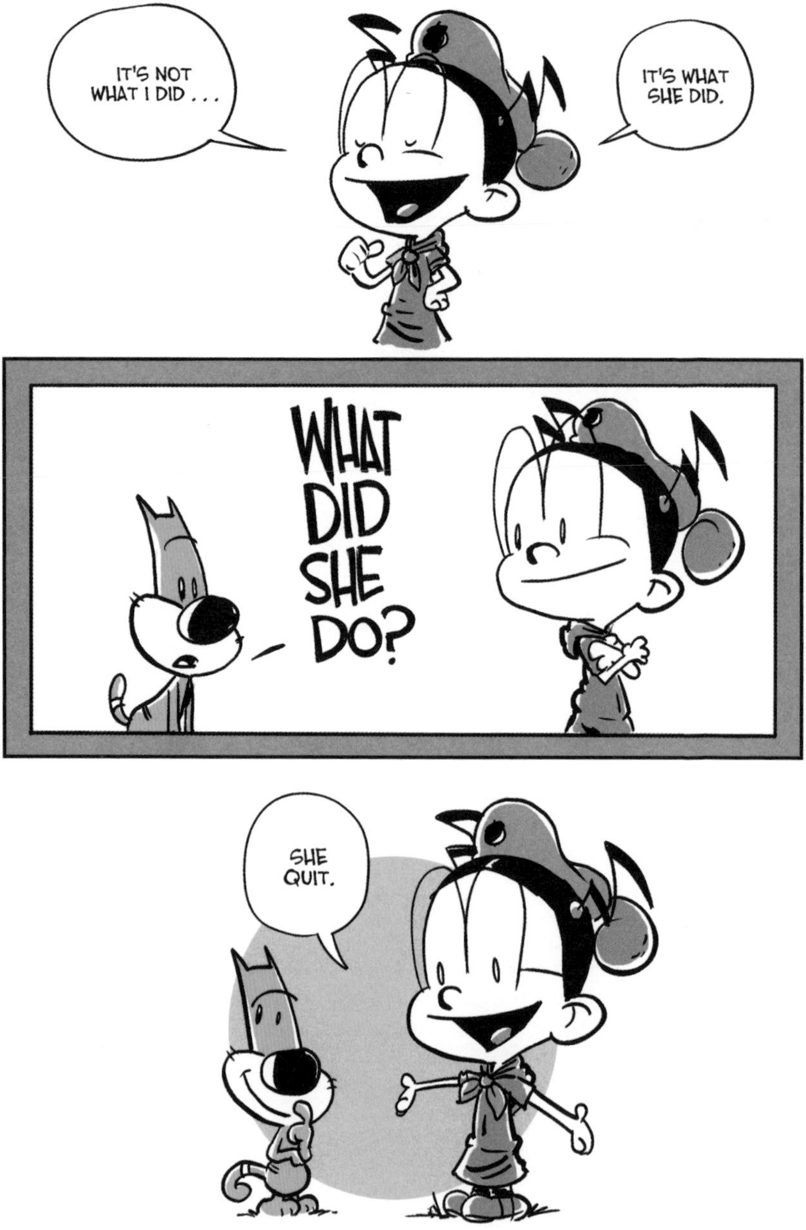
IT'S NOT WHAT I DID . . .
IT'S WHAT SHE DID.
WHAT DID SHE DO?
SHE QUIT.

Getting to KNOW FRANK CAMMUSO

FRANK LIKES
1. TRAVELING WITH HIS FAMILY
2. COOKIES (ALL KINDS)
3. DRAWING COMICS
4. PLAYING LEGOS WITH KHAI

FRANK DISLIKES
1. TUNA FISH
2. MAYONNAISE (ALL KINDS)
3. SHOVELING SNOW
4. CAMPING IN A TENT

FUN FACT: DID YOU KNOW . . .
THAT FRANK CAMMUSO WAS ONCE A BOY SCOUT?

SPECIAL THANKS TO . . .

Ngoc and Khai, Kathy Leonardo, Nancy Iacovelli, Hart Seely, Tom Peyer, Maggie Lehrman, Charlie Kochman, Katie Fitch, Chad Beckerman, Morgan Dubin, Judy Hansen, and finally to all the folks who recommended I get a CINTIQ.

For more fun stuff about Salem and Whammy Check out my website at . . .

WWW.CAMMUSO.COM

In Memory of My DAD...

WHO TAUGHT ME TO NEVER GIVE UP.

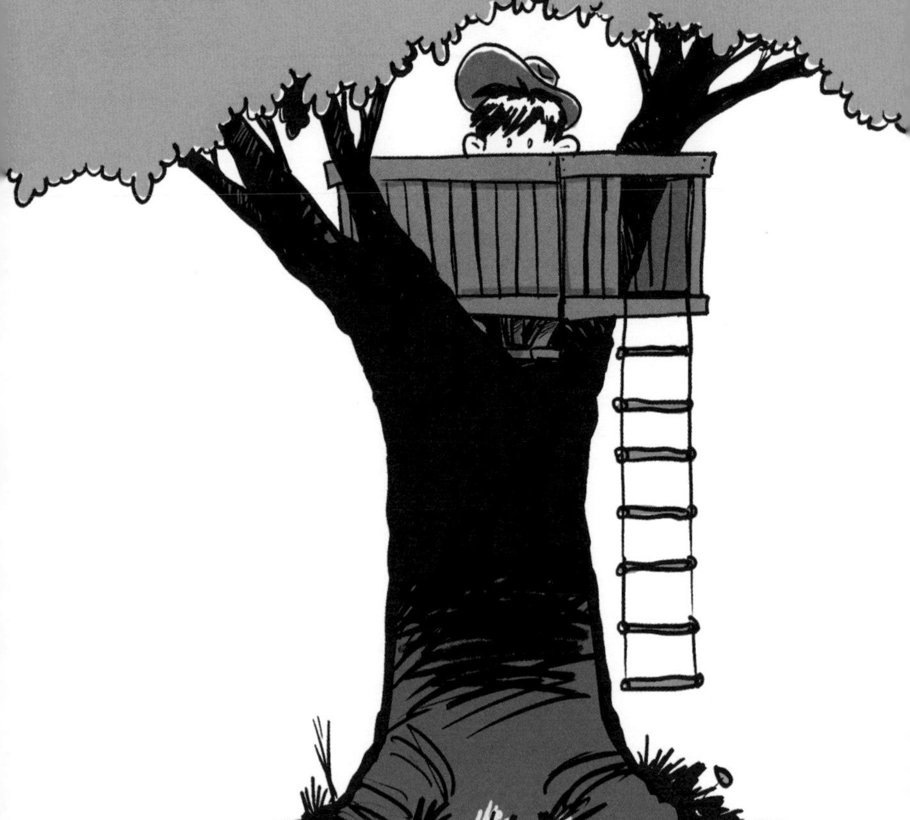

TREE-FORT BUILDER, HORNET SLAYER, SCOUTMASTER.

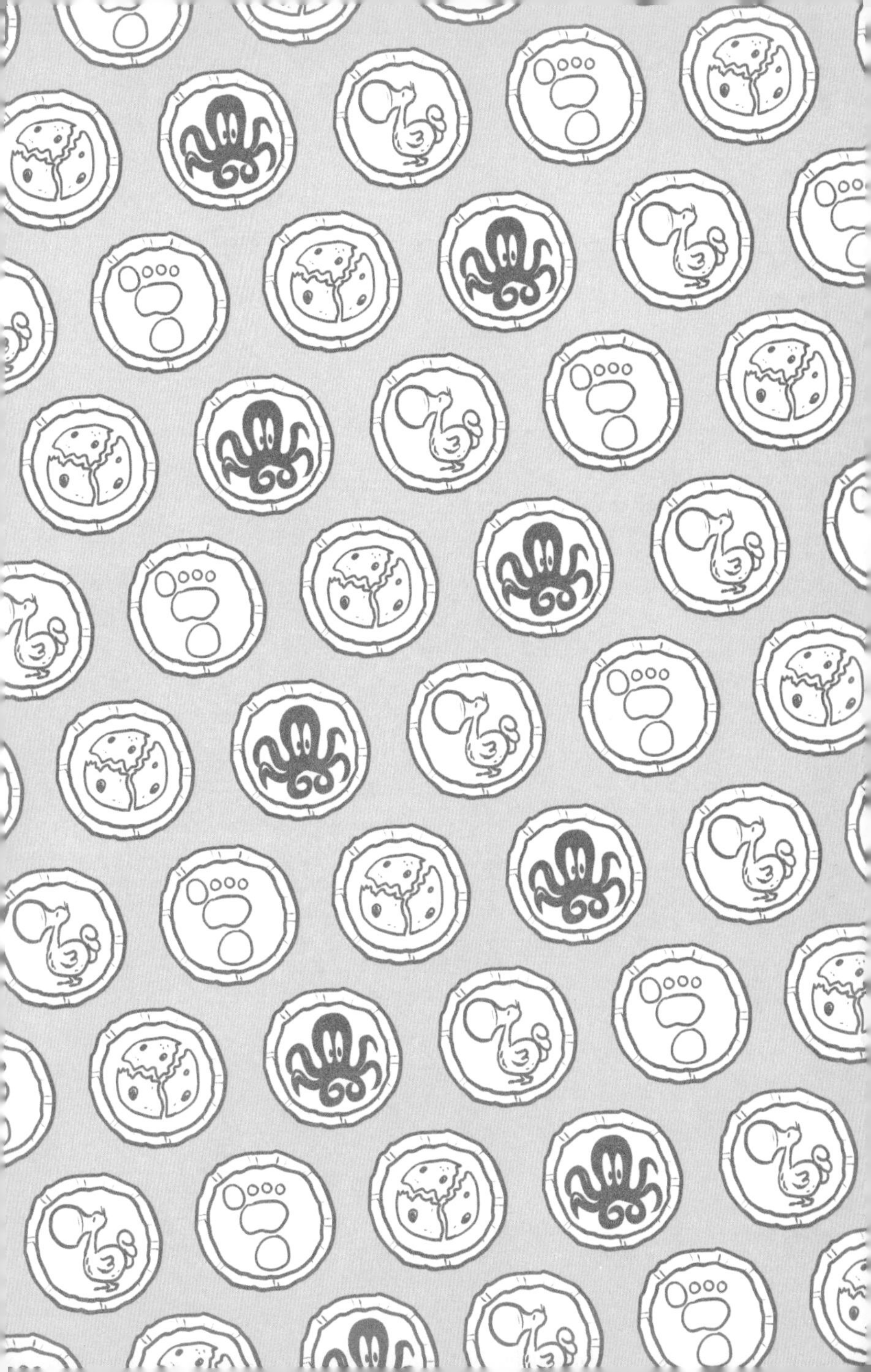

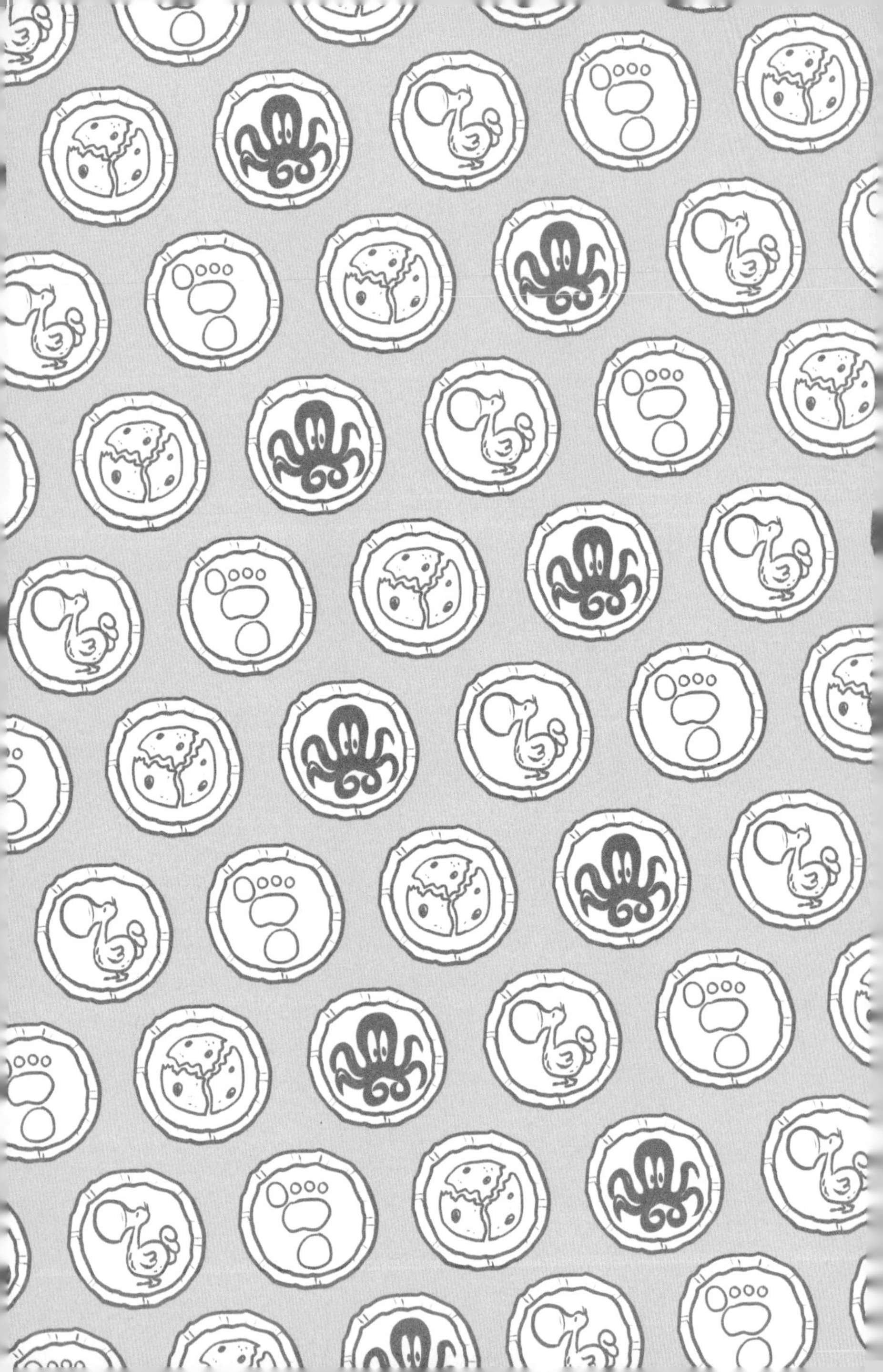